TIME FOR FRANKIE COOLIN

BILL GRIFFITH

TIME FOR FRANKIE COOLIN

RANDOM HOUSE NEW YORK

Library of Congress Cataloging in Publication Data
Griffith, Bill.
Time for Frankie Coolin.
I. Title.
PS3557.R48918T5   813'.54   81-19247
ISBN 0-394-52123-4   AACR2

Manufactured in the United States of America
98765432
First Edition

For those in the trades—
and my father and T. J. H.

The day shall not be up so soon as I,
To try the fair adventure of tomorrow.

—WILLIAM SHAKESPEARE

NOTE

Common ethnic names, real street names, real
neighborhoods, real suburbs—all are used in
the story that follows. But despite the edge
of realism, this story of Frankie Coolin and his
time is fiction and is not intended to bear any
resemblance to that of any person, living
or dead.

— B.G.

TIME FOR FRANKIE COOLIN

1

The G came around again to Frankie Coolin on Thursday, just when he was taking the last of the radiators out of the six-flat he had bought in June.

There had been a dozen other jobs that were more important and now it was October and there really wasn't much time left to strip the old building of the pipes and radiators. The building was empty at the moment but Frankie Coolin intended to hustle in new black tenants before the weather turned cold.

Two of the G stood there and showed him their plastic cards with their color photographs on them and their names and the outline of the Justice Department seal. Coolin took each card in turn and examined it as though they were showing him three-dollar bills for the first time.

Coolin met them in the vestibule by the front door, which was still not painted. There was sweat in a sheen on his face because he had lugged a radiator down out of the next-to-last bedroom of the south apartment on the second floor. He had figured on heaving the radiator over the railing on the gray, wooden back porch, dumping it in the littered back yard by the alley. The dirt in the yard was pockmarked with other depressions caused by other radiators thrown down in this way. But the back door of the south apartment was jammed shut and when Frankie Coolin started whacking at the jamb with his hammer, the ancient wood began to split and show its white insides. Cursing the door and the radiator and his own bad luck, he had wrestled the radiator down the front stairs.

The G were about the same height. Coolin gave them back their cards. They looked like wallpaper patterns, he thought, stamped out over and over in great sheets at the G school and then rolled up for shipment. They didn't wear glasses and their hair looked as though it never grew; they were solid without having weight around the middle and their clothes were neither too expensive nor too cheap. The only thing that made them stand out at the moment was their surroundings.

The neighborhood was black, it was black for miles in every direction. It was the middle of the afternoon, the most aimless time of all in the ghetto. Black women, fat and shuffling, walked down the cracked and broken sidewalks and packs of vicious, hungry dogs slouched down the alleys, upsetting garbage cans and casually fighting each other in the search for food. The G had taken up positions in the middle of the narrow vestibule, hemmed in by the unpainted walls and the radiator and now Frankie Coolin himself. They looked as though they did not want to touch the walls. Frankie Coolin smiled as they put the cards back in their pockets and stared at him. He saw how out of place they were, in this slum, in this narrow vestibule. Frankie Coolin owned three buildings on two blocks and this was the fourth. He had picked them up at county tax sales for nothing and slapped bright paint in them and rented them out—after he made sure all the heat radiators and steam pipes were pulled out.

"We talked before." It was the G in the gray suit who shifted his weight slightly from one black Florsheim to the other.

Frankie Coolin realized he had already forgotten his name. Gribbs or Tibbs, something mushy.

"I seem to remember. You want to talk down here or up in the second floor? I got the north flat finished on the second floor, it's nicer."

"How could anything be nicer than this?"

"Whatever."

Gribbs or Tibbs in the gray suit looked at the steam radiator. He drew back his polished right shoe slightly. "You were carrying out this radiator. I saw a radiator in your truck outside. I thought you owned this building. You doing a wrecking job here instead?"

Gribbs, Coolin thought, deciding. "Winter's coming." He touched the pocket of his flannel shirt for a cigarette and found none. That was usual. Gribbs watched the gesture but did not respond to it, even when Coolin looked at him.

"You take out the heat, your tenants are going to freeze," said the other one. Coolin had talked to him before as well.

Coolin had not liked him and vice versa from day one, especially when he found out the guy was from the Des Moines office of the G. Des Moines. A hick, he had hair like hay.

"Space heaters," Frankie Coolin said.

"What are you talking about?"

Frankie Coolin smiled. "You got slums in Des Moines or only farmers?"

Garwood, that was the name. Gribbs and Garwood. Garwood with hay for hair and a brown suit that came off the same rack as Gribbs in gray.

"I know what space heaters are."

"Well, if you were looking out the window of your command car coming out here, you probably noticed this is the low-rent district." Coolin reached at his pocket again, found nothing, and rested his foot on the radiator. "When kids grow up from here, they got something to tell their grandkids about. You know—'When I was a kid, we were so poor'—that kind of stuff. So what am I going to do about heat? I can't heat these people. I'm not charging them half a throw a month, you know."

Garwood blinked and kept staring.

Coolin made a wide gesture. "Look, when gas heat didn't cost nothing, the gas reader comes around every other month, sometimes he doesn't come around at all. Heat was practically free. When I was a kid on the West Side, you didn't pay for gas. Nobody cared about gas. And then the Arabs raise the oil and naturally the wise guys in the gas company said they might as well jack up the gas price too. So that puts me in the middle, see? There's three people involved. There's me. I rent flats. There's them, my brothers out there, they rent from me. And there's the gas company where there didn't used to be. I don't want to be in the middle so I don't get between them and the gas company. They want to rip off the gas, fine, just don't involve me in it and I am involved if I give them the heat and the gas company collects from me and I got to collect from them. The way it is now, it's simple. I pull the boiler out of the basement, radiators, everything and then the guy rents from me wants to sit around in the middle of winter with the windows open and space heaters on full blast, that little meter going around like a Ferris wheel on the Fourth of July, sweat coming down off his face, so hot they make it in here they sit around in their underwear with the windows up, you can grow tropical plants in here—well, it's up to them. This way the gas man doesn't come around and say, 'Hey, schmuck, I got a bill for twenty-three thousand dollars last month for your six-flat, come up with it.' You see what I mean? I leave my people alone, they don't bother me and the gas company and them can work it out. I just want to be an innocent bystander."

"You haven't been innocent for a long time," said the G from Des Moines, shifting his weight back from the left Florsheim to the right. His shoes were brown with little tassels where the laces should be.

"You keep saying that," Frankie Coolin said.

"It keeps being true," said Garwood. Coolin stared at him, shrugged, looked down at his brown boot on the radiator.

"We thought you wanted to tell us what really was stored up there," Gribbs said.

"I told you that."

"Tell us again, only try to get it right this time."

"Every time it's right," Coolin said. "I got the same thing to say I said last time. Just play the tape back and you don't have to drive out here every time to talk to me. Saves you time, saves Uncle gas."

Garwood from Des Moines blinked again. His face was blank.

Gribbs said, "A conservationist. You make me proud of you."

"Thanks."

Gribbs took a half step forward, pushing the polished toe of his right shoe closer to the dirt-encrusted radiator. He stared down at Coolin.

Coolin could smell the soap and aftershave. Old Spice, he thought. Or maybe just a government brand they issued at G school, the same place agents got their suits and shoes and haircuts.

"I want to talk about something different this time," Gribbs said. "Just to add variety."

"I like a change."

"I want to talk about something about your tax returns for 1978."

"That was a bad year for me."

"You aren't dumb."

"Thank you."

"That was the year you listed your losses from the warehouse fire. On the returns."

"Sure. I know that. I mean, I don't do my own taxes, you know. I can't keep up with it, you guys keep changing the rules every year. I got a Jew."

"Losses," Gribbs said, letting the repeated word drop like a radiator falling from a second-floor porch.

"Kappelman. He says it was all right to list losses."

"Big losses, Frankie. But not a thing about television sets stored in the warehouse."

"I don't know about TV sets. I don't store TV sets. I had losses, I'm in the trades, I got buildings I own, I'm trying to rehab, provide a little decent housing—"

Garwood said, "This don't look like a historic district."

"I think you're being prejudiced," Coolin said.

Gribbs broke the tangent. "TV sets, Frankie."

"You checked the returns. I list my losses neat. Everything is going up, even losses got to keep up with inflation. My wife went to the store, she comes back and bacon is two dollars a pound. Remember bacon was thirty-nine cents a pound. I mean, what is the stuff but fat from pigs? Two bucks a pound for fat from pigs, I could have got steak for that a couple of years ago."

Garwood interrupted. "You're just playing the hard guy. Very, very hard, very tough guy."

Coolin let a sigh blow over his lips. He was thirsty and he wanted to go to the truck and get a beer out of the cooler but he wasn't going to do it while they stood there. He didn't look at Garwood but turned to Gribbs. He tugged at the peak of his battered black Sox cap, the one he had found in the litter of the truck because he had to get his six-month inspection sticker that morning. His lucky cap.

"I'm not a hard guy," Coolin said to Gribbs as though Garwood had disappeared. "Just a little guy, I got a couple of buildings, I got some skill in the trades. I hustle for myself, you know? Who's got time for this, for you guys coming around all the time. What are you guys going after? You after me? The G must have a lot of dough, sending out you two guys over and over all the time, just to give me a hard time. For what? You think I deduct too much on my returns? I claim too much in that fire? You want an amended return?"

"You want to amend your return?" Gribbs said.

Coolin made a face and shook his head and sighed again. It was like playing stickball in the alley. Everything was so constricted, no one could hit swinging out for fear the ball would pull right or left and break a window. It was the way the cops talked, all of them, city and G. Stupid. They danced him to the point of lying to them or saying something that wouldn't be healthy in the long run. Coolin wasn't dumb, like Gribbs said.

Garwood pointed it out. "You know you lie to us, to federal officers, you know that's a felony."

"I heard that. That's what makes you guys less fun than regular cops. Especially you, Garwood, with that Sony taped to your chest."

"Mr. Garwood to you. Mister."

"Whatever you say. Your wife lies to you about the milkman, is that a felony too? You lock her up?"

Garwood did not blink this time. For a moment, a flush colored his face and then it was gone; for a moment, the federal veneer slipped and then it was adjusted back over the pale skin and the flat eyes. "You're getting dumber by the minute," Garwood said. But it sounded lame to the three of them as soon as he said it and it made it worse.

Coolin closed his eyes for a moment. This didn't do him any good. He opened his eyes. "Look." His voice was soft. "I ask you guys fifty times why you come around to hassle me. For Christ's sake, I got work here. I got maybe only three weeks left to finish up this building or I eat it for the winter and the bums move in and burn me out."

"You know a lot about fires," said Garwood.

"Yeah. Maybe you could use another income tax fire." This was Gribbs.

"So if I'm a big shot from downtown with my connections in the Hall and I come out here and rehab these buildings, they put my picture on the front page of the *Trib*. But if I'm only Frankie Coolin, then fuck me, right?"

"You're screwing yourself," Gribbs said, stepping around the stronger word that Coolin suggested. "You want to know what we want?" He let his voice fall to a confidential whisper, as though they weren't standing in an empty building or Garwood didn't have a very sensitive tape recorder whirring away under his coat.

"Sure. That's what I said from the start. Either you guys got a smoke?"

Garwood stared at him and then blinked.

"Shit," Coolin said. He tapped his flannel shirt pocket again. "I run out."

"I'll bring a carton next time," Garwood said.

"Make 'em Luckies."

Garwood turned to Gribbs and said, "This guy doesn't want to listen. He's a comedian."

"I want to listen but I want a smoke too," Coolin said. "OK. It's your dime."

"You had those TV sets there. You knew they were there. In the warehouse. That's why you rented the space in the first place. And you knew they were hot."

"I thought you were going to say something new this time."

"What else did you have up there, Frankie?"

"I had in there what you know I had in there, what you saw on my '78 return. I had my own shit there. I didn't have no TV sets. Look, I don't even give the shines heat, you think I'm providing them TV sets?"

"You were keeping the stuff for someone else."

"I don't do that, you know that. Ask anyone, I don't do charity work. Go to the Salvation Army on Ashland. I work by myself, you guys know that, you been following me in that white Pontiac. Ask around."

"What about Kennedy?" said Gribbs.

"What about him?"

"Your wife's cousin."

"I know the man."

"He was storing the TV sets, right?"

"Was he?"

"Come on, Frankie."

"I don't know nothing about it."

"We know enough about it, Frankie."

"Is that right? You know enough? Then what the fuck you coming around here? You get paid to hassle me, right? Did I vote wrong in the last election? You want to nail Kennedy, you got enough, nail away."

"You don't seem to get it for a bright boy," Gribbs said. "We ask you if you see Kennedy and you tell us you don't see him, don't work with him, don't talk to him."

"I see him around. He's my wife's cousin. You see everyone around after a while—"

"You don't talk to him, right? Is that right, Frankie, am I getting it right?" asked Garwood. He was hustling now, setting Coolin up.

"I see him, what do I do, not talk to him? You want me to avoid seeing him, I can handle it. This guy is no great friend of mine. Friends you can choose, relatives you got to take. I was down by the Bohemian's place maybe a week ago Thursday, I see him, if you mean seeing him like that. I see lots of guys at the tavern. I see you more than I see my uncle, you guys are becoming like relatives, maybe I'll invite you over at Thanksgiving, you can meet the rest of the family. Hey, Garwood, how long do those tapes go before you gotta change the side? Can I see your machine? I wanta get a machine for my kid for Christmas, he's going to college, he could use it."

Gribbs went on. "You saw Kennedy at the Bohemian's tavern, you don't talk to him, is that right?"

"If I knew you guys were out in the parking lot watching me, I would have invited you in." Coolin smiled. His teeth were white in the sun-dark face. "You guys got expense accounts, right? We could have had a couple of beers."

Garwood blinked again. Gribbs sighed, stepped back away from the radiator, and looked around him. The vestibule had grown stuffy with the presence of three bodies breathing and sweating. Gribbs opened the door for a moment. The air carried a musty chill. He shut the door. "Maybe," he said at last. "Maybe we all ought to just go someplace like the Dirksen Building, just go down and have a little talk, the three of us, until we get all this straight."

"Aw, man. I got shit to do here. You think I'm working like a Polack because I need exercise? The doctor says I'm in better shape now than half the guys he sees that are half my age."

Garwood said, "What did Kennedy have in the warehouse?"

It was an old question, an old trick, and he sounded tired of it.

"In where? We're talking about the warehouse now, not the tavern? In the tavern, I think he was drinking the usual, Walker and water. I don't drink whiskey, I never did."

Garwood let the words explode then, as though they were mines laid down a long time ago. "You know what he did. You know because you were part of the scam, you stupid little prick. Hard guy. You're so fucking hard, you can break like ice. You won't be so fucking hard when you start spending winters up at Sandstone. And they don't have space heaters in Sandstone. Uncle pays for all the heat."

"Well, that's the G for you. Got all the money in the world."

"John Q.," Garwood said. "Just a taxpayer."

"Sure. And you're public servants, right? You feel like public servants? You wake up in the morning and you think to yourself how you can go down and serve the public today? I bet I feel more like a taxpayer than you feel like a public servant."

Gribbs said gently, "This isn't going to help you." Another slight, nearly microscopic step towards the radiator. "You know it isn't, Frankie. You know we don't waste our time. You know we're moving, you know how careful we do it." The voice had taken on the quality of a voice remembered or heard in a dream. "You know we're coming down closer to it every day. You know us, Frankie. We don't play."

Coolin blinked now, in an imitation of Garwood's flat-faced way of staring at statements. "Sure. You want a beer? I got a six-pack in the truck, in my cooler."

"They don't serve beer at Sandstone," Garwood said.

"And they don't ask you to work up a sweat lugging radiators down the stairs either, right?"

"Very hard. Very hard," Gribbs said with sadness.

"Not hard," Coolin said. He ran his thick fingers under his White Sox cap and through his brown hair. Lucky cap. Bought it the night down at Comiskey Park when the Sox took a twi-nighter from the Yanks. Lucky all the time. Even this morning when he found it under the seat and the inspection station passed the truck one more time without a word, without

Frankie having to grease the inspector even though he knew there was something wrong with the manifold. Another six months safe.

What would happen six months from now?

He stared at Gribbs and patted his empty shirt pocket again. He thought of Uncle Brian coming out of Sandstone. He and Rose had driven up to Minnesota to get him out of the place. He looked old when he came out of Receiving, it was only two years in the joint and it wasn't as though Sandstone was a max joint or anything. Some of them kidded it was a country club but Brian didn't look like it was a country club. He had looked old and Frankie and Rose had been shocked but they hadn't said anything. He stayed old until he died.

Lucky cap, Frankie thought, touching the black bill again. "Five times guys like you come around. Five times. When you stop coming?"

"When you tell the truth, Frankie."

"I don't lie to you, man."

"You haven't done anything but lie to us," Gribbs said quietly.

"Oh, boy." He couldn't stop thinking of Brian. "Why you want to do this to me? There aren't any crooks left in the world? You go down to LaSalle Street and get some of those stock market creeps running dope like stock options, you could fill every fed joint from Sandstone to Danbury. You know what we got in Chicago, Garwood? I don't want to blow your mind but we got the Outfit here, there isn't a dago in the world isn't tied to the Outfit. You got the Outfit and if that ain't your cup of tea, you got killings, you got back jobs every day practically, and so what are you guys doing? Sitting in the parking lot at the tavern, watching drunks come in for their daily fix. I think I'm dealing with the minors, here. You guys are Double A or something, right? You practice on me and then you get to go in the big time, right? Down to Sarasota for the winter tryout."

"Bad guys are all over the place. Like clams."

"I agree, I just made that point. You're pounding on me because you think I was a fence for the stuff you say you found after the warehouse fire, right? You follow me all the time, for weeks, you see me fence? Am I fencing? Who am I going to fence to? Shines? I had tools in that building, I had my building materials in that building, roofing supplies. What did I say it was worth on my return? I forget. I rent some space in that prick's warehouse, I had to; you see the neighborhood around here, what was I going to do, store it in the basement? Or you think I should store it in my basement at home? I got a panel basement, I got my old man lives down there. In the old days, who gives a shit about building material? You can leave it on the site, a kid comes by and steals some two-by-fours, who gives a shit? Now everything is gold. You got to keep everything locked up."

"TV sets," Gribbs said. The voice was still quiet, still relentless, the cadence slow and easy. Just like a dream. Coolin looked around. The building was musty with fifty years of abuse and neglect but a bright, strong smell of cheap paint came from the finished apartments upstairs: paint and dust and the smell of new wood to replace the old; the dank odor of new plaster on old ceilings recently fixed. It was his world, his smells. He looked at Gribbs and knew Gribbs would never understand it.

"It was a big warehouse," Frankie Coolin said. "You found television sets. I didn't go up there that often."

"TV sets. In cartons."

"Not mine."

"In the space you rented."

"That prick that started the fire, he probably was moving everything around in there. That's what I told you up front. This is bullshit and you know it, I told you what I had there. You said the firemen found it, insulation rolls and some asbestos firewall panels. I listed it all."

"And TV sets," Gribbs said again. "We found TV sets."

"Someone else was storing TV sets."

"Frankie." Gribbs said the name and then said nothing more.

Garwood picked it up. "Remember 1977, that wonderful year?"

"Remember? How can I forget? My brother John had a triple bypass operation, he still looks like shit. They cut his legs open to get the veins out for his heart, he goes around to the taverns and wears loose pants so he can pull up his cuffs and show everyone the scars and make everyone sick."

Garwood said, "That was the year we got four eighteen-wheelers hijacked at the Flo-Thru truck stop on I-55 down near Joliet. Four in six months, bim bam bim. You know what two had on them? TV sets. Sixty-four pallets. Cases and cases of Sony TV sets in from the Coast. You know what a Sony goes for? Even hot?"

"I don't buy Jap sets, I buy American."

"You're dumb. They're all made in Japan anyway."

It was Gribbs's turn. "Two truckloads, Frankie. And what do we find when Kostner Warehouse burns down one night?"

"That was a torch job, that fire, you guys know that."

"Nobody is talking about the warehouse."

"You guys got your priorities all fucked up. A guy torches a building, that's still a crime, isn't it?"

"They got city cops for that. That's not federal."

"Listen, it ought to be. The only time a cop clears a torch job is when he sees the porkie running from the scene with a Zippo in his hand."

"You don't have faith in law enforcement," Garwood said.

Gribbs broke in again. "Frankie, we are talking about Sonys in cartons on pallets in the warehouse. Some with water damage, some not. Lots of Sonys and very hot."

"After a fire like that, you got to believe it."

"This guy is smart, you know that?" said Garwood. "A regular wise guy, so goddam smart he's a pain in the ass."

"I told you what was in my space. I told you in person, I told the cops, I wrote it down, I put it on my income tax. Sometimes I get the feeling we can't communicate anymore. You want me to send you a singing telegram too?"

"Nobody is going to rent space in a warehouse to store the crap you said was up there. Insulation. Who the hell stores insulation."

"There were other things."

"Radiators?" Garwood asked.

"Sure. Radiators. A couple. Didn't I put that down on my return? I was waiting for my price, I was working a deal. I gutted that building kittycorner from here where you turned up the one-way street about three years ago. You know what pipe goes for now? Radiators are gold, you can't get radiators. Fifteen bucks a foot."

"For ugly shit like that."

"You must have been raised in California. They heat cheap, you can't get heat cheap like that any more."

"Not as cheap as space heaters, huh?" Garwood said.

"Space heaters I explained," Coolin said. "Nobody wants to pay any more so you got to get out of being the middleman. It's like the mope who ends up holding the check after a big meal. I don't want the gas company on my ass. They call me up, say they want to cut off the heat, I say, 'Hey, ten-four, turn it off.' I give a shit. If I'm responsible for heat, I got to raise the rents to pay for it and they say I'm gouging and they get the do-gooders come down here marching on me. They put my name in the *Tribune*. Look, I'm just a little guy, trying to hustle a buck, you know that. I pick up shit, these buildings are shit, I put them back together, I paint them, I fix the toilets, make it nice. You think everyone in the world is making twenty grand a year? You got poor people, you got to stash them someplace. So I make it nice and I don't charge them an arm or a leg and I still got to carry a piece to collect rent on the first of the month. You think the city wants to give me a medal? They can stick it. I just want to be left alone is all."

For a moment, Gribbs stared at him without a word. They could hear each other breathing and then the silence was broken by a shout from the street. The shout was answered by another and then more silence came until Gribbs decided.

"Sit down, Frankie."

Coolin sat on the radiator. Time for the commercial. All the rest of it was play. Gribbs had been the good cop, Garwood the bad cop. He knew the routine.

"We peeled that operation at Flo-Thru, you get me?" The voice was mild, the words were delivered softly. "We peeled until we found an inside man and an outside man. How did they take the rigs? How did they move them out? How did they get rid of the shit? How did they dump the trucks? You know how it goes, Frankie, one thing leads to another. We do things careful, we do things nice. There was money made all along the line. Working broads took the drivers upstairs for a little shower and blow job and then the truck just disappeared. Crude but interesting and the only mistake was greed, they took too many trucks too fast. One thing leads to another and now we just about have this little puzzle all put together on the card table. Stop me if I'm boring you."

"Actually, this is very interesting."

"Shut up," said Garwood.

Gribbs went on as though no one had spoken. "Guy named Visconti, you know Visconti, don't you, Frankie? Guy named Visconti leads us along to a guy named Kennedy who turns out to be your relative and then it all begins to fit, after the fire I mean. Until then, we didn't have clue one because we didn't know where they were dumping the TV sets. And now there's Frankie Coolin with his warehouse space and there's the TV sets and there's Frankie's cousin—"

"My wife's cousin. I'm no kin to him except by marriage."

"You and him," Gribbs said slowly. "Just like that. Frick and Frack. You sat on the shit while he hustled buyers."

More silence. Frankie Coolin touched the peak of his baseball cap as though he were giving a signal and then let the hand drop.

"I didn't have anything to do with what you're talking to me about and you both know it. If I was such a big shot making dough, setting up whores in a truck stop, you think I'd be busting my balls hustling radiators down alone in this building in the middle of spook town? You want to see my truck? You seen it. I got a '75 Ford three-quarter-ton F-250, you seen it, it's got rust on rust, the fenders are coming through, I just got it through the inspection station. By spring, I'm going to have to shoot it or pay a shine ten bucks to steal it. You want to come out to my house? You seen where I live. I got seven rooms, top and bottom, when you count the room I built for the old man in the basement and that's not even a room. I got two baths but one is in the basement where the old man lives. I got a daughter, Peg, at Holy Rosary, I got one kid, Mickey, he's at DePaul, he should graduate in June but now he wants to be a lawyer, so I got another three years to pay for him. Maybe he'll go in the FBI, that'd be all I need. I don't care though, I don't grudge him, he wants to go to school so he doesn't end up like me busting his nuts on radiators up and down the stairs. And I got the old man in the basement, I told you, that's a book in itself. This guy is like a bird on my neck. My wife, I told you she got cataracts last year, I had to go to the bank for it to get the money. Thank God everything turned out okay but it was still money up front. You want me to go on? You didn't bore me, I'll try to keep it interesting for you. My nephew Joey is supposed to be here today helping out with me, he says he wants to go in the trades, the fucking kid wants to be a bricklayer, he couldn't lay a wall to save his life. Not a bad kid but you think he was a general contractor. You don't see him around here, do you? He had to take the day off, he wants to see the Cubs play the last series. The fucking Cubs of all teams, I wouldn't go across the street if they gave me a ticket. But what about me? You think I don't want to take the day off, go out to Hawthorne, watch the ponies, maybe even go to the ballgame myself if the Sox was in town? Hey, what kind of an asshole am I? Why am I working? Joey's got the right idea, fuck off, that's what it's all about. Maybe you think this is bullshit but I'm telling you straight and you're telling me about blow jobs in truck stops. I work my ass off, man, because all the good stuff is taken, they got no room for me in the club; maybe you guys don't know there's a recession out here and it don't mean dick if you can't shake that stick.''

Coolin paused and looked at them. Gribbs had not moved and Garwood's eyes were glassy.

"I tole you about my brother from day one when you're telling me bullshit about hijackers. I'm telling you about Joey's father, the kid out at Cubs' Park. My brother John was a roofer, now he can't climb to the top of a basement window. He sits on his fat ass at home all day when he ain't in the joints, drinking beer in the kitchen. You know about roofers? I never met one that was crazy about working in the first place but now with his heart, my brother can't work, he's drawing federal checks. You know why he was a roofer? He could of come in with me, even if he's a lush he could have come in with me. I never met someone so fucking stupid, that's why he had to be a roofer, but no man fifty years old should be on a roof in July. I got to thank God I got my health because if I didn't, this whole thing I'm trying to tell you is going to collapse. I'm not looking for a tag day for me but you guys don't get it in front.

I pay my taxes, I hustle a buck, no one gets hurt, I'm putting more in Uncle's kitty than I take out. So why the fuck don't you guys get after some shines? There ain't no welfare cheaters left? You know why. You go after a guy like me because you got me by the short hair, I'm stuck, I got a house, I got family, I got problems, I got buildings. You say, hey, this is an easy asshole, this guy is sitting in shit and thinks it's roses, let's wash him off and trot him down. I think this is a horseshit way to treat me."

"You've touched my heart," said Garwood.

Gribbs blinked and spoke. "What about it, Frankie? What if we don't have to want you? What if we could all talk about this problem and maybe work something out? Shit, like you said, we don't have to go after you but you're sitting in the middle of it and we can't walk around you. You said it yourself. You're easy, you're too easy not to clean up and trot down."

Coolin looked at the hands on his lap. He stared at the blackened knuckles. He waited like a patient.

"Everything you say is true, Frankie, let's say," Gribbs began. "Hey, you got problems, we got problems, everyone's got obligations. You got your health, you got to work every day. Right? Am I right? I can sympathize, believe me. You see it that we're coming down too hard on you, that we aren't being fair. Believe me, I can see it from your point of view. But you got to see our side, too. My side, Garwood's side, Uncle's side. We found all these Sonys and we've got a hijacking case that is nearly four years old. We've got to do something about it, right? I mean, there it is: interstate theft, right? Maybe if the warehouse hadn't burned down and the fire department hadn't reported on the Sonys, we would have been able to drop the whole thing. Not everything gets solved and we wouldn't have to lose a lot of sleep over it, right? Personally, Frankie, I know what you're up against and I'd rather not be interested in you. Personally, I'd like to leave you alone. I think you can see that. But the Attorney wants some action, the Special Agent in Charge wants some action, and you know how it goes. I think you could give us a little cooperation now, talk a little bit with us now when we need it, and I could go to the Attorney and we could work something out. Definitely. I definitely can say we can work something out and get off your case, totally, wrap this whole thing up."

Coolin stared at Gribbs, at the mask of sincerity painted on the flat, pale face. "Thanks." Cops never got it. "I guess I would like the part about your not bothering me but I can't help you. I don't know nothing about it."

"Shit. This is shit," Garwood said. "This is a waste of my fucking time."

Coolin waited.

"Crapola, Frankie. This is just crap. I'm sick of it, sick of this shit. You take us for fools, you know that. I hate that, I really do. You insult Gribbs, you insult me, a little while ago you were insulting my wife. I don't have to take this shit. I'm not going to take it. I'm going to get your ass, you little mick bastard, you smart son of a bitch, you'll be a great-grandfather when you get out."

"Is that right?"

"Count on it, you son of a bitch. You just sit there on that fucking radiator, you dirty fucking thief, you sit there and you think about Minnesota. You know how cold it gets there in Sandstone?"

"I know, I know. I told you before my uncle was there. He told me. He caught cold up there lots of times."

"That's what you get when you leave the windows open," said Garwood.

"Just like the shines."

Gribbs pressed. "Your kids, Frankie, you got to think about them. Your daughter, the boy at DePaul, wants to go to law school. I hate to think about them, how they're going to feel. They're going to be ashamed, you know? How's that going to make your boy feel?"

"I hope he feels bad if the time comes."

Garwood made a noise in his throat that was half a snarl. "The time is coming. It ain't if, Frankie, it's when. You're bringing it on yourself."

"Well, I hope that doesn't happen. I'd feel bad."

Garwood blinked. "You're right, Coolin. You're going to feel bad."

"I don't know what you want me to say."

"Sure you do."

"No. You know that. You know I got nothing to say. You know more about it than me and you know I got nothing to say."

Gribbs shook his head sadly. "Stand-up guy. You think someone's going to put up a statue for you for being a stand-up guy? Noble, Frankie. You're noble."

"I try to do the right thing."

"Shit," said Garwood.

"How long?" Coolin said. He said it softly.

Gribbs seemed startled and stared at Frankie's dark eyes, which were partly hidden by the shade from the baseball cap.

"I mean, how long do I got? I got things to do, to set up."

"What are you talking about?"

"Garwood says there's nothing I can do about it so when are you coming down? When is it going down?"

Gribbs made his face flat again. "What are you talking about?"

"Time. When does it come down on me?"

Garwood smiled for the first time. "You know we don't tell you anything. It doesn't work that way. You talk and we listen."

"Yeah. Thanks."

Garwood kept smiling. "It might be next week or maybe next year. Maybe in a couple of months. Maybe December. You aren't going to know until you see the guys waiting for you in the driveway."

"Nice. You do it at the house? Nice. A class act, come up the street, right to my house."

"You could avoid all this."

"You know I can't."

Garwood said, "We usually come right to the house, see the family, the kids, the neighbors. We try to get you at home because that's the best place, a guy doesn't want to start shit right in his own home. Maybe the neighbors see it but that can't be helped. Cuffs. When we put the cuffs on, you belong to us."

"When they wantcha, they gotcha."

"That's it, Coolin."

"I can't handle it."

"Come down and talk to the Attorney. Make your deal."

Quietly: "I can't."

"We could figure out a way. We have the Federal Witness Program."

"Sure."

"We could help you."

"No. You couldn't help me."

Gribbs buttoned his suit coat. "You want it that way, Frankie, that's the way it's going to go."

"You know I don't want it that way."

Gribbs shrugged.

Garwood pushed open the outside door. The street was in shade now, cold and bare and ugly. Damp clouds clotted the sky.

The G walked down the steps of the wooden stoop to the broken sidewalk.

Light, fading in afternoon, danced briefly on the broken glass of a smashed whiskey bottle on the bare, black dirt parkway between the walk and the street. The parkway was festooned with dried dog droppings.

They got in their white Pontiac and started away and Coolin watched them through the open door, sitting on the radiator in the bare hall.

Typical. Typical G. Dull bastards.

And hard. Don't forget hard. Harder than they had to be because nothing could stop them. When they wantcha, they gotcha. Nothing to stop them.

2

"Game over early?"

"I left in the sixth."

"They win?"

"No."

"Figures. Gimme a smoke."

Joey extended his pack of Lucky Strikes to Frankie Coolin.

It was four P.M. and they were sitting in the middle of the bar which was rapidly filling with customers. Most of the men —and they were all men—were dressed like Frankie, in flannel shirts and Levi's and steel-toed boots. Their eyes looked tired and bloodshot and their faces were colored red by sun and wind. The bar was not very dark; it smelled of stale beer and stale cigarette smoke. The once-white ceiling panels were stained yellow, like teeth. The dark plastic paneling was greasy to the touch. Behind the bar, along its length, a dark and dusty mirror reflected their faces as they drank beer.

The Bohemian waddled down the back of the bar, over the wooden slats on the floor, holding a foaming glass of beer in his left hand. He put it in front of Frankie on a green Old Style coaster and absently scooped up change from the pile of bills and coins in front of Joey.

Joey smiled as he lit a cigarette. It was an old, nearly unconscious trick of Frankie's: his uncle never put money on the bar unless someone asked him to do it.

Coolin took half the glass in a long swallow that made the back of his throat cold and tingling.

"What score, Joey?"

"Three zip down. Kingman strikes out in the fifth with the bases loaded. Same old shit, another year down the toilet. They ought to back up the truck next year, you know that? Get rid of some of these guys. Hey, I had a good seat, down in the lower boxes, right over the first base dugout. It turns out the usher down in that section was Larry O'Neill. You remember who I mean?"

"Larry? You mean John D.'s kid? He's an usher down at the park? That's a skirt job, ain't it? Why doesn't he go to work helping out his old man, the poor old bastard."

"He says he was going to college, I was talking to him. He's in Loyola."

"I was going to say, if he was in DePaul, maybe Mick knew him."

"Yeah. Anyway, there was tons of empty seats so I took one. Jesus, it was cold out there for drinking beer."

"Aw, Christ, I'm sorry to hear it, Joey. I really feel bad about that. I was nice and warm in the building pulling radiators which you were going to help me on. I should have gone in your place so you could have watched the game someplace warm, on television."

"Fuck, Uncle Frank, I didn't know you were pulling radiators today, I would have helped you."

"Come on, Joey, what do you think? You think I was going down there to pull my wand?"

"O'Neill says he's been working all the Cubs games but I never seen him."

"I wish he was working the Bears game, he say anything about that? I gotta get an in somewhere, I need an arrangement since they expanded the seating at Soldier Field; shit, I'm sitting up now where you get nosebleeds, you need oxygen up there."

The Schlitz beer clock on the chain from the ceiling spun slowly above the bar top. It read 4:15, which meant it was really 4:05. Most of the regulars were in the place now and the bar was filled with voices and smoke. They sat on backless barstools of red leather and chrome legs, hugging the seats with big butts, leaning with elbows extended on the bar top for support in the usual stance of beer drinkers. Their red faces got more red; smoke worked its way up to the ceiling and hung there.

"You gonna stiff me tomorrow too?"

"I'll be there, Uncle Frank. I just wanted to catch the last game."

"We got two more radiators to take out and then we can

finish the painting. I did some plastering on the first floor on the south side. Hey, I went out to the truck to get my other six-pack about two this afternoon, I was watching that house, you know the one I guessed was a whorehouse? I saw the pimp coming out and I'm watching him, he's humbugging up and down the street; what an asshole. He was looking for his mama, I seen her leave about ten, I think she blew him off."

Joey blushed and Coolin smiled.

There was a joke between them about Joey's alleged virginity. Coolin had told his brother, John, that his son was still unfucked. John Coolin, the roofer with the bad heart, had pointed out that Joey was just a kid. It was true. Joey was just twenty with big shoulders and big hands and a broad face that made him look older. The Bohemian had never carded him, from the first day.

Coolin said, "I could make a deal with the shine pimp for you." He slid his glass forward across the bar and the Bohemian took it to the tap.

"I don't want to fuck no nigger broad."

"They're the best."

Joey grinned again.

"I'm telling you, Joey. I've had them all. The best. I think you're just prejudiced."

Joey kept grinning and blew out the smoke of his Lucky. Coolin took the fresh glass of beer from the Bohemian.

The Bo kept the glasses clean and served decent corned-beef sandwiches at lunch but everything else in the place showed signs of neglect. The previous owner had left a stuffed owl on the back wall which was now perched over the Stroh's beer sign. The Bo had a cat, a black and white tabby named Kaiser, who took a nip out of the owl from time to time and the owl was a little bare in places. Kaiser killed mice in the basement and sometimes bigger game. The Bohemian had asked Coolin to lay a patch of cement in the basement two winters ago during Frankie's slow time. Coolin had gone down the basement steps to survey the job and come upon four rats sitting on the foundation ledge near the front wall. He returned upstairs without a word and gave the Bo a price. Normally, he would have turned down the job because he didn't want to mess with rats but this was his home bar—his wife, Rose, said it was his home—and it would have made it bad between them to refuse the Bo. He made the price high but the Bo agreed to it. Coolin then got off the hook by farming the job to his son-in-law, the one married to Rose Two (as she was called). Andy was a cement finisher by trade and did the job without complaint. Coolin took twenty percent off the top as contractor. Once Andy spoke quietly about the rats and Coolin said all rats were cowards and if you whacked one with a shovel, the others would know you meant business and leave you alone. Until the job was done, Coolin avoided his son-in-law. And the bar, which was harder.

Coolin tasted his second glass of beer and stared across the bar top at the dusty, dark mirror. He saw tired eyes. And he saw they were afraid. For a moment, he yearned to talk about it all with Joey or the Bohunk. Just a moment.

"You been here long?" he said instead.

Joey looked up at the beer clock and waited for the clock face to come into view. "Twenty, thirty minutes."

"You seen Pat Kennedy?"

"Naw."

"Hey, Emil," Coolin said to the Bohemian. "You seen Pat Kennedy in here today?"

"Yer cousin?"

"He ain't my cousin but that's the one."

"You could of meant Kennedy the oil man."

"Not that Kennedy. Pat."

"Kennedy names are all the same to me. He was in at lunch, I think. Maybe it was yesterday. No, today's meatball sandwiches so it was today because he had a meatball sandwich."

Emil the Bohemian had an accent like gravel poured down a chute, rough and rasping and relentless. He claimed he was a native-born American from Berwyn but no one believed anything he said.

"He say he was coming by tonight?"

"What am I, his secretary?"

"I thought he'd say, you got nothing but time on your hands."

"He didn't say."

"When's the pool open?"

"Soon as I finish the lines."

Emil was drawing squares on a piece of posterboard for the weekly football pool on the Bears game.

Joey said, "What d'ya want to see Kennedy for?"

"I got business."

"I hate painting the worst. I thought you were going to be painting today."

"Naw, I got to get the radiators out first, I told you, or I just gotta go back in and finish around them. You should see the paint I got. The shines are going to be in shine heaven. I got twenty gallons of paint off Nolan by his warehouse, this is all pink and bright blue, it looks like it would give off sparks. He says it fell off a truck and to make sure, he put dents in some of the cans but it was good stuff, Sherwin-Williams, the best; I got it for three bucks a gallon. If Nolan'd had any other colors but pink and blue, I would have brought some by the house for Rose, we need to paint the bathrooms."

Joey stared at his beer. "I really hate painting. It's the one thing I hate. Dumb, you know?"

"Everything's dumb, tell me about it."

"Well, I told you I was going to help so when are you going to be by tomorrow morning?"

"I'll be by around seven."

"Which means you'll be by around eight."

"No, Joey, I got to hustle tomorrow, big day tomorrow. Big plans." Coolin tasted the beer. He only drank beer and maybe a glass of wine at Christmas. He drank beer all day long when he could but he never looked drunk. He once told Rose he needed beer because there wasn't enough white blood cells in his system and the beer made up for it. He thought she believed him.

"You got to hustle? What does that mean, Uncle Frank? You got to hustle means you're sticking me with the painting, don't it?"

"When did I stick you? I ain't going to stick you." In fact, he was. He had hustled a plastering job in a private home weeks before but the old woman who owned the place wouldn't give him an advance against the job until he actually started the job and right now he needed cash. He would stick

Joey in the ghetto building and handle the plaster job in the morning.

"Look, I told you I don't want to be in a shine neighborhood alone when you're out drivin' around."

"Come on, Joey. You think they're going to bother you? They don't bother me. You got a worse neighborhood up around Wrigley Field where you were in today. I work in a shine neighborhood before I work with the hillbillies and porkies. How long I own my buildings down on the West Side? I never had no trouble except that once and that wasn't trouble. Look, I even was doing work during the riots. Tomorrow morning, I'll level with you, I got to go downtown, there's going to be a good winter job coming up at the VA hospital and I got to talk to Connors about it because he's subcontracting right now. He's gonna get me in for the winter. Hell, I'll get you in too. It's an investment for you, Joey."

"Inside job."

"Warm, inside—with nurses."

Joey grinned. "How long?"

"Half an hour tops. I'm meeting him at Mitchell's on Jackson, cup of coffee, we talk and set it up and I'm back."

"You never did nothing in a half an hour in your life."

"Swear to God, Joey, I got to meet him at ten." Frankie Coolin's voice was flat with sincerity, unemotional, as though he expected misunderstandings. "I drop you by the building and we get a start on the third floor, pull out the last radiators, and I go downtown and do my thing. I'll be back by at eleven and we can break around one or two. I gotta show you this shine place on Crawford, you get ribs there. We can have some beer, ribs, only shines can make ribs, you know?"

Joey grinned again. "You're crazy drinking in a shine tavern."

"Hey, they don't bother me. They ist my brothers."

"You look like it."

"Maybe we get you laid tomorrow after work."

"Aw. Come on."

"OK?"

"Sure. You talk big. But don't stick me all day in the joint by myself like you did that time."

"What happened that time? Nothing happened. I pick you

up at séven and we come by here and get some beer and ice for the cooler and we go out. I'll even leave you my piece, I'm only going to be gone a half hour."

"OK. But don't stick me," Joey said, already resigned to it. He signaled for another glass of Old Style beer.

Coolin's piece was a .357 Colt Python six-shot revolver which he kept under the seat in the truck. He had moved it for the truck inspection that morning, which is why he had found his lost White Sox cap. He had picked up the piece from a guy on Taylor Street after he was hijacked one night off the Eisenhower Expressway on the West Side six years ago. It was winter and he had been working at a winter job for Salvatori Brothers and he was trying to find a restaurant address to dump a load of beef. Two kids had jumped on the running boards and they both had pieces and acted very hard. He let them take him, take all the money, take the truck and the meat. The worst part had been explaining this to Gino Salvatori who didn't believe him because he had known Frankie Coolin from the old neighborhood when they were both city street kids. He had sweated out the story until the cops stopped the kids two days later when they were knocking over another truck. Frankie had sweated because the Salvatori Brothers had friends and relations in the Outfit and trying to convince Gino that he didn't jack the meat himself was not working—after all, Gino knew Frankie. After that, he had asked his wife's brother's cousin to get him a good piece but the obscure relative, who was a cop in the Deering district in Bridgeport on the South Side, tried to dump a hot pistol on him. He picked up his piece from a reliable source that Gino Salvatori steered him to. After he got the piece, he had practiced with it one night, shooting out lamps on Fifth Avenue in the West Side. And one night, about three years ago, he had come to use it. He never told anyone about that.

"You think the brothers are going to come into the building and eat you?" Coolin smiled, suddenly playful.

"I just don't like them, that's all. I'm prejudiced."

"Nothing wrong with that. They don't like you. But you got the problem that you grew up in the suburbs and you think the shines are some kind of bad dream. You never seen one, you never talked to one. You never even seen one till I took you down to the city to work."

"What do you mean, I never seen one? I seen plenty."

"Kids come out of the suburbs, they either get afraid of them or in love with them. Keep it simple in your mind, Joey. Nobody likes shines and shines don't like nobody. They don't like me in my building and I don't like them. We respect each other, but they ain't afraid and I ain't afraid. I don't want to hear you talking about being afraid of them. You want to be in the trades, you got to work in the shine neighborhoods, that's all. You ain't never going to make no money out here pouring sidewalks for some old Bohemian. You want to hustle, you gotta take a chance. You never even had a black piece of ass, right? I told you—"

"I don't want to hear this stuff."

"Hey, we could set up a jar behind the bar, take up a collection for you to get your first blow job."

"I told you—"

"Make it a pickle jar. If everything else fails, you can use the pickle." He laughed.

"That's all bullshit, Uncle Frank, you know that. I just don't like to get stuck in the building. You get in a tavern somewhere and get all beaned up and you forget that I'm out there."

"I'll leave you my radio with the beer. In case you gotta spend the night."

"You think it's funny."

"Listen, I take a laugh when I can get it."

"Don't stick me."

"Trust me."

This time Joey laughed as well.

Emil the Bohemian brought two more beers and looked at the bar for change. It was gone. He looked from one to the other. His face was pasty and dark and his eyes were startling in their clarity and blue color. It was as though someone else's eyes had been set in a tired, old man's face.

"You never buy a drink, Emil, or what?" asked Frankie Coolin.

"Look who talks. How about you? You never buy. You make the kid here buy all the time."

"The trouble with you Bohunks is you got moths in your purse, you should let them out sometimes for air."

"This is a business. Who pays?"

"Hey, Joey. Can you get it? I left my wallet in the truck."

"Hey, who elected me chump?"

"We all did. It was a secret vote."

Joey laughed and pulled a five out of his old leather wallet.

Frankie said, "Hey, make change for a dollar, I gotta make a call."

"Christ. Is there anything else I can do for you? You want me to take a piss for you too?"

"Later. I can always hold it for the first five beers."

Emil dumped change on the counter. Frankie took four dimes and went to the rear of the tavern. There was a single green-sided pay telephone mounted on the dirty plastic paneling near the lavatories. The doors of the lavatories were marked "Kings" and "Queens." Piles of Old Style beer cases formed a cardboard telephone booth around both sides of the phone and made it private.

On the wall above the phone was a schedule of White Sox games for the year. The schedule was used as a scratch pad. It contained bits of phone numbers, an occasional comment on life, and an offer from Mary to perform sexual acts.

Coolin dropped twenty cents into the machine and punched out the numbers he knew so well.

"Yeah."

The voice, a woman's, was guarded as always.

"Kennedy there? This is Frank Coolin."

Silence. In the background, a television set was tuned to an afternoon children's program. Steps in the background, muffled sounds, and then a male voice, deep and suspicious.

"Yeah?"

"Frankie."

"Yeah, whaddaya want?"

"I want to talk to you."

"It's your dime."

"I don't want to talk on the phone."

"Oh." Pause. "I gotta go over by the high school because my kid's practicing in football. I was gonna drop over and watch. Why'n't you come out and see him play."

"What the fuck I wanta watch your kid play football? This is important."

"Hey, fuck you, right? I got things to do. I tole Tommy I was gonna see him practice, I'm gonna see him practice, you wanta see me, you know where I'm gonna be."

This was wrong. Coolin felt the anger in his gut but it was wrong. Oil on waters, he thought.

"Hey, I didn't know Tommy made the team."

"Freshman. Decided he wanted to go out and the coach says he's got what it takes. I guess I didn't tell you that when I seen you but I thought you knew that."

"I ain't seen you for a while, Pat."

"Yeah, well this is my busy time. I was by the Bo's today for lunch, I had a meatball sandwich. He raised the price on them again, the sandwich, and I don't give a shit what you say, that son of a bitch has got more cereal in those meatballs than he's got meat."

"Yeah. Yeah. Well, I been busy too, I'm in the joint now."

"Is that right? Tommy is playing middle lineback on defense."

"Terrific, Pat. You'll be saving up for knee scans."

"Yeah, well, I know you had some problems with Mick but Tommy's OK, he's strong, you know. He wants to play, he plays, that's the way I figure it. I was a kid, who had time to go out for football? You hadda hustle. I was working when I was his age."

Coolin closed his eyes. Pat Kennedy talked about his childhood as though he were the only man who had ever had to work when he was a kid. It was a moral position with him and he wasn't interested in anyone else's story.

"But money," Pat went on. "They want you to cough up, you know, that fucking school? Fuck. This is the last one I send to a Catholic school, they practically want you to pay for a chance to take a piss between classes and that's not counting what they shake you down for for the building drive and for Christmas and all that. Last one, I told my wife that. I don't care if they got to go to school with shines, I don't care if they turn out atheists I told her, I ain't dropping money down a rathole just so that some nun can get up and start telling them to love their colored brother or something. You pay to shit, I swear to God, and where does it get you? You send your kid to school and one day he comes home and tells you swearing is a sin. Or he comes home and asks if it's okay if he can bring some jig down to the house on Saturday. I told Maureen that when she came up with that shit, I said the day a fucking nigger crosses that door, is the day I burn the fucking house down and I mean it."

"Well, that's the way kids are nowadays."

"Not while they eat my bread, they aren't. They love niggers so much, they can go to school with them over at the high school where they bus them in, and it won't cost me nothing."

"Everything costs money, Kennedy. I'd like to organize a tag day for you but I got my own problems."

"Yeah. Well, you got two in the Catholic schools yourself."

"College, Pat. That's a different game with Mick in college. You pay, I pay, everyone pays but college is the majors, Pat."

"Not the jigs, Frankie, not the jigs. They got shines on the fucking freshman team with Tommy, you think they ain't got a scholarship? You tell me where a jig gets the money to go to that school and I'll kiss your ass at high noon."

"Enough about them, I been with them all day, I want to talk about the other thing, Pat. I got to see you."

"Yeah." Pause. "Well, you know where to find me. I'm going by the high school in a half an hour."

"I'll meet you there. You be there now."

"Yeah." They broke the connection without another word.

Coolin's stomach started to rumble and he forced a belch. It was Kennedy. Kennedy was an asshole, he thought.

He put more coins in the slot and punched another number.

"Coolin residence." The voice sounded like a wind chime.

The trouble with Rose was that she kept living more and more in a dream world. Now she was saying things like "Coolin residence" on the phone and she started calling supper "dinner" and the icebox "the refrigerator." They had known each other all their lives, coming from the same West Side neighborhood, coming from the same class of tenement Irish without lace curtains. But Rose didn't believe that anymore. Slowly, over the years, she had made another world that was precise and polite and kind and full of family warmth. There was nothing wrong with it except that it did not exist. She made Coolin feel helpless when he was trapped in her fantasy.

"Me," he said.

"Oh," she said. Rose seemed surprised by his calls though he had called her all his life. "You want your messages?"

"Anything important?"

"There was a woman who called, I think she called before, about a plastering job."

"Yeah, I know about that, I'm taking care of that tomorrow. That's taken care of. Anything else?"

"No, not really. The *Tribune* called and they want us to subscribe to the paper, you want to subscribe again?"

"Hell, no. That goddam paperboy was dropping the paper off at noon."

"It's nice to have a paper."

"You want a paper, get a paper."

"Well, I wanted to know if you wanted a paper."

"I get the paper on my way down."

"OK."

"I won't be home for supper."

"I can hold it. I made chops and sauerkraut. You want a potato with it?"

"I got to see a guy. You can keep the chops in the oven for me. You get the chops at the store or from Gino?"

"Gino. You told me."

"Yeah. I got to see a guy. Everything OK, then? The kids OK? The old man?"

"Yes. Everything."

They waited and listened to the silence buzzing on the line.

Another big talker, Coolin thought. You think no one ever used a phone before. Take an Irishman out of a bar and he clams up. Like Kennedy. Like Rose. They think phones are tricks.

"Well, I'll be by around seven, maybe."

"Okay," she said.

Suddenly, in the silence of that moment, he wanted to tell her.

He closed his eyes instead, hidden in the cardboard alcove formed by the Old Style beer cases. He wanted to cry and tell her that two G had come around again, for the fifth time, that this matter was hanging over him and it was getting worse, like cancer. He wanted to tell her but she couldn't have done anything, she would have just worried and that would have made two of them. He wanted to tell her so that she would hold him and soothe him and say it was all right. He kept his eyes closed because he felt there were tears behind them.

Man, I don't want to do no time.

"Frank? Is everything all right?"

"Sure." There, the voice was all right; for a moment, he was afraid he would not be able to talk to her. "I got hold of Joey, I'm taking him down with me in the morning."

"Good," she said.

"If we're lucky, we'll be finished next week."

"Good," she said.

Good. Hi. Fine. Yeah. Nobody talked. He came to the tavern for talk and everyone watched the baseball game. Sometimes he thought everyone was going dumb.

"I'll see you when I see you."

"OK."

Pause.

"Frank?"

"What?"

"Nothing." Another pause. "I'll see you when you come home."

"Anything wrong?"

"No. Nothing."

For a moment, he felt they were both lying to each other, but it would never be solved on the phone. They broke the connection.

When Coolin returned to the bar, Joey had taken his folding money off the bar top and left a small pile of change. Coolin's glass was half full and he finished it in two swallows, standing next to his stool. The bar was full and loud; it always got louder as the week neared an end. On Mondays, the bar was half empty and quiet.

"So, seven I'm coming around your house, Joey?"

"Yeah. Just honk, I'll be ready."

"How's the old roofer?"

"Same as always." Joey rarely talked about his father, John, who was Frankie Coolin's brother. And Frankie rarely brought

up John's name, as though there was a bond between uncle
and nephew that mention of the father's name broke.

"He feeling all right?"

"Yeah. Who knows? He had a job this week, doing some
work on a porch that was rotted out. I had to give him a hand
last night, he was fucking it up."

"John ain't no carpenter."

"He ain't no roofer neither."

Frankie stared at Joey for a moment, at the confident big
face and the frank Irish eyes staring out at him. He liked Joey
sometimes more than his own kid. Maybe not *liked* him more,
but felt closer to him, as if they were the same kind. It was too
bad about John; he had blown it a long time ago with his kid.

"OK, Joey. Say hello."

"Sure."

They hit the door together and crossed into the cinder-and-
gravel parking lot. The Bohemian's place was on a block of
homes, an existing zoning variance from the days when the
suburbs had been nearly rural.

Bullshit, all of it, Frankie Coolin thought as he climbed into
the rusty green Ford pickup and slammed the door. The only
clear place on the bench seat was where he sat. The rest of the
cab—seat, floor, dashboard—was littered with hundreds of
maps, odd sheets of paper with phone numbers scratched on
them, old newspapers and invoices and bills, shreds of Mc-
Donald's hamburger containers and empty Coke and beer
cans. He turned the key in the ignition and listened to the
engine grumble into life.

Fucking winter coming, he thought. He pushed the engine
into high idle for a moment and then pulled into first gear.

Winter. And all I do is bullshit with assholes.

Slowly he pulled out of the lot onto the shoulder of Butterfield Road. He waited for a break in the traffic and then moved
into the narrow and busy artery and headed west for Hillside,
through the town, under the expressway viaducts into DuPage
County.

Coolin had come here from the West Side of the city long
before, when the blacks swept through the old neighborhoods,
block by block, after the Second World War. The west suburbs

had grown up in a hurry after the war and they were visual extensions of the sprawl of Chicago now. It was quitting time in a dozen factories that lined Mannheim and Wolf roads and cars from the factories streamed into old, narrow suburban roadways that had been built for rural traffic. Overhead, in the darkening sky, minute by minute in relentless march, planes from O'Hare Field boomed above the rooftops.

He pushed the green Ford pickup into the parking lot next to the high school athletic field and climbed out. He had to slam the door twice to make the lock catch.

Pat Kennedy was there, standing on the near sidelines, looking like a coach in his brown felt hat and light nylon jacket. Frankie came beside him without a word and watched the scrimmage. Kennedy's kid was in the process of sacking the quarterback with a vicious and illegal pull across the throat.

"Looks like Dick Butkus looked, don't he?" said Pat Kennedy.

Light was fading fast. The western sky was streaked red and clear against the line of clouds overhead. The wind had a damp chill to it. The sounds of the jets whining up into the sky from O'Hare kept pounding.

"Look at that hit, is that a hit?"

Coolin stood next to Kennedy and stared across the field at the boys grunting and cursing and slamming into each other with all the joyful hatred of their flexible, youthful bodies.

"He's looking good, huh, Frankie?"

"He looks okay."

"OK? Your fucking ass OK. Fucking A he looks OK. He looks better'n OK."

"OK. What do you want me to say? He looks like Butkus? He don't look like Butkus."

"Sometimes you talk like an asshole."

In the next play, the quarterback threw a flat pass over the line and Kennedy's kid dumped him very hard. One of the coaches whistled and went over to the kid.

"Late hit," Coolin said.

"Late hit, my ass. They want to put skirts on the quarterback next." Kennedy was a fleshy Irishman with blue-green eyes and a big belly straining under the nylon jacket. He wore a small diamond ring on the little finger of his right hand and a gold wedding band on the appropriate finger of his left. His hands were soft.

"Why you think he blew the whistle on him, it wasn't a late hit? Jesus Christ, this is scrimmage, not the Super Bowl."

"You gotta play hard."

"Tell me about it."

"You don't know shit about football."

"Yeah. I forgot that I was the dope bet a C on the Bears last week and dropped it."

"Hey, they fucked up, I could of won. I had gone into the over-under on the game but I had it made and they fucked me up. The Bears don't got a quarterback, that's all there is to it."

"Kennedy, they didn't have no quarterback when the season started."

"Well, I got news for you. This is the year."

"Sure."

Again, they stood quietly. They heard the football sounds: pad against pad, breath delivered in grunts, shouts, bodies against bodies, feet thudding over the hard field.

"I hear you picked up another building."

"That was June."

"You got people in it?"

"No. I'm still working on it, I couldn't do it over the summer, I had some good jobs. I'm busting my balls."

"You gonna get it ready by winter?"

"I got the radiators out. I'm painting now, I got Joey to help me."

"How many radiators you got? Maybe I can do you some good on the radiators, I got a guy now looking for some pipe."

"I already got a guy."

"OK, fuck me, excuse me. I was doing you a favor."

"Is that right? You were doing me a favor?"

"What's that mean?"

"You know what it means, Pat."

"Things are tough all over, Frankie."

"Tell me. You're still driving that Buick, I see, that thing must have been invented by the Arabs."

"I get ten, eleven. Listen, I don't give a fuck what gas is. Gas can be five bucks a gallon, I give a fuck, I ain't going to drive a fucking Jap cheesebox. Them Jap cars, you hit one of them, they're like hitting wet toilet paper. Like those lanterns the slants make."

"I didn't say it wasn't a nice car. A Buick always was a nice car."

"Yeah. Hey, look at that, Frankie. The kid's got guts, ain't he?"

"He hits good. He's gotta watch the late hit is all because they'll come down after him, get the knees."

"Like Butkus."

"Like a lot of guys. Like Mick got hurt."

"He's a big kid."

"Butkus was a big kid. Mick had size on him."

"We're talking apples and oranges, for Christ's sake."

More silence. The lines hit again and again, with the sound of pad on pad, body on body, in the cool, darkening afternoon. Everything came together in the moment: sound, light, feeling, Frankie thought. Then, more whistles and the coach gathered them around for the afternoon sermon.

Kennedy looked at the ground for a second. "Well."

"Yeah. 'Well' is a good word. Two of them came down to the building today. This makes five times for me, Pat."

"Oh."

"Yeah. Oh. Another good word. They got very hard this time when they came to the commercial."

"That's the way they talk. They talk that way."

"Yeah, you're right about that, they talk that way. They were talking about Sandstone that way."

"They're just trying to scare you, Frankie."

"Is that right? Shit, I ought to bring all my problems to you, you see right through them. They're trying to scare me, Pat? Well, they're succeeding. I got scared, all right. You forget I went up to Minnesota when Brian came out. I saw him, I listened to him the whole time while we were driving back. He didn't even want to stop for a drink, for Christ's sake. He just kept whispering about it."

"God rest him. I saw Brian after he got out too. Brian was a very sick man, Frankie, even before he went in."

"Maybe so, but his health didn't get better inside the joint. What the fuck am I gonna do?"

"They mention me?"

"Yeah, your name came up."

"You bring it up?"

"No, they were talking about Flo-Thru and your dago pal."

Pat Kennedy looked across the athletic field at the players whooping around the coaches. On the other side of the field, a priest stood at the sidelines in an old-fashioned black cassock, his hands behind his back.

"They talk about what they were going to do?"

Frankie Coolin stared at him. "Sure, man, what the hell you think they were coming by for? They want your ass, they want your friend's ass, they want to take my ass too. We can have three-handed pinochle games in the day room when we head north."

"I ain't gonna go to no joint. I ain't gonna do no time for this, you believe it."

"Who is, then?"

"What'd they want you to do?"

"What do you think?"

"But what did you say?"

"What do you think I said?"

"I hope you were stand-up."

"Do you?"

"You were standing up. Wouldn't be good not to stand up."

"What are you going to do, give me a medal? Pat, what if they come down on me, what the hell am I gonna do?"

Kennedy looked at him. Kennedy's face was fleshy but pasty and cold, like a cold meat pie.

"Well, Frankie, maybe you got to think about that. Maybe we gotta face facts. What if they come down?"

"Face facts? Man, I'm forty-nine years old, I don't want no time no more than anyone does. What about Rose and Mick and Peg? What the hell would they do?"

"Who says anything about time? If they come down, fight it is all. This is a free country."

"Don't talk like a fucking alderman, Pat. Not to me. Save that civics shit for your kid."

"You got a mouth. Get a mouth for you."

"Lawyers eat too. What am I going to pay him with?"

"Get a, get a Public Defender."

"I want a P.D., I might as well plead. If I need a mouth, I want to win the fucking case."

"I know a guy."

"Hey, Pat. Am I still talking English or what? Am I coming through to you? I can hear my own voice but maybe it's not working right for you. I said what would I pay him with, not a name. Names are a dime a dozen. Even Mick is going to be a lawyer now, they let him in, they let anyone in. Pat, we are not talking about a DWI or fixing a parking ticket down at traffic court, we are talking the G, man. Feds. The real thing. We are not talking a thou to a shiny suit to fix a DWI."

"You're getting worked up."

"You oughta be worked up too. What are you on, Valium? You taking dope or what? That was your shit in my stall in the warehouse."

"You threatening me or what?"

"If I was threatening you, I'd knock you on your ass. You never were shit with your hands, Pat, not when you didn't have that gut on you and not now."

"I ain't worried about hands with you. I got friends."

"Everyone's got friends, you mick bastard. Don't lay shit on me."

He was hot again. He wanted to fight Pat Kennedy and punch him in the gut and watch his eyes go sick and then club him hard on the back of the head. He wanted to push the old man down and beat the shit out of him and pound that pasty face until it was filled with blood. As soon as he realized it, the moment passed. Rage became sick, gnawing fear.

This is serious, he wanted to scream, everyone is walking around in a daze and this is serious.

"This ain't getting us over our problem," is all Coolin said at last.

"You ain't part of it, Frankie."

"I sure the fuck didn't know what you were putting in the warehouse, if that's what you mean."

"You tell them that?"

"Tell them what?"

"That I was putting stuff in the warehouse."

"I didn't tell them anything."

"Don't tell them anything or you gonna have another problem."

"Don't get on that again, Pat. Don't get on it, will you?"

"They got diddle, Frankie. They talking indictments to you? They talking counts? They got shit, they're flapping their lips, they ain't gonna indict nothing."

"They want your Irish ass, Kennedy."

"They want all they want and they don't get nothing."

"If they wantcha, they gotcha."

"Yeah? Well, you keep your fucking mouth shut about everything. I guess maybe you want me to say that to you, is that right? OK. I said it. Open your fucking mouth and you'll get a plaster asshole."

"You want to talk cheap threats, you fat turkey, you go ahead. You play hard on me, your son will be working to support his crippled father because I'll drop you like a bird drops shit. So fuck you and your talk. I got to get a handle on this, I figure you got some ideas, I come over to talk to you and I get gangster dialogue. What kind of cheap shit is this?"

"You got a mouth on you, Frankie, you keep it up and you ain't going to do yourself any good."

"You said there was no problem, I just keep my mouth shut and rent the space. And then your kraut friend torches his own fucking warehouse and I'm sitting there with shit on my face and you tell me to keep grinning."

"I'm going to take care of that heinie bastard too."

"You couldn't take care of a load of shit in plastic bags."

"Some people are already talking to Kostner. I don't want them to talk to you."

Kostner owned the warehouse. Everyone knew he had the place done but you can't prove arson. Kostner said he didn't know nothing about anything except that Coolin had rented the space on the fourth floor where the firemen found the Sonys. If the torch had been done right in the first place, no one would have found anything. Coolin had told Kennedy that all his life he had dealt with mental cripples and now he was being screwed by a jerk who couldn't even torch his own joint.

"Look. I got the name of a lawyer from downtown. You want a name?"

Coolin said, "Who?"

"Guy named Klein. Arthur Klein."

"A kraut?"

"A Jew."

"That's better."

"You want to make a city fix, get a mick lawyer. You want to make a federal fix, get a Jew. This guy is very recommended."

"Recommendations are things you get on credit applications. Is he gonna get me off?"

"Hey, Frankie, one thing at a time, you don't know what's going to happen in the first place. You know there ain't no sure thing with the G. They come down with fifty or sixty counts down at you, what the hell can I do about it? You can take some time if it comes to it. The family is going to help you out, you know that in front. You're tough, Frankie, you always were tough even when you were playing football when we were kids. I always said you were tough. You could take time, you know you could take time. This isn't like Brian, Brian was a sick man and he was a lot older than you. You ain't sick."

"And I ain't crazy. The next thing you do, you're going to sell me life insurance. If I had a nickel for every time you try a cheap hustle on me, I'd own Butterfield Road. I come here because this is not a game, this is the fifth fucking time the G comes around to me and they aren't running a credit check. You tell me shit like take it easy, what's a little time in the joint, I can stand a fall, I can take it. Fuck that shit. Those weren't even my TV sets. What do I got? I got a Motorola at home, so fucking old all I can get is black and white reruns on it. You think maybe some day I don't want a Space Command, sit in my chair at home and turn the dial without even getting up, like they got in the tavern? No, I don't have it, I don't have nothing. What I got is a set fifteen years old, the kids are ashamed to watch it. You got a fucking house full of television sets, I'm surprised you're not blind, you drive that fucking Buick deuce-and-a-quarter like a shine pimp. What do I get? You think Frankie Coolin is just a dumb turkey down in the trench, fuck him, right? He don't want nothing, he can do time. Well, think again. I got that blind old man down in the basement always banging on the basement ceiling with his stick and two kids in Catholic schools, fucking college for Mick and now he wants to go to be a lawyer. You bitch about high school, about how much it costs, wait till you send your kid to college. But I'm the chump, right? 'Take the heat, Frankie, you can handle it, you can get used to it.' You sound like a doctor telling me it ain't so bad to die. You ain't like me, are you, Kennedy? You got your fat gut and pinkie ring and fucking car. Well, you ain't class with all the rings in China. You tell me I can take time? I can tell you that you are a fuck-nosed pussy if you think I'm sticking for it."

"You got a half a thou out of it."

"Why don't you say five bills, it sounds like less?"

"Plus your rent you got for the space in the warehouse. I said I had to store some stuff, you didn't want to ask me questions about it. You're no virgin, Frankie, you been laid before."

"Which is why I know when I'm being fucked."

"Look, we both got fucked up by Kostner. I put my shit in and you put your shit in and he does a torch."

"Hey, Pat—"

"Knock it off, Frankie, knock it off. Tommy's coming over. Don't say nothing in front of the kid."

The kid was big, all right. Dusk had stolen up on them. The planes were still spinning out into the sky like shuffled cards.

Pat Kennedy said, "What'd the coach say to you?"

"He says I was hitting late."

"That's shit."

"Yeah. See me when I nailed that fucking queer quarterback?"

"Watch your mouth, Tommy. What the hell you using language like that for? You see, Frankie, the way it is? Catholic school, they talk like dagoes. Yeah, I seen it, Tommy, and you keep on doing it. If you don't hit them first and hit them hard, pretty soon the coach says to himself that you ain't doing the job. You gotta give a hundred ten percent because nobody else is going to give it to you unless you take it."

Bullshit, Frankie Coolin thought. Everyone wants to bullshit. Nobody wants to face up to it. He stared at Tommy Kennedy and saw the mean pig eyes set in the flesh of another pasty Kennedy face. The kid ate like a pig as well; he had watched him at Andy and Rose Two's wedding last year.

All Frankie said was, "You got speed for your size, Tom. How much you go now?"

"Hunnert twenty."

"Hunnert twenty and you're just a freshman. Man, you got speed for that size. You gotta watch for the blindside hit, I saw you play in eighth grade, you lay on the quarterback too much. Like your old man says, you got to go after it but you can't get them mad, they're going to cut you. This is just practice. Save it for the big one."

"Yeah, just like they got Butkus. You look like Butkus out there," said Pat Kennedy.

"Who the hell is that?" Tommy said.

"Butkus," Coolin said. "He played middle linebacker for the Bears. For Christ's sake, you must of heard of Dick Butkus."

"Oh, yeah. I saw the guy on the beer commercial."

"Frankie, we gotta head home, Ma's waiting supper for us. You want that name again, the guy we were talking about?"

"Yeah. Sure. I guess so. This is a good name, Pat?"

"Gold," said Kennedy. "On LaSalle Street downtown. A very heavy guy. Art Klein. Arthur Klein."

"I never heard of him."

"Well, he ain't running for office so maybe that's it or maybe you never needed him before."

"Thanks," said Frankie Coolin. There was a bitter edge to the word. Pat only smiled and gave a little wave with the pinkie ring hand and the boy clumped after him in cleats across the parking lot. Coolin stood and watched them. The boy sat on the bumper of the car and took off his cleats. Then Pat Kennedy said something to him and started back to Coolin.

"Don't call me no more. Maybe they got my phone wired."

"I thought of that."

"I mean it. You gotta get me, leave it with the Bohunk for when I come in and I'll call you."

"You think they don't have my phone wired too?"

"Well, we could arrange a meet."

"Fuck it."

"Come on. Don't be that way, Frankie. I was just fucking around with you before. If you can't fuck around with your family, who can you fuck around with?"

"I ain't family to you, you're Rose's cousin."

"Well, same thing." Pat shuffled his little feet and shoved his hands deeper into the pockets of his trousers. "Hey, I know what I wanted to say to you. You want some cheese?"

"What?"

"Cheese. I got a contact, this guy is a wholesaler. He's got some of the best cheddar you ever seen, not that shit you get in the grocery, this is the real stuff. They make it in Wisconsin, see, but they ship it to New York to age it, they call it New York sharp cheddar but that don't mean anything because they make it in Wisconsin. This is aged eighteen months, I ain't shitting you, this is really good stuff. I like cheese, I was talking to him, I met him at the Bo's. You like cheese?"

"How much?"

"Buck fifty a pound. Beat it."

"It's a good price. How much do you pay?"

"Buck fifty, same as you. I'm trying to do you a favor is all. The thing is, though, you gotta take a catch weight on it, might be fifteen pounds, he said."

"Fifteen pounds? What the hell am I gonna do with fifteen pounds of cheese?"

"You got a family, you got mouths to feed."

"Fifteen pounds feeds a lot of mouths."

"OK, Frankie. It's nothing to me. I was just mentioning it."

"Buck fifty. I wonder what he gets it for."

"You don't want to ask."

"Doesn't sound bad."

"Doesn't sound bad? You know how much cheese, just ordinary cheese like the shit you get in the grocery goes for?"

"How do I get it if I get it?"

"You tell me, I'll tell him and I'll drop it off by the tavern and leave it in the Bohunk's cooler."

"Maybe once. All right, I'll go for it once. Now, don't go no twenty, thirty pounds on me."

"Might be fifteen, sixteen, might be fourteen, thirteen. He said. Around there anyway. You see, it's a catch weight."

"When you gonna drop it?"

"This is Thursday, I see the guy tomorrow if I see him, he could have it to me Monday and I'll put it in the cooler."

"OK. I'll see what I can do with the stuff."

"You pay me when you get it. I'll pay him in front."

"Sure." Coolin was thinking about Willie Oboe. Willie lived in the top apartment in the first building he owned. Willie was a minister on Sundays and a hustler during the week when he wasn't working at the post office. And Willie wasn't working at the post office even when he was there. Willie could hustle the stuff for three bucks a pound and Coolin could sell it to him for $2.20. Maybe.

One year, by accident, he got hold of a pallet full of cartons of toilet paper. Six hundred rolls. He sold it all, mostly through Willie Oboe. Rose said she couldn't use any of it because it wasn't soft enough and because it was all white and didn't go with the bathrooms. Frankie pointed out to Rose at the time that the old man who used one of the bathrooms was blind but Rose had already put it out of her mind.

"OK. Frankie, I'll see you around. Don't get so worried about everything. You gonna worry every time a cop hassles you, you ought to be doing something else."

"They haven't talked to you, I can't understand it."

"They did, they did, they came around two months ago and the first thing I did was I called my lawyer. You don't have to fuck around with these guys, you gotta do things smart when you're in business. I got a lawyer, I got an accountant, I got things set up."

"You're a living example to me, Pat."

"Well, you got to get things set up, too."

"Yeah. I got to do that. You think I could get a secretary to ride out with me on the job and keep my appointments straight for me? You think? Of course, she'd have to sit in the bed of the truck because I keep all my important papers on the front seat."

"Don't forget the name I give you. Arthur Klein. I'll even call him myself in the morning. You go down to see him."

"Yeah, sure, fine."

"Take it easy, Frankie."

"Yeah."

"And I'll get that cheese."

"Yeah. Fine."

He watched Pat walk away and climb in the car. Pat was short and he had a booster cushion in the car so that he could ride tall. He claimed it was for hemorrhoids. Coolin watched the car pull slowly out of the lot.

He felt sick, maybe it was the beer, maybe he had forgotten to eat lunch. He opened the truck door and slid inside, pushing away the sandwich wrappers that had slipped into the cleared spot.

For a moment, he just sat there, resting his big hands on the steering wheel and gazing at the green of the hood, staring into the dusty finish as though it were a crystal ball. Kennedy wasn't worried, nobody was worried. The world was spinning along and everyone was whistling. Except Frankie Coolin.

He turned the key in the ignition and listened to the engine shake into life. He eased the gear into reverse and pulled back in a slow circle, then pushed it into drive and shot forward to the edge of the road. He waited for traffic to part.

And then, in the dusky light, he saw them. Across the street. In a Pontiac Firebird colored white.

Two men in two suits alike without hats, one gray and one brown. Sitting in the front seat, watching him. G.

3

Rose's Pinto wagon was in the driveway when he got home, so he had to park the green pickup on the street in front of the brick bungalow. The village had an overnight parking ban so he would have to move the truck later; maybe he would use the excuse to go to the tavern for a beer and a little talk. Maybe he'd just come out and drive west until morning and never come back.

Frankie Coolin slammed the truck door twice to catch the lock and trudged across the uncut lawn to the front door. For the hundredth time that brief summer, he noticed the storm door didn't fit snugly in the frame any more. Everything had to be fixed by winter.

He unlocked the door and went into the front hall and then left into the living room where the sounds of the television set came from. Peggy was in the big armchair and Mick was slumping on the couch. Howard Cosell's voice boomed from the set.

They didn't greet him when he entered the room; Frankie sat down on the edge of the glass-topped coffee table and looked at the screen. "You think you guys could turn the sound up? I don't think Gilleys' across the street can hear it."

Mick made a face and didn't move. Peg stared at the screen. Frankie reached over and turned the knob down and Cosell faded.

"I wish we could get a second set. I want to watch what I want to watch," Peg said. She was sixteen and not pretty. She watched television a lot.

"Life is hard," Frankie Coolin said. He took off his baseball cap and threw it down on the coffee table next to him. His eyes did not leave the screen. The two teams lined up and the ball was snapped into play.

"I didn't know there was a game tonight. How come?"

"Lions and Jets."

"Who's up?"

"Lions fourteen-zip over the Jets in the second," Mick said. "You watch this guy Sims, he's got some good moves. He's light. They got an awesome team this year."

Awesome. It was the current word for football. Mick knew the slang. He played high-school ball until he tore the left knee. The coach told Frankie Coolin it was too bad because Mick might have gotten a college scholarship out of football. Coach was right; it was too bad. The doctors and hospital collected three grand from Coolin because he wasn't carrying his own hospitalization at the time.

"I mean it," Peg said. "I don't know why I don't have the choice sometime. I don't get a vote to watch what I want to watch."

"This isn't a democracy," Mick said in that little smartass voice that got on Frankie's nerves. He had developed the voice in the past year. He'll grow out of it, Rose said. It's a phase. Everything's a phase, Frankie said, living is a phase. How long is this phase going to last?

"It isn't as though we can't afford another TV set," Peg went on.

Coolin stared at the screen at the replay of the play he had just watched. He tried to concentrate. He felt like a stranger in this room; he always did, from the first moment they moved into the house.

"What do you say, Dad? You could get a color set and we could use the black and white. I could watch what I want to watch?"

He said nothing.

"Why can't we even talk about it?"

Talk. It was her big thing now; people should talk things over, discuss things, communicate and verbalize. Another phase.

"OK, I can see this is a waste of time."

Mick said, "That's what the Jets are saying." He snorted a laugh that was just as unattractive as his voice. Coolin felt irritated suddenly.

"How come the car's in the driveway, I couldn't park the truck there?"

Silence.

"Who had the car last?"

"I did," said Peg.

"I tole you a hunnert times to put it in the garage because I got to have the truck in the driveway so I can get out in the morning."

"Well, I was thinking about using it again."

"What? You were thinking about going out again? Forget that, it's almost eight o'clock, where you gonna go in the car at eight o'clock? You got school tomorrow."

"Over by Darlene's house."

"What? Two blocks? You mean two blocks you need a car? Why don't you trade in your legs for wheels."

"I get it," Peg said. "I got no rights. I just don't exist. I get it."

"I can't hear the TV," Mick interrupted.

"Knock it off, both of you," Frankie Coolin said.

"Mick can have the car, he picks the TV show, he drinks beer—"

"I have pain in my head," Frankie said.

"Yeah, shut up, Peg," Mick said.

"You shut up too. God, you drive me nuts. Where is she?"

"In the basement."

"Doing what?"

"Laundry," Peg said.

"Everyone lives like niggers in this house, you know that? How come no one does things when white people do things? She does laundry at midnight and sleeps all morning and she's up with eggs at three A.M. And you with that stereo on at seven in the morning last Saturday, I don't want that again."

"It wasn't loud."

"We could have used it during the war to destroy Tokyo. The point is you wanted to hear records and you wanted the rest of the world to join you."

"At least she's doing the laundry for you."

"Yeah. If we waited on you, Peg, to do anything around here, we'd be wearing cobwebs. You guys ate, right?"

"Sauerkraut," said Mick. "Ugh. I don't know why she makes that stuff."

"You mean she didn't give you a menu? What's wrong with her?"

"I hate sauerkraut. She knows that."

"I'm really sorry, Mick, I really am. Life is so goddam hard sometimes."

He said nothing.

Peg smirked.

"And chops," Frankie said. "I bet you hated chops."

"I'm not crazy about pork."

"Pork makes me break out," said Peg.

"From now on, we'll have T-bone. OK? I really feel like an asshole about this, making you kids eat meat and sauerkraut. How about some rice like a goddam Iranian."

"We aren't hostages," Mick said.

I am, Coolin thought. He got up and didn't speak. Cosell was snorting on the set. He went down the hall into the kitchen and looked around in the half-darkness. Rose always left the little light on over the built-in stove. He turned on the ceiling light and went to the refrigerator and opened the door and removed a can of Old Style. He popped the top and took a swallow and looked around the kitchen again.

Rose kept neither a neat house nor a sloppy one. Dishes sat drying in a rack over the sink; a black iron skillet was on the stove, filled with congealed grease from the chops.

They had moved into the house twenty-three years ago, from the old flat on the West Side of the city.

He thought about the flat, about the summer afternoons spent sitting at the old oak kitchen table, in the back of the flat, the screen door letting in the first breeze of the sultry day. He remembered kids making noise in the alley below the second floor of the flat. He and Rose. They would make plans over the table, over endless cups of coffee, talking about buying a home in the suburbs. All the things they intended to do.

Plaques on the yellow walls of her kitchen now: Rose had a passion for collecting shit, according to Frankie Coolin. One asked God to bless this house and another suggested that the Road might rise up to meet you. The third said: No Matter Where I Serve My Guests, It Seems They Like My Kitchen Best. A dream world, Frankie thought.

He felt uncomfortable in the empty kitchen. When there were people, during the hustle of the morning, he didn't think about the house or about the family surging around him. Now he felt isolated from Peg and Mick. Even from Rose. The house, with its plaques on the walls and kitchen cabinets done in fruitwood Formica, seemed out of another part of time to him. It was as though he were standing at the edge of a dream he could not enter.

He heard the front door slam shut and, in a moment, the sound of the Pinto starting. He went to the hall and listened. The football game was still on; Peg had taken the car after all. He felt a surge of anger and then let it die. Maybe he shouldn't have said anything to her at all.

He opened the basement door. The washer and drier were both on, humming and thumping from below. He listened to the song Rose was singing, a song they had not heard together for thirty years.

He went down the steps. The basement was foreign territory as well because the old man was there. The Old Man. His father, now eighty or eighty-one years old, so old he could not remember. It seemed to Frankie that the old man had shrunk in the past few years or his bones had gotten smaller. He remembered his dad as such a big man. Coolin's mother had died ten years before and it had been hard on all of them, made harder by the old man's reaction to it. He had been distracted by grief for months; he was like a child. Kate, Frankie's sister, had wanted the old man to sell his house in the Austin neighborhood of the city because blacks were moving in and it was becoming a dangerous area for an old white man. But he had resisted. Just grief, he had said once to Frankie, I have a grief in me is all. But Kate was stubborn and pushed at him to move in with her, to spend the rest of his days as a visitor in someone else's life. Frankie Coolin said nothing. John had joined Kate in the assault on the old man's privacy. And then Rose.

Kate would say: "I was cleaning over by his house, he's got everything out, papers on the kitchen table, he's got no room to even eat, I don't think he even eats. There's dust on the frying pans, Frankie, I feel ashamed."

"Why? You ain't cooking for him."

"You don't care what happens to him, what people think about us leaving him like that."

"He doesn't want to live with you."

"The toilet, you should have seen the bathroom, it was filthy. The toilet was all stained, I swear to God he must take a crap and leave it in there."

Frankie would say nothing. Kate was bossy and John went along with her, from the time they were all children together.

The battle went on for two years and the old man held out against them. He accused John and Kate of wanting his money, which was perfectly true. Everyone had too many bills, too many kids to get along; and the old man, at the end of his life, sat in a paid-up house with a bank account to choke a horse.

Rose also came around to Kate's point of view after a while. The women took turns cleaning for the old man in his house and cooking him a hot meal once in a while. Once during the two years, black teenagers knocked him down on the street as he walked to the tavern for his morning shot and beer and the women had kept at him for weeks thereafter, talking about the decline of the neighborhood and how he wasn't safe in his own house. The old man, for his part, started carrying a gun again, the gun he had used when he was a barn boss on the old transit lines in the early days. Coolin, who said nothing during all this except to tell Rose to keep out of it, admired that last bit of information handed him by an outraged Kate.

"He'll get himself killed."

"He'll take someone with him," Frankie Coolin said.

He might have held out forever except he started to go blind. The process was not so gradual for the old man. A dimming, day by day. Consultations followed and glasses and tests but the blindness grew. His fading vision won the battle that Kate and John and Rose could not.

He put the house up for sale and sold it to a black couple. The black man, ironically, worked for the Chicago Transit Authority and the two of them talked sadly about the decline of public transportation in the city. The old man had shown the black buyer where he kept his gun and the other alcoves and secret places of the house. Then he put all his money in CDs and went to live with Kate.

Kate hounded him day and night for money, sometimes with subtlety, sometimes with loud tears. Frankie couldn't stand to visit his sister anymore—even at Christmas time.

And then, a year later, one February morning, the old man

appeared at Frankie's house. He stood on the stoop and rang the bell while a cab driver struggled with his bags and cardboard boxes. He was moving in, he told Rose, in his flat, Irish accent. Rose took him into the kitchen and sat him down and made him coffee. The old man passed the morning sitting in the kitchen, talking to Rose in his sweet, strong voice, telling her nothing of Kate or the row that had impelled his arrival; he spoke instead of County Clare where he had come from, of the fairy rings hidden in the tall, green grass in the fields down by the wide Shannon beyond their farmhouse windows, of cattle that grazed along the narrow roads, and of meeting his wife in the village of Doonaha so long ago at a dance in the church.

Frankie Coolin had missed it all. He had left early that morning for a wrecking job and when he got home in late afternoon, the old man was sleeping in the spare bedroom.

So sweet, Rose had said, entranced by the gentle, rolling voice that had rarely spoken to her for so long.

"Yeah, a charmer. It's just terrific but where the hell are we going to put him? I didn't want him here in the first place."

"Your own dad."

"Yeah. I know. I'm a bum."

The problem of lodging the old man in the little bungalow and of keeping his few possessions—photographs he could not see, old letters he could not read, a wooden chest which he claimed to have brought with him from Ireland sixty years before—persisted all that spring while Frankie hustled jobs and ran his first building and tried to spend as little time at home as possible. He avoided the house in hopes that the problem there would fix itself in his absence, like the broken storm door. The old man was broken too.

One Saturday morning, as they sat at the kitchen table and arranged not to speak to each other, Frankie stared at the old man drinking his coffee and thought of a solution.

"The basement," he said.

"What?"

"The basement, Dad. We got a basement with a lot of room, we ought to use it. We put the ping-pong table down there when the kids were younger and they never use it anymore and there's just shit sitting on it. We fold up the table and we got a lot of room. I can get Andy to help me, we can put up some interior walls, insulation, panel it nice—nice paneling, I can get a deal on it, not the cheap stuff—and I put a radiator down there and hook it up to the boiler just like upstairs. You'll have it all to yourself."

"I'm not a potato," the old man said. "I won't live in a cellar."

"Not a cellar, for Christ's sake. This isn't the old country, this is a basement. You been in the basement. It's nice down there, cool in the summer, warm in the winter when I put in the radiator. It's dry since I put in the sump pump. I'll put in a door, make it like a room. You got your radio, you'll have the place to yourself."

"I won't live in a basement, boyo," the old man had said.

Rose, at the stove, had said, "But Frank, the basement will be too dark." And then she paused, remembering the old man's eyes.

"Look, Dad. Either you move down there or I do. I can't stand living on top of each other like we've been doing because it's crazy. We got three kids still at home and we got them until Andy and Rose Two decide to finally get married or go shack up some place, and we got you, we got us and nobody's got privacy—"

"Don't say 'shack up,' " said Rose.

"Whatever. I'll even put a shower down there for you and a toilet, right off your room, like a private apartment or something, I got this toilet out of the last building I wrecked."

"What am I going to do with the laundry?" Rose asked.

"We got a big basement, I ain't going to take the whole basement for this room. The only thing we got to do is get rid of that goddam ping-pong table nobody wants to use."

"I got my canning."

"Put your canning some other place, put it in the garage, I don't give a damn where you put the canning, all you want to do is can those pickles and nobody can eat them, they're so salty. Dammit, Rose, Dad, the only way we can live with each other is to get out of each other's way."

"We had ten of us there was in a three-room house when I was a lad—"

"Terrific, Dad, and you all ate potatoes three times a day.

It was so great that the first thing you did is take a boat to the new country."

"There wasn't work, there was troubles in those times." The old man said it gravely as though he had never said the same thing before.

"OK. I got it wrong as usual."

"You don't have to put me in the cellar. I can go back to live with Kate then, she wants me money, you know that, but that's all right, I'll just go back to her and leave you to your precious solitude."

"Oh, God." Frankie had put his cup down softly. "You aren't going back to Kate or over to John's house either because John doesn't work all day and they don't have a pot to piss in and Kate will drive you crazy. You stay here."

"John takes a drop," the old man allowed. "He's on the roofs all day."

"John's in the tavern all day," Frankie said.

"John's got troubles," the old man said.

"Everybody's got troubles." But he knew the old man was weakening. They talked and talked all morning until Frankie got sick of it. The next morning, while they were all at church for the eleven o'clock mass, he started on it in the basement. He made the interior walls with some care and Andy helped because it gave him a chance to see Rose Two in her own house. They were very serious with each other though Rose thought her daughter was making a mistake limiting herself to someone who was only a cement finisher; Frankie thought that Andy might be too good for Rose Two but said nothing. He wanted her married off.

All these thoughts flooded back to him as he walked down the narrow steps to the basement. Soon, sooner than he expected, all the kids would be gone. And the old man would still be alive. The old man had fitted into the room like a glove. He had become the Old Man in the Basement. In the afternoons, when he wanted to nap, he would bang on the ceiling with his cane to silence the house.

Coolin had told Rose: "This is like living back in that old flat again. Remember when the people downstairs banged the steampipes because we were making too much noise in the bed?"

Rose remembered and kissed him in the middle of the day. They had remembered the pipes because the creaky old bed with the springs made noise when they made love in the afternoon and in the morning, at the odd times, not like now when they only made love in the darkness. He would be up on those mornings, half-dressed and ready for the job, and she would be in bed and look at him in the half-light of the red city dawn; and reach for him and he would stop buttoning his shirt and come to her, on the bed, moving over her. Rose had been so much smaller then, her belly pale and flat. He had kissed her belly, her pink nipples, and kissed her wide, salt-tasting lips, and moved over her, into her. Those mornings. He had listened to the eight o'clock factory whistles from Crawford Avenue in her arms. He had always worked for himself; he had always hustled in the trades; he had never answered a factory whistle.

Thump, thump, the old washer sounded in the basement. Sometimes, Frankie Coolin thought, nostalgia overwhelmed him. Maybe it was because he was so scared right now, because the answer didn't seem ahead of him but behind him.

"You're back," Rose said flatly. She was sorting clothes on the table. The laundry area was smaller now. Beyond was the door that led to the old man's room. "I heard the truck and I thought I heard the car just now. I want you to look at the washer, I think there's something wrong with it."

"I'm looking at it, it's working."

"Don't you hear that thumping?"

"Sure. You put too many clothes in again."

"Maybe I ought to call out Sears."

"Don't call out Sears. You know what they want to charge? Wait till the thing breaks down finally, you want to call someone and I'll call Longo over, he can fix it."

"Who took the car?"

"Peg."

"Why'n't you stop her?"

"I told her not to go out. I'm the invisible man."

"I put the chops in the refrigerator."

"I had a beef sandwich on the way here."

"It's behind the milk. You want some sauerkraut with it?"

"I said I had a beef sandwich."

"Why do you eat stuff like that when you know I got food waiting for you at home?"

"I was hungry."

"The old man is sleeping. I heard his radio and then he turned it off."

"He can sleep through anything, he can sleep through you washing clothes in the middle of the night. Why do you wash clothes in the middle of the night?"

"I've got to do it sometime."

"But it's the middle of the night."

"Besides, there wasn't anything on television."

"There's never anything on television."

"Mick and Peg are fighting about the television again. I came down here to think."

"You get driven out of your own house," he said.

"It wasn't that but Peg gets on my nerves when she's like this. She has problems. I think I want her to go to the doctor. I think she has problems."

"Everyone has problems," Frankie Coolin said.

"And your sister came by."

"Terrific. She was checking to see if the old man had died yet?"

"I wish you wouldn't talk like that."

"I got a bad mouth, I been with niggers all day."

"I wish you wouldn't use language like that. You know I don't like that word."

"You ought to see the reaction the shines have."

"Peg was after me for the car and I said I didn't want her driving around at night like this so she takes it anyway and you let her. How can I tell her one thing and you let her do it."

"I don't let her do anything, what am I gonna do? She's sixteen, you want me to spank her?"

"I wonder if she's taking dope."

"Why not worry about the Pope's underwear, Rose. You make things up to worry about."

"You'd be surprised, you think you know everything but you think that kids don't take dope now? Even in the Catholic school? You'd be surprised what's going on."

"She still talking about this boyfriend of hers?"

"No. That's what's worrying me."

"I hope he's white."

She glanced up sharply from the table full of groceries. "Frank. Don't say that."

"I got all the radiators out but two and my back is killing me, I was going to take a bath but now you're washing clothes, there isn't any hot water. I saw Joey over at the Bo's and he says he's gonna help me tomorrow and then I saw your cousin, Kennedy. We watched his kid scrimmage."

"Kevin?"

"No, this is Tommy. Kevin doesn't play football, he's the one with the glasses."

"Oh, that one. I get them mixed up, I don't know why. Tommy is the one made a pig of himself at Andy and Two's wedding last year and the way he talked back to his father, I tell you I'd give him a cuff."

"He's a little shit but he looks pretty good on the line. He's going to get his knees popped, he likes the late shot."

"I still want to cry when I think about Mick's operation."

"So do I, every time I get the tuition bill from DePaul. He could have had a scholarship."

"DePaul doesn't have football."

"Rose, there are a thousand places in the world he could of gone."

"I'm glad he's going to a Catholic school."

"He could of gone to Notre Dame. Now, that would have been all right, that would have thrown your cousin Kennedy's fat nose out of joint with his pinkie ring. He wears rings like a dago alderman. Well, that's down the sewer anyway. Maybe I'll have one of the chops—"

"I'll warm it for you."

"I like it cold."

"You shouldn't eat cold pork."

"Rose, you just cooked it, there's nothing wrong with it. It's raw pork you shouldn't eat."

"I don't know. I don't trust pork."

"Then why do you buy it?"

"It's cheaper and you don't like chicken."

"I hate it, in fact."

"So what am I going to cook? It can't be meat, meat, meat every night."

"Sure."

"And then Mick wouldn't eat because he said he didn't like pork. I wonder why I cook?"

"He eats what you give him or he don't eat."

"Well, I told him that but he's a big boy now."

"Not that big."

"I went to the doctor today."

"Why?"

"My checkup."

"Rose. You go to that quack five times a year and there's nothing wrong with you. Why do you want to do that to yourself? You always worry about it—"

"Well, it's better to be careful, you should see him once in a while yourself."

"I don't mess with doctors. Look at John. They sell him on this triple bypass and the guy isn't worth a shit now, not that he was a ball of fire in the first place. And then I read in the *Trib* that they say half these operations you don't need in the first place."

"John'd be dead if he didn't have that operation."

"He's alive now, you mean?"

"He said I was run down."

"Is that right?"

"He ran a blood test on me."

"And you're pregnant."

"No. Sometimes I feel tired is all."

"Hey, sometimes I feel tired too. Is this your last load? Maybe I can take a bath."

"Yeah, I just wanted to do some of these things."

"OK, you got a clean pair of jeans in there? I got to go downtown tomorrow."

"What are you doing?"

"I got to see a guy."

"A winter job?"

He thought of the lie he had told Joey. "Sure."

"I hope you get a good inside job this winter. You aren't young like you used to be."

"Neither are you."

"Frank."

"Joke."

"Frank." Lingering, eyes bright.

He followed her up the stairs to the kitchen. They closed the basement door and Rose went to the refrigerator and pulled out the chops.

He sat at the kitchen table with another can of beer and watched her drop the chops into the frying pan and turn on the gas stove. Heavier, he thought, but the legs still young. She always wore dresses and skirts because she said she was too heavy to wear slacks and jeans and she didn't want to look like some of the women shopping over at the Dominick's store. He thought she wore dresses because of her legs.

"We're out of cheese," she said and wrote the word "cheese" on the blackboard near the sink. Rose was constantly organizing herself and the blackboard was her answer to forgetting things.

"Something wrong, Frank, you're so quiet."

"I'm tired with the radiators and Joey finked out on me, I thought I was gonna break my back."

"You get Mick to come by and give you a hand, he's off on Fridays, he's only got four classes a week now. He could give you a hand."

"No. Mick should study. Besides, he's worthless to me. He's lazy and it's just as easy for me to do it myself as make him do it."

"Well, he ought to help you. Is Joey going to be there tomorrow?"

"Joey's all right, he's just got the idea in him that he's still a kid and he can fuck off when he wants. Well, good luck to him."

"Don't use that word. Would you like some of this sauerkraut or not?"

"No. Just the chops."

"I could give you some cottage cheese with it."

"With chops?"

"Well, just some vegetable."

"That's not a vegetable."

"You just eat meat and bread."

"It's better than potatoes three times a day."

"We got no mail, just bills and junk. I talked to Two, she said she can't come over tomorrow because Sean has got something." Two was what they called their daughter Rose, to distinguish her from her mother. When their son was born, Rose wanted to call him Frank but Frankie said no. He said he was the only Frankie Coolin there was going to be in the world.

"What's he got?"

"Sounds like another cold."

"Kid is seven months old, he gets nothing but colds."

"I told her to give him oatmeal for breakfast."

"She gives him that shit food because that's what she wants to eat for herself, some fucking Frosted Horseshit or something and she won't put him on the tit. Milk on the tit is better than stuff out of the bottle."

"I don't like that word."

"Did Longo open the drain for you in the tub?"

"He was by. You want to take a shower instead of a bath, I think there must be enough hot water."

"OK. I guess so, I can eat my chops and watch the game. I'll give Mick the truck keys and he can move it in the driveway after Miss High-and-Mighty decides to come home. I ain't going to talk to her, Rose, you got to talk to her, you know that."

"I'll talk to her."

"She says she wanted to go by Darlene's house, you ought to call to see if she's still there."

"I'm not going to call and embarrass her."

"How do we embarrass her when we call? Well, I don't want to get into it. Oh, yeah. Cheese, you said you were out? Don't get none at the store. I got some coming to me, through Pat Kennedy. He said he got a deal on it. Cheddar cheese."

"Not too strong because it doesn't melt right when it's too strong."

"I don't know what kind it is but the price is right. If it don't melt, it don't melt. Pretend it melts."

"You're the one wants to eat grilled cheese all the time."

"Well, pick up some Velveeta then for the grilled cheese."

In the blue bathroom with the blue towels and blue toilet paper and blue shag toilet-seat cover, he stripped off his clothes and stuffed them in the wicker hamper, then reached through the blue shower curtain and turned on the faucets. The room filled quickly with steam from the hot water while he shaved. Sometimes he shaved twice a day, just to feel the cleanness of the razor over his face, just to make it seem that morning was here and he was beginning again. He climbed in the tub and closed his eyes and felt the jets of water pound at his body. He was lean still with only a slight flab of belly. His face was very red from the sun of thirty years, his hands were red and broken and scarred. Only his body was pale. He soaped his dark brown hair with bar soap and then his body and turned and let the water run over him.

He thought about the Sonys in that moment. He hadn't even known they were there. He knew something was going on but he didn't want explanations. And then they found the Sonys.

He opened his eyes and looked at the bar soap. It was blue. Blue fucking soap, he thought. He rubbed the bar against his face and pushed the suds into his eyes until they stung.

What would the joint be like?

But this was impossible; he couldn't do time. Not that he couldn't take it. He could take a lot of things. He could take it, but how would Rose make out? And Mick and Peg still at home? And the old man? And Joey for that matter because it was a cinch that John the roofer couldn't help him; he couldn't help himself.

Cold, the G said, they said it with pleasure. And then they were sitting across the road, waiting for him to come out of the high school parking lot. Kennedy probably didn't even see them, he was so smug, so goddam sure that nothing was going to happen to him.

Mostly, he thought, it would be stupid inside the joint. That's what Uncle Brian had told him. After you got settled in and got your territory straightened out with the shines, it was stupid and dull and all the time the guards were moping around you like your mother. You couldn't get a drink to save your life unless you were willing to deal with the niggers and Brian wouldn't do that. You could get pot, you could get that from the guards, and downers from the hospital. So he took drugs and slept. He slept away days and nights. He did time.

That's all you can do, Brian had told him, is make the time go away. Watch television and sleep; work in the laundry and sleep. Sleep and sleep and don't look at the calendar. Take your pills like a good boy and stay down, stay buzzed down.

Two fucking years.

Goddammit, Frankie Coolin thought.

4

Frankie Coolin thought he had made a mistake as soon as the secretary opened the door off the reception room and led him down the thick-carpeted hall to Arthur Klein's private office at the end. For example, he noticed the paneling on the walls was real wood. And the carpeting had to go for forty dollars a square. And the recessed lighting in the ceiling was unguessable.

And then he saw Klein and was certain he had made a mistake or that Kennedy had hustled him. The attorney sat behind an oversized teak desk, in a huge black leather chair, his back to a window wall that gave an impressive, if slightly surrealistic view of the Loop from the twenty-ninth floor.

Klein had to go three hundred fifty pounds, Coolin thought. He was as big and sleek and unmarked as a grotesque baby.

"Sit down," Klein suggested in a surprisingly small voice. "Miss Dobbs. Do you want coffee, Mister Coolin?"

"No, thanks."

The secretary left the room, letting the mahogany door close silently behind her. Arthur Klein did not stir. He sat silently and stared at Coolin with mild, large eyes that seemed neither benign nor shrewd. In a three-piece sky-blue suit, he reminded Frankie of Mayor Daley.

"I received a call from your friend this morning."

"He's my wife's cousin, not my friend."

"A distinction I will accept. You have some need of my services?"

Frankie didn't answer for a minute. "Listen. I think maybe this isn't going to work out."

"That's a possibility but we have yet to explore it." The eyes narrowed slightly. "What's the beef, federal or local?"

"Federal."

"Before we begin, before you disclose one iota of information, let us talk about the most important thing."

"What's that?"

"Money."

"I can't talk about that right now because I don't know what this is gonna add up to; maybe nothing is gonna happen."

"Mr. Coolin. If you thought nothing was going to happen, you wouldn't be talking to me."

"Well, there's that."

"When the time comes, when the federal officers actually have you in their care, when the bracelets are locked over your wrists, the meter begins at that moment, do you understand?"

"Sure. That's only fair. What do you figure this is gonna run me?"

"The final payments would be difficult to ascertain even at that moment, though I could give you a rough guess once I see the bill of particulars. I can assure you that nobody can give you a better estimate than I."

"You mean the indictment."

"Precisely."

"So what's the charge?"

A faint smile. "As much as possible, as much as the market will bear, Mr. Coolin, and any attorney who denies that is a liar or a fool. If he is a fool, you don't want to retain him; if he is a liar, your confidence in him will be eroded."

"Is that right?"

"Mr. Coolin. I am a successful attorney which means I not only win a goodly proportion of my cases, both local and federal, but it means that I am well fed and that I have a wonderful home and a wonderful, socially adept wife and quite nice children and I belong to three clubs."

"I'm glad to hear it, I like to hear you're happy."

"Five."

"What? What did you say?"

"When that day comes—and Mr. Kennedy seemed to imply that your problem would require immediate consultation with me—when that day comes, I want five thousand dollars in front, as a retainer against the eventual fee."

"I'll see you around."

"Goodbye, Mr. Coolin."

Frankie got up but Arthur Klein still did not budge or make any gesture to stop him.

"How would I get five grand?"

"That doesn't interest me at all."

"You play a hard game."

"Life is hard."

"Yeah. I can see that. I can see the calluses on your hands from here, I can see how hard it is for you."

"Let's not have class epithets. They demean you and place you in the position of a street urchin throwing mud at a passing carriage. The mud will wash off, Mr. Coolin, but the urchin will still be groveling in it."

"You talk like a book. Would you win?"

"There is every possibility."

"A sure thing I'm looking for."

"Every possibility."

"Man, for five grand, you ought to be able to talk better than that. I can fix a DWI for a grand and have the thing expunged."

"Driving While Intoxicated is a local charge and anything within reason, short of murder, is fixable locally. Perhaps even murder in the right circumstances. But we are talking now about fixing the federal government and I can assure you that in my experience, the federal government is beyond fixing. It wants nothing, it needs nothing; the bureaucracy is indifferent and therefore its arrogance is unchecked."

"Well. What if we lose?"

"Then I will try to get you the smallest possible penalty."

"And what does that mean?"

"Exactly what it appears to mean. There are no mirrors, no tricks, no lies. There are no miracles, you know. Clouds do not part, light does not fall down from heaven. This is not a motion picture, Mr. Coolin. We labor in the vineyards, all of us, and we hope for our rewards at the harvest."

"Except you get paid when you walk into the vineyard, not out."

"Five grand is earnest money, Mr. Coolin, a gesture of your good intentions. It is a down payment. Successful or not, it will cost you more than that."

"You want blood, too? Five is a lot of money to a little guy like me."

"Five is a lot of money to a big guy like me, Mr. Coolin. Even in these times. It is, at last count, seven ounces of gold, for example, as absurd as that may sound."

"Where would I get five grand?"

"I told you that doesn't interest me. If you are a thief, steal it. If you are a murderer, kill for it. I suppose you would get five grand to save your life."

"Five grand is a lot of money."

"Five years in Marion maximum prison is a lot of time."

There was a silence.

"They never talked to me about Marion. Man, I don't want to do no time in that monkey cage down there. They didn't talk about that."

"What did they talk about?"

"Sandstone."

"A country club."

"I don't see people lining up to go there. I don't see them advertising in the travel section of the *Trib*."

"Well put, Mr. Coolin. Sit down. No, over there, I can see you better."

"You could turn your head."

"I move as little as possible."

"I can see that."

"Well?"

"OK. Let's start off saying I give you the story of my life. Pat Kennedy sent me over, Pat Kennedy called you, I never heard of you in my life. Maybe this thing I got to tell you about is involved with Pat Kennedy too or maybe not. Where do we stand with each other?"

"No mirrors, no lies."

"I don't get that."

"I have ethics, Mr. Coolin. I stand with my client."

"So is Kennedy your client?"

"That would not be ethical, would it? To advise you in a matter that would involve one of my clients."

"Life isn't ethical. Ethical is that piece of paper on the wall, like things in doctors' offices. It only means you probably clean your needles before using them again. If I had a dime for every doctor—"

"Yes, I'm sure, I'm sure. You look to me like a man of

resource, Mr. Coolin, and I am willing to bet that when the time comes, you will come up with the five. And so I am willing in turn, being a man who relies as much on instinct as intellect, to invest the next fifteen minutes of my life in listening to your particular tale of woe. I can assure you that everything you say will be held in confidence, but I perceive that my assurances will not be accepted. I can see that; I can even understand that. So I won't waste my breath, though it's perfectly true. These walls have heard a lot of stories just as dreadful as your story, I can assure you. I am certain of it as the priest is certain that he has heard every sin in the confessional."

Coolin studied him for a moment and tapped his flannel shirt pocket. It was empty; he left the cigarettes in the truck.

"Yeah. Listen, I want to ask, if you don't move, how do you get around court? You got bearers?"

"I rarely go to court."

"Terrific. How do you arrange that? You get them to come to you?"

"Very little of substance is ever done in court, Mr. Coolin. The business of the law is in preparation, in planning, in negotiations, in bargaining, in making friends and making contacts. Standing in court, saying your little piece to judge and jury—the theater of trial work—is the least of the matter in most cases, Mr. Coolin."

Again, Frankie Coolin fidgeted in the leather side chair in front of the teak desk. He looked out the window wall and saw clouds beginning to shroud the Loop towers. It was going to rain in a little while. Friday afternoon just after three, and Joey was alone out in the West Side, painting the second floor south apartment, carrying the piece in his back pocket. Frankie had stiffed him after all.

"Fourteen minutes."

Coolin thought about it and decided. He hated to make a decision, to commit himself, because it was not in his nature to eliminate options. Yet the fat man was forcing it. The G was forcing it. He hadn't slept all night. He had lain in bed with Rose snoring gently next to him. He couldn't tell her, he couldn't tell anyone. The only one he could talk to was Kennedy and Kennedy was in it too and Kennedy was a hustler.

"OK," Frankie Coolin said and he told Arthur Klein nearly everything. He did not tell him about the deal with Pat Kennedy or his vague and guilty knowledge of what was really in the warehouse. He told Arthur Klein more than he had ever told the G.

When he was finished, they just sat there looking at each other. Finally, Klein spoke. "Do you know, Mr. Coolin, I like this story." The lips barely moved. "It is so instructive of the way the government can operate. They have, in their plodding way, a certain genius about them. Here they have expended countless man-hours on what is, on the face of it, a piddling act of venality."

"I didn't do nothing."

"In a moment. Let me go on: if this had been a matter for the city cops, they would have dropped it a long time ago. Like murder. I happen to know of at least three former clients who have literally gotten away with murder in the course of their occupation because it is too hard, too much trouble, too complicated for the cops to get them. The locals must weigh the worth of pursuit with the worth of eventual reward. This is cost-efficient. The government, on the other hand, has all the money in the world."

"And Kostner-torched his own place."

"Precisely, the little twist to the story that intrigues me. Do you see where he stands? If the locals had the time and money and sheer stubborn determination—no, let me say if they had a tenth of these qualities and monies—as the federals, Chicago would be as safe as houses."

"Yeah. Well, I'm glad you find this so fascinating. I like to be entertaining. You see I got a problem."

"More clearly than you understand. You have neglected to mention your involvement with Mr. Kennedy but I can infer it. I'm surprised Mr. Kennedy sent you to me. He must be involved."

"Why?"

"Because you were worried about him. About his relationship to me. Let me set your mind at rest. Mr. Kennedy received my name in the first place from another client of mine whom I will not mention to you. This gentleman is a wholesaler of sorts, dealing in meat and cheese and sometimes in areas in which he has less expertise. He took a chance and the chance nearly took him. He beat the rap, in the parlance of the streets, and perhaps he has learned his lesson. Mr. Kennedy received my name from him. I do not know Mr. Kennedy from a man in the moon."

"Well, I didn't mention Kennedy to you."

"But he is the key to our mutual trust, Mr. Coolin. He is obviously the fixer in this. What favor did you do for him?"

"I rented the space for him."

"Yes. I see that. You understand how much better it will be for us if we trust each other."

"Trusting a mouth is hard."

"Of course. All your life I presume lawyers have pursued you, dunned you, sued you, threatened you. But now the shoe is on the other foot, Mr. Coolin. I am on your side. I am your great weapon in this matter. And to begin, I will tell you one thing that I understand in my gut. Mr. Kennedy is not your friend."

"I never said he was. He's my wife's cousin."

"And what does your cousin expect of you?"

Coolin stared at the bland, baby-blue eyes set in the porcine smoothness of that unwrinkled face. "I don't know."

"You do, Mr. Coolin. He expects you to be a stand-up guy. I rather like that vulgarity. Stand up and take it. Be a stand-up guy. And what does the government expect you to do?"

"I don't know what they expect but I know what I am going to do."

"No. You do not know, Mr. Coolin. You haven't a clue to what you are going to do because you have done nothing yet. You are at the crossroads, you are confused, you are uncertain. I will tell you what the G wants you to do, Mr. Coolin. Sing. Speak. Tell your story."

"Yeah. Sure."

"Yeah. Sure. Exactly. And you won't do it."

"I don't say anything." Coolin saw neither sympathy nor amusement on the face. Nothing. Like talking to a cloud or a sponge.

"Then what will you do?"

"I don't know."

"Yes. That's the intelligent answer at last."

"I don't want to do no time."

"No one wants to do time. Time is never pleasant."

"No. I mean, I really don't want to do time. It isn't that I couldn't do time. I could stand time. I could do it. But I don't want to. I really don't want to. Not for something like this that I didn't really have anything to do with."

"I sympathize."

"Fuck sympathy," Frankie Coolin said. "I'm not coming at you like some fag on his hands and knees whining about it. I can take it if I got to take it. That's not the point. I got commitments, I got family, I got two kids still at home, I can't even explain about the rest of them, about my nephew or my brother who's a bum and nothing coming in, or about my son-in-law who's all right but he don't know how to hustle on his own yet. I mean, it's complicated. If I had to do two, three years, it would all collapse, you see?"

"The indispensable man."

"Well, fuck, someone's got to be."

"You can always make money; you can't make time."

"Well, if it comes down to it, I can stand it. I don't want it but I can stand it. I'm just scared about it."

"You can stand it and that is why Mr. Kennedy is so certain you will be a stand-up guy."

"I don't know what Kennedy thinks."

"Of course you do, Mr. Coolin. You are thinking about it right now. You are sitting there on my chair in your little uniform of the tradesman, the construction worker, you are sitting there on that chair in this wonderful office with a view, listening to this fat Jewish lawyer talking to you and as you listen you are thinking about so many things. You are thinking, 'Why did Pat Kennedy give me the name of this yoyo?' You are thinking it as surely as I am sitting here, on the other side of this desk which cost three thousand four hundred dollars, thinking, 'Why do I see more clearly than I see this desk that Mister Coolin is going to take a very bad fall?' Do you see that, Mr. Coolin? Pat Kennedy is counting on you more than your wife or your children or your hapless brother. Mr. Kennedy, who is not your friend, is so certain that you will take the fall that he gave you the name of a lawyer. I think something very dreadful is going to happen, that is what I think."

"Jesus H. Christ." Frankie Coolin's voice was soft.

Arthur Klein nodded slightly. "Precisely."

Frankie Coolin said, "The cheese man. That dirty fucking prick. He was standing there laughing. He wanted me to buy cheese from him. He gets the name of a lawyer from the cheese man and then he hustles me for cheese."

"I don't understand any of that."

"Nothing. The thing that surprises me still is that he gave me your name."

"It surprises me as well. You are afraid this is a trap; I am surprised because it is not, because I know who and what I am, Mr. Coolin. I am a terrier at the rathole and I win because I work harder than anyone else. That is why I have my home on the North Shore, why my wife—"

"Yeah, is wonderful, and you got three clubs."

"Exactly." The voice changed now, each word counted, the cloud blew away, the fat man inclined his body a quarter of an inch forward. "Mr. Kennedy is a foolish man because I am his Waterloo. I am a winner, Mr. Coolin, no matter what the rules of the game and when that day comes, when it comes, you will be my client. This is not guile on my part, Mr. Coolin. If it comes down to it, the bottom line is reached, when it comes to the litmus and the benchmark . . . when we reach that final point, Mr. Kennedy will hang by the balls before you do. I am certain—no, not certain—I am reasonably sure that you will not hang, Mr. Coolin."

"But what do you think? I mean, that isn't going to cost you anything, to tell me what you think."

"Everything costs. Time is money, even your time. But I will tell you what I think, yes, I will. You are in a fix, Mr. Coolin. You are contained in a box partly of your own making. You are down for the count but not out yet."

"And the G? They're going to come down on me?"

"Inevitably." The word made everything black for a moment. Coolin closed his eyes, opened them.

"Even the *federales* do not come into the open unless they have superior firepower. The war is not declared until it is won. The government officers have shown you their hand, Mr. Coolin. They are so certain they have all the best cards that they have shown you their hand."

"Yeah. I can see that. They have."

"Perhaps, in the depth of his black soul, Mr. Kennedy feels a trace of remorse. Yes. Perhaps that's why he suggested me. The human factor, it is always beyond mere calculation."

Coolin did not understand. He stared at the fat man as though waiting for him to speak again. And Klein did: "Remorse for what he has done? Or remorse for what he is going to do?"

"What? What are you talking about?"

"Nothing. Nothing for now. I have developed an affection for you in these few minutes, Mr. Coolin. Perhaps it is your naïveté."

"I ain't naïve."

"In some matters, no doubt, you are wise." Pause. "Perhaps your house. You own your home."

"What?"

"A second mortgage. For the five grand."

"Put a mortgage on my house to pay a lawyer."

"One idea. I'm trying to help you out. It's one thought. Normally, I would not offer suggestions of this sort. But this matter intrigues me, it is beguiling, I must say that. I would like to see how it all turns out."

"I'm glad you find it interesting. It intrigues me too."

"Good. I'm glad it has your attention."

"Well. I'll think over your generous offer."

"Do. Do. But time is fleeting, Mr. Coolin. Your time, in any case."

"You think so?"

"My professional instinct tells me so. The old viscera. The gut reaction. I think the moment was passing very fast when you were visited yesterday by the two gentlemen from the Federal Bureau of Investigation. Yes. Passing. I think it is down now to a matter of an appearance before the grand jury and then the indictment. In fact, I am sure of it. Let me see, this is October fifth. I should think, this is my best guess, that the indictment will come down before Thanksgiving. Possibly until Christmas but I will bet on Thanksgiving or earlier."

He said it like a man discussing the price of meat. No. With less passion.

"Nice timing. Not a sentimental bone in their hearts, indict a guy at Christmas."

"The governmental heart bleeds judiciously."

"Nice."

"Mr. Coolin, to be frank with you, and I am not intending a pun upon your given name, but to be frank: a Christmas under a cloud as a free man is infinitely preferable to a Christmas in even such a country club as Sandstone Federal Penitentiary."

"Well, I guess you can have a beer once in a while when you want it."

"Yes. A beer. You can have that as a free man."

"I'll think about it."

"Yes. Do think about it. Do that. And do let me know. But I would not delay if I were you. No. Not at all."

Frankie followed the corridors to the elevator. No bullshit, he thought, there wasn't bullshit now.

Klein had confirmed his private terror.

5

A thin black man with a wide mustache and a balding brow was waiting on the stoop of the building when Frankie Coolin got back to the West Side. It was late afternoon and the neighborhood was starting to come alive for Friday night. The streets were filled with kids. The man gave Frankie Coolin a little wave when he saw him.

"Man, I been looking for you."

"I been around, you must of not been looking too hard."

"Say, Frankie, I come by this afternoon, you got this white dude up in there, he be painting or some shit like that. I say where you are and he say, he say nothing. Man, I seen that cat was shaking and he had a piece on him. So I say I wait for you out here."

"It's my piece."

"I don't know who owns it, Frankie, but I thought your white dude was gonna shoot me with that piece, he was nervous like, you know?"

"He pull it on you or what?"

"No. But he was nervous. I tole him you and me got business."

"We got no business, Willie."

Willie stared at him for a moment and then spat on the stoop. "You talk bad, you know, Frankie."

"That's because I am bad. OK, what the fuck we got to talk about?"

"We got to talk about the association. We got to set things straight."

"Is that right? I give you twenty-five bucks two months ago for that blackmail bullshit, I don't want to hear any more shit about the fucking association."

"Listen, Frankie, I didn't blackmail you. You wanted to give to the association, dig?"

"Tell me about it."

"Besides. I ain't asking you for money now because I got to talk about what the association is now come up with."

"So what's that that they come up with?"

Frankie waited on the steps.

"We was talking about these properties that you own down here, about maybe the improvements that you says you was going to take care of especially on that building over on Arthington."

"I took care of the toilets. I had Scottie out here in July, he went through that building like shit through a goose. Pardon the expression. He found they were throwing hairbrushes down that toilet on three. You know where the MacNeils live?"

"Yeah, I know about that. I tole them that. But we ain't talking about that."

Willie stared hard at Frankie Coolin. The two men were of similar build and height. Willie's skin was very black; his eyes were large and white with red tinges around the dark iris.

"We talking about Scottie. We talking about that white dude you got up there in that building painting those apartments."

"I'm glad he's working. You like the paint?"

"I don't like that pink, that's a nigger color."

"I thought you'd like the pink."

"You just want to get me going, you want me to be talking about something else."

"I don't want to be talking about anything with you, Willie, because we got nothing to say to each other. I give you twenty-five bucks and you give me one of those bullshit decals to put on the doors in my buildings so that we don't get hassled by your fucking association and so you don't call up the building department on us."

"That ain't so much money for so much protection."

"Look, Willie, you want to fuck around, everyone can fuck around. If you want to get the building department down here on every fucking building, we can get them down here and they can shut me down and I'll take the sinks and tubs and toilets out and burn the places down. You want to be a hard guy about these buildings, I don't need the hassle right now."

He stopped because he realized he was getting mad again. He never got mad. It had all started with the G yesterday. It had kept up with Kennedy and with Klein, the lawyer, this afternoon. And now even Willie Oboe was getting his goat.

"I ain't talking about you burning down no buildings."

"Sure you are. You want to be such a Ralph Nader, then go ahead, see if the city is going to rehab these fucking buildings for you. I'm making a little money on these—"

"You making a lot of money. Don't give me no bullshit, you ain't jiving me, man. You come down here to make a lot of money or you ain't coming down here."

"I come down here because I love you people."

"Don't jive me, mother."

"I ain't your fucking mother, Willie; if I was your mother, I would have drowned you."

They stared at each other for a moment, letting the hostility show in their eyes. And then Willie Oboe made a gesture of dismissal with the back of one black hand.

"Ain't any use getting like this."

"I don't need this kind of hassle on Friday."

"We wasn't talking about no jive-ass building department anyway. Did I say building inspector to you? Shit, did I ever say anything about a building inspector to you? They white anyway, what's a nigger got to say about a building inspector? They come down here and you give them twenty-five bucks and they don't find no violations less we out here with Jesse Jackson or someone like that to get the TVs out here."

"All right, what were you talking about?"

"I'm your friend, Frankie, you see it or not. You all the time come by with these peoples like that dude Scottie what you brought down here."

"He works cheap."

"Shit, ain't work as cheap as a nigger works and you know it. Now, you come down here and that's right because you owns these buildings. I ain't saying you can't come down here. I got respect for you; you trying in these buildings, I understand that. I tole that to the association when we were meeting the other night. I say, 'Frankie, he ain't a bad white man. He come down here at least.' I say, 'Ain't that so, Mrs. Cletus? Ain't that right last December when the pipe broke down in the basement and you calling me up and I calling up Frankie out by his house out in the suburb, I say, Frankie, come out here, and he come, ain't that so, Mrs. Cletus?' You see, I talking for you, Frankie."

"I appreciate it."

"No, you don't appreciate it. Why you got to make everything so hard? I just come by to talk to you and you got your white cat upstairs he wants to pull a piece on me. I tell you, Frankie, I know he don't mean nothing, he just being nervous, but if it was someone else was down here and some white cat pulls a piece, I got my piece too. That cat be dead, Frankie."

"Just so you don't blow that smoke at me, Willie. Don't fuck with me."

As they talked, they began to dance up and down the steps. First Frankie Coolin circled above Willie Oboe and then they reversed positions so that Willie Oboe was on the top step of the stoop.

"You take this cat, Scottie, he come down here because you tell him, 'I got some toilets need fixing.' I seen him, you remember, that was one scared white dude, he looking up and down ever' time someone come into the room with him, he keeps putting his back against the wall, he can't hardly work on those toilets."

"That ain't a bad idea to keep your back to the wall."

"Shit, Frankie, you ever have any trouble coming down here?"

"You remember when the Washingtons moved out? You remember that?"

"They took the refrigerator."

"They hustled that icebox down the steps and up the alley. Took my fucking icebox to the new building they moved into. They owed me two months' rent, I don't let anybody go two months on me but I figured they were all right and you told me they were all right."

"I tole you that because I thought they were all right. I didn't know they needed no refrigerator."

"So they took my icebox. You figure that was all right, huh? They need an icebox, take Frankie Coolin's icebox out of the building."

"I didn't say I thought it was all right. I just said I didn't know they needed a refrigerator."

"Everybody needs something, doesn't mean they take it."

"Now, Frankie, what you think people do they need something? They got to take it, don't they? You know it yourself. Where the hell you get the refrigerator in the first place?"

"That's my business."

"So they take the refrigerator, wasn't nothing to you, you got it back."

"I got it back because I got my piece and because I'm not afraid." Frankie Coolin said it so flatly that he nearly believed it himself for a moment. And then he thought of Arthur Klein. He shoved his hands in the pockets of his jeans because he suddenly felt cold, standing on the stoop, watching the street.

"Never said you were afraid," said Willie Oboe. "I'm the one tole you where they moved to and we went and got it back."

"And when Washington pulled that knife—"

"You pulled your piece. Shit, I seen the face on that nigger when you pulled your piece on him, I thought he was going to take a shit right in his pants."

"I thought I was going to shit in my pants too."

"But everything be cool, wasn't it? We got that refrigerator out just like that. Even got Washington to help us take it down the stairs."

"That was nice of him considering he stole it in the first place."

"Man, I tole you in front. He needed a refrigerator. I tole you that."

"I don't care what you told me. And what does this got to do with the plumber?"

Frankie Coolin waited. He had met Willie Oboe four years ago. Willie rented one of the apartments in the building on the corner and had complained about the electrical overload in the apartment. Frankie ignored him until the day the story appeared in the Chicago *Daily Defender* about a white slumlord operating a dangerous building on the West Side. Willie Oboe had sent a copy of the black community newspaper to Frankie Coolin's house and Coolin went down to the West Side that night.

They had met in Tort's blind pig, an illegally operated tavern off Campbell Street which kept its own hours and which paid no taxes. The blind pig was in Tort's basement and

Frankie Coolin and Sgt. Michael Cork from the Monroe Street police station were the only two white men who ever went into the place. It was a fair place to drink because Tort did not permit violence, because Michael Cork kept the peace outside and because the price of beer was thirty cents cheaper than anyone else would charge.

Willie Oboe had explained that he only wanted the building fixed up and Frankie Coolin had given him a lesson in the economics of operating a slum building.

"You want me to fix it up right, I can fix it up right," Frankie Coolin had said. "I do what I can. OK, you can't run a dishwasher and a TV off the outlet, what the hell, that building was thrown up in 1905, they didn't even have TV then. But you got to make compromises. If I do everything all at once that needs to be done to fix the building, you can't afford to live there."

"What are you meaning?"

"What I am meaning, my man, is that I can fix anything up and then I got to charge. You pay a hundred five a month. You want to pay three-fifty? You got that kind of bread? You got it and you want to live here and shit, I can fix anything up for you that you want, hot and cold running whores or anything. But you gotta pay if you wanta play and that's what that is about. You're poor people so you got to live in a poor building and that's it. When you get your bread, you'll blow off this neighborhood faster than you can say Jackie Robinson and you know it."

"I still only talking about the electrical work."

"Listen. I'll go look at it but I don't need this shit in the paper about slum buildings and all that. I don't need the heat. Look, you're a busybody, you got these people stirred up. Why don't we cut a deal?"

It had been the critical moment in their relationship.

"What you got in mind?"

"I got to have a manager down here in the first place."

"Yeah? What's it pay?"

"It don't pay nothing."

"Nothing for nothing gets you nothing."

"Maybe it takes care of the rent though. Maybe if someone is getting a little subsistence for the rent from welfare, maybe he can handle the rent and still handle the money for himself."

"How much rent you say you charge me?"

"Hundred five a month."

"That's not enough," Willie Oboe said.

Frankie stared at him. He understood what Willie was saying.

"I thinks you got to go up a little on the rent. Say one-fifty a month."

"All right. Hundred half."

"But I ain't working for you, dig?"

"Sure."

"I get complaints, I call you and you take care of it, dig?"

"I dig."

"Man, I ain't messing now."

"But you got to get these people to calm down and I don't want to see no shit in the *Defender.*"

"Don't worry 'bout that now, now that we understand each other."

They had managed to understand each other and their peculiar arrangement for four years. Frankie Coolin even understood—in a way—why Willie Oboe started his Arthington and Neighborhood Tenements Association.

"I got to look to my place in the area, you dig?" Willie Oboe had explained.

"Sure. Whatever. You're just hustling."

"I ain't hustling you."

"You can put that in the bank, Willie." The voice had been flat. "You want to hustle the brothers, feel free."

"I mean, you got to join the association, dig?"

"I don't join. Nothing. Lions Club, Rotary—"

"Man, you don't have to go to no meetings."

"What's it cost me?"

"Twenty-five."

"Twenty-five what."

"A year."

"Put me down."

"All right." He pulled out a sheet of paper. "You got a check or what?"

"I'll catch you Friday."

"Hey, shit, my man, I know Friday."

"The eagle don't fly until Friday. And that's something I

wanted to tell you about. You can call this outfit anything you want, but it ain't tenements association. Tenements are buildings. Tenants are people."

"I know that, Frankie."

"Just so you know."

"Look here, I ain't representing no people, I'm representing the buildings they live in. We want decent buildings."

"Fine. Get me some decent people and I can get you decent buildings."

"You prejudiced, you know that?"

"So are you, Willie."

And so it had gone. And now Willie Oboe had a new scam. Frankie Coolin waited on the stoop. He knew it was coming and he could see the rough edges of it but he was waiting for Willie Oboe to define the scam.

"You must have a bad time, you know. Going out there in the suburbs and getting some of them white boys to come down here and work on your buildings."

"They'd rather be working in Oak Brook," Frankie Coolin said.

"Right. Right." Willie was smiling and nodding. "I mean, I bet you can spend half a day trying just to find someone to come out here. That Scottie cat ain't gonna be out here no more."

"He will if he wants to get paid."

Willie laughed, flashing teeth again, bobbing his head. Too agreeable, Frankie Coolin thought. "Right, right. You a hard man, Frankie, but you gotta be hard."

Frankie waited.

"Now, dig, I was thinking about this just now, when I was upstairs and this nervous cat with the piece was painting. I be thinking about it and saying, 'This ain't right.' I mean, you working on these buildings all the time to keep them up and I appreciate it—"

Frankie didn't speak.

"But I was thinking, if you had some cats from down here to be working on the buildings, that would be easy for you, right? I mean, get some of the brothers to do some of the work for you, they right here in the area to start with, they could be doing that ole monkey painting that cat is doing up there and

I know two mens personally they could clear out your toilets for you."

"Yeah. They'd walk away with them."

"Aw, now." Exaggerated frown. "You know I don't mean them kind of people, I never gave you one reason to say something like that to me, never in all the time we knowed each other, did I? Man, I mean quality cats, you dig? I mean some people that could come over in the middle of the night some night when you got a leak in the hot water heater down to the basement, they could put the fixup on it and you wouldn't have to drive out like you done last winter during that snowstorm and get stuck here for two days."

"I had a good time, a few drinks over at Tort's and Mrs. Cummings made supper. It wasn't so bad."

"Shit, who you jiving?"

"No, Willie, who are you jiving? You want to be contractor on maintenance around here now, right? You get the bodies and I pay you, right? Pretty soon people around here would think you owned the buildings."

"Nothing wrong with that, Frankie. You know there's nothing wrong with that. That's why you got me managing them in the first place."

"Look, you're like a smoke alarm. You tell me there's a fire but you don't put it out. I like the arrangement the way it is and you should like it too. You just do your shit and drink your JB and Bud on Friday night and I'll do mine, okay? I really can't use a hassle right now."

"Because of them mens."

Frankie waited, stared into Willie's eyes.

"The mens come by yesterday was the same ones what come by before."

"You're the eyes and ears of the world. You should have been a reporter or something."

"I see what I see. I see the mens come by yesterday. And I know what they is."

"What is they?"

"They heavy." Willie Oboe stared back just as hard as Frankie stared at him. "They is the FBI."

"Is that right?"

"What you done to get the FBI on your case?"

"I don't have the FBI on my case. They are on your case, Willie. They been coming by asking me about your little church over on Madison."

"Aw, shit, that's jive. I don't pay no taxes. I don't know no one pays no taxes."

"They said this year they're going to get one guy in the ghet-to and make an example out of him. You the man."

"Shit, Frankie, you and me go back, don't we know each other a long time? You don't have to jive me. I got eyes."

"You got big eyes." Frankie paused. "I can't shoot the shit with you all day, stud. I got things to do, people to see."

"Shit, now, Frankie, I thought we could have a couple of Buds down to Tort's, we could talk out on this problem."

"Look, Willie, hustle somebody else. Hustle the sheeny owns that corner building, maybe you can get him to have you set up a labor pool for him. Why are you always hassling me?"

"No one even knows where that Jew lives. He ain't in the phone book. We tried to get on his case."

"He's smarter than I am then. I should have got de-listed when I first bought a building over here, then I wouldn't have to listen to all this shit all the time. You think you got me by the balls just like everyone else thinks they got me by the balls, because they think I'm sitting out there with a wife and kids and house and mortgage and all the rest of the crap. Well, you ain't got me and no one else does. Not yet." The anger was up in him again and he realized he had doubled his fists. What was he going to do? Hit Willie?

Willie stared at him. "Frankie. I ain't hassling you."

"What's this shit about maintenance? I got my brother's kid up there now; that's who that white dude is that you want me to put him out of a job for some colored guy I never saw before, so you can cut a commission and make even more easy money than you're making."

"Shit, man, I don't make no money."

"Yeah and Tort gives away JB these days."

"Man, that ain't money. That ain't money. That's drinking money. I'm talking about money."

"I know what you're talking about and you think it all comes from the same place. Well, Willie, I ain't got it to give any more." He was still angry and his voice was rising and he was aware that there were a couple of black men standing on the sidewalk watching him. But he didn't care. He felt the frustration crushing him.

"Man, you wrong to lay that on me," said Willie. "Man, you so wrong."

"Tell me about it some other time when I could use a laugh. I ain't got the time right now."

"You could get trouble."

"I don't want no trouble," Frankie Coolin said in a lower voice. "I don't want to hear about me getting trouble, not with these buildings and not someone hassling my tenants. I don't want to hear word one about shit going down in my buildings. I mean that, Willie."

"Is that right? Is that right, my man?"

"I ain't your man, Willie, and I ain't your brother and I ain't your momma, so you can cut all that shit out in front."

"Hey, brother—" It was one of the black men—young, tall, in a leather coat—calling from the sidewalk. "You got some trouble, brother?"

Willie turned. "Ain't got no trouble, brother."

"Thought you might have some trouble with this white cat."

"Ain't no trouble, brother."

"All right, brother."

"All right, brother. Amen."

The two on the sidewalk still stood and stared. Night was drifting in over the narrow street. The sounds of children— skates on sidewalks, yells in gangways, shouts from the roofs —were all becoming louder and more hollow.

Frankie Coolin stared at Willie Oboe.

"Hell, Frankie," Willie said at last, flashing a grin. "Hell, man. We got no hassle with each others, we be friends too long for that. Man, it's just those FBI cats got you going."

"I got no problem with the G."

Willie grinned.

"I got no problem," Frankie repeated.

"Sure, man. They be coming out here to see if they could rent an apartment, that right?" Willie Oboe laughed and the two black men on the sidewalk watched him laugh. "They going to integrate, that right?"

"Sure," Frankie said. It was draining out of him, he realized;

Willie wasn't going to push it. Not now, in this place, at this time. But it would still be there, waiting for its chance.

"Man, you a liberal."

"And you a man of God," Frankie said. "You ought to turn Catholic."

"Shit, then I'd have to wear a collar and I couldn't fuck."

"Everyone can fuck. The opportunity is always around."

"You can say that, Frankie," Willie laughed. He put out his hand and Frankie took it in a temporary truce, but Willie had never brought up the idea of handling the maintenance before and Frankie felt frightened. The door had been opened. He wondered why.

The G, Frankie Coolin thought. Willie thinks I'm going away.

He stared at the black man on the stoop for a moment without speaking. Yes. He figured Frankie's time was up. Maybe it was. Maybe he would need someone like Willie Oboe after all.

"Take it easy," Frankie Coolin said, wanting to break off the contact. He started up the steps of the stoop to the unpainted outer door.

"You be careful, Frankie, your boy in there is very nervous with that piece."

"He won't shoot me."

"Shit, he might. It's dark in the hall and we all looks alike in the dark." And Willie laughed.

"That's all right, I won't smile," Frankie said. "Take it easy." He opened the door.

"I'll just take it," Willie said, still smiling.

Coolin paused. It was something that he might have said.

6

ohn was in the Bohemian's tavern when Frankie Coolin and Joey hit the door. It was dark outside and later than normal for them; but it was Friday night, and the place was still crowded with the after-work crew. Stacks of money were on the bar in front of each stool and the golden glasses of beer on the bar top caught the dim light and made the place seem warmer. Voices were loud and someone had put money in the jukebox for the first time that week. It thumped and groaned a cowboy song.

"What the hell is my dad doing in here?" Joey said, his voice framed with disgust. He had been angry with Frankie Coolin back at the building but he had finished painting one apartment. He handed Coolin his piece in the building and told him about the appearance of Willie Oboe; Coolin told him who Willie was.

John Coolin was fat again but pasty, the same pasty color he had assumed after the operation three years before on his heart. He looked like a dead man. His eyes were dull and his nose was red. He wasn't supposed to drink beer, the doctors told him. He wasn't supposed to do shit, he told Frankie Coolin once. Joey did not look like him at all but John Coolin told his son that he would, someday, after he worked twenty or twenty-five years on the roofs. Joey had said he would never do a roof job, not even on his own house.

"Hey, Joey. I didn't know you was working with Frankie today." The voice was slurred and soft, the voice of a sick man who drank.

"Yeah. We been painting. I been painting, I mean."

"I had some business."

"Is that right, Frankie?" John said.

The Bo put up two glasses of beer and Frankie took one and drank it until it was drained and hit the bar hard with the bottom of the glass. The Bohemian took it back for a refill. "You buying, John, or what?"

"OK, OK, I'm buying." John Coolin reached for his wallet and pulled out a five and put it on the bar. "I never see you pull money out of the pocket," John said.

"You got that right, John," Frankie said and smiled. "It always tastes better when you're buying, John."

"Then it must taste good a lot of the time because it seems like I'm always buying. How'd you like working with the niggers, Joey? Frankie show you around, take you over to that tavern he goes to over there? He introduce you to his nigger friends?"

The voice was sneering and mean. Frankie smiled and sipped his beer. "Niggers don't bother me," he said.

"Yeah, Frankie loves niggers, he can't get enough of them. After we move out here to get away from the niggers, Frankie still has to go down into the city."

"They got green money just like white people," Frankie said at last. He held the beer and the smile on his face. The smile was pasted on, Joey saw.

"Yeah, Frankie is a big shot down on the West Side, they think he's a white god or something."

"You got that right, John. What've you been doing today?"

"You want to know what I been doing?"

"You been drinking," Joey said.

"Listen to it, Frankie. I got to take shit like that from my own kid. If it wasn't for my heart, if I was the man I was, I'd knock him on his ass."

"Take it easy, John," Frankie said. "The Bo don't want you to have a heart attack right here."

"I could have a heart attack after today, you know that, Frankie? I could just drop dead after today. And maybe not just from my heart either. Maybe I could just drop dead because I'm ashamed."

"Ashamed of what?" Joey said. He signaled for another round of beers and pulled a twenty-dollar bill out of the pocket of his jacket.

"Of my own brother, for Christ's sake, my own fucking brother. I was in the house, sitting in the kitchen and your mother was over to the Hillside shopping center because they got a sale at Goldblatt's, your mother doesn't have enough shit in the house, every time she gets the throwaway paper, she sees a sale and she's got to go over and get more shit. That's what we need in the house is more shit. She's got shit on the shelves, she's got shit in the closet, she's got it stored in boxes in the basement, she's got it in the garage, she's got shit coming out of my ears and she's got to go and get more shit."

Joey's face hardened as his father spoke.

"Shit, shit, shit," John Coolin said. "My life is surrounded by shit. She's got twenty salt-and-pepper shakers."

"She collects them," Joey said.

"Twenty. She's got plastic ones and glass ones. She's got wooden ones from when we were up in Wisconsin two years ago, they got deers on them. And when you go to find a fucking salt-and-pepper shaker in the house, one that works, you can't find one because of all the shit there is. I never seen so much shit in my life."

"Well, everybody's got to have a hobby," Frankie said mildly. "I drink beer."

"You drink beer, that's funny. You drink beer, I suppose I gotta laugh. I was sitting in the kitchen and then there's someone at the door. The dog is barking, that fucking dog is dumber and lazier every day of his life. I shush the dog up and I go over to the door. I don't like to hear doorbells in the middle of the day."

"It wakes you up?" Joey said.

"You see the bullshit I got to put up with, Frankie? You see why I got a bad heart in the first place?"

Frankie waited. He had not moved for the last few seconds. He wanted to know who was at the door; he knew who was at the door.

"You know who was there? Fucking FBI men, Frankie. Two fucking FBI men. They show me their identification and they come in the house and the fucking dog starts yipping and one of them is afraid of the dog. He keeps saying to me, 'That dog going to bite or what?' That fucking dog wouldn't bite a rabbit if the rabbit was sitting in its mouth. That fucking dog don't bite nothing that's for free. Steaks he can bite and he can bite canned dog food but he can't bite dry dog food. I told him that dog wouldn't bite a flea."

The G, Frankie Coolin thought, and the thought drowned out John Coolin's voice for a moment.

"You know why these guys are coming by my house, Frankie? But you know, don't you?"

Joey looked at his uncle, his eyes open and puzzled.

"They weren't selling raffle tickets," Frankie said.

John frowned. His face was unshaven and puffy. His eyes did not glitter. His dark hair was matted and dull.

"Make a joke, Frankie. You see, Joey, when it gets too heavy, Frankie makes a joke, like everything can be laughed off, like nothing means nothing. When we were kids, he was like that. Joke, everything is a joke. He and Heinie Dorfman got me once down by the railroad tracks and they tied me up, for Christ's sake, I was a kid about nine years old and these two pricks tied me up and they put me in a boxcar, in a fucking boxcar. When the train was by the siding there over by Lake and Halsted. And so I'm in this fucking boxcar and there's rats in there, I swear to God. A big fucking joke."

"It was pretty funny," Frankie Coolin said.

"Yeah. Funny if I'd of died, then Frankie would be really laughing his balls off. So the train takes off and I'm trying to get out of the ropes and finally, I push myself out of the car over by Crawford and I roll down the embankment. There I was, nine years old, and I'm tied up."

"You never told me that," Joey said.

"He didn't want to because he was ashamed," Frankie Coolin said.

"Sure, everything is a joke," John Coolin said.

"If you look at it the right way," Frankie said.

"This guy was going by in a car and he stopped and untied me. He asked me who did it. I could of got you into trouble instead of me. But I'm the sucker, see Frankie laughing? I'm the sucker. I go home, I walk back home over to where we was living then, and I'm late for supper so the old man gives me a whack and Frankie is laughing there, I thought he was going to shit."

"It was funny," Frankie said. "You can't hold a grudge forty years."

"I can hold a grudge as long as I want," John Coolin said. "You gonna buy a beer now or you going to do your song and dance again? Your uncle is the cheapest bastard I ever met, I seen sheenies got more open pockets than your uncle is got. He spends all day with the niggers, robbing the niggers, and then he come out here and he tries to rob his friends. Your uncle is always robbing someone."

"There's always someone waiting to be robbed," Frankie said, the edge of irritation suppressed by his mild voice.

"Well, maybe now it ain't going to be so funny. Those guys weren't selling no raffle tickets. They were asking me questions. You know how long they were talking to me? They were talking to me about an hour."

"Is that right, John? What were you telling them for an hour that was so interesting?" Mildly but with the blade of a warning drawn across the neck of words.

"You want to know that, don't you, Frankie? You see, Joey, you think Frankie is a ballbuster, you think Frankie is such hot shit that you can't wait to go out and work for him down in nigger town and learn all that nigger shit and nigger talk and all that shit. You think Frankie is so fucking hot and I'm going to tell you something. Frankie ain't so fucking hot." He paused as though he had made a profound point. "In fact, Frankie has just about got his balls caught in the ringer, I think."

"Is that right?"

"And that crook that's your wife's cousin, too."

"We aren't talking about Rose," Frankie Coolin said. "I don't want to hear that."

"We aren't talking about Rose," John agreed. "Your wife is like a saint, she's got a crown waiting for her in heaven for just putting up with your shit for twenty-five years. She's got a crown, Joey, that woman is a saint. A saint." He said this very loud and the Bohemian stared at him from the middle of the bar.

The Bohemian said, "You want the Saints? I never took a bet on them."

"I ain't talking about the Saints," John said, slamming his hand down on the bar and coughing. He coughed when he became excited. "I am talking about a saint, that's who I am talking about. I am talking about Rose Coolin."

The Bohemian waddled down the boards. "Rose? Frankie, is something wrong with Rose?"

"Nothing's wrong with Rose. Bottle Nose here is just getting a little crazy. Give us three more, Emil."

Joey smiled.

"Bottle Nose?" John said. "Oh, that's funny. Isn't that funny, Joey?"

Joey grinned.

"Funny, my own kid thinks that kind of shit is funny. You got a mouth on you, Frankie, you always did and now you're going to get your ass in trouble because of it. You're not the only one's got a mouth on him."

"What did you talk about? With them?"

"We talked about you, naturally. What the hell do you think they came by the house for? They want to talk about salt-and-pepper shakers?"

"If they did, they would of come to the right place."

"We talked about you and where you keep your building material. And we talked about how much money you got. You know, things they like to talk about. We talked about Pat Kennedy, too."

"What did you talk to them about? You don't know nothing about me or my business," Frankie Coolin said. His voice was hard and low. Joey stared at him. He had never heard Frankie Coolin speak with this voice and it was a voice that Frankie had never used with his brother John.

"Maybe I don't and maybe I do. I know something's been going on, I should of put two and two together. I should of known something was going on."

"John. What did you talk about."

"They keep wanting to know about you and who you know. They want to know about your buildings down in nigger town. They want to know about your nigger friends. I said, hell, I don't know nothing about his nigger friends except he's got them." John Coolin smiled. "You got nigger friends and sheeny friends and Outfit friends. You got a lot of friends, Frankie, I hope they're all around to help you out when the time comes."

"What's going on, Uncle Frank?"

"Nothing's going on, Joey. I don't want to hear that you talked diddle shit with them, John."

"Is that right, Frankie?" John Coolin belched and poured beer down his throat and belched again. "You're always the tough guy, Frankie."

"I get as tough as I have to be."

"You think you're such a big shot." The voice was mean, full of little shards of glittering hatred. "Joey tells me about 'Frankie done this' and 'Uncle Frankie is going to do that.' 'Uncle Frankie.' Well, I tell you, Uncle Frankie, that you are in shit up to your collar. I am telling you that it is hitting the fan and you are standing in front of it. The big man. You own buildings. Big fucking deal, you own a couple of slum buildings full of whores and pimps down on the West Side. Full of niggers. You are such a big man."

"Lighten up, Dad," Joey said. "Christ, who needs this?"

"You telling me to lighten up, my own kid? You can mind your own fucking business, kid, the day you start telling me what I can say and what I can't say; I'm still a big enough man to knock you on your ass and you believe it."

Joey made a face. "Just take it easy." He sipped his beer. "Christ." He sipped it again.

"You," John Coolin said, turning to Frankie. "You got this kid's eyes so wide that he'd believe the Pope is a Jew if you told him."

Everyone was beginning to bristle. The noise in the bar seemed at a higher level. A week's worth of frustrations was being drowned in beer up and down the bar and some of it was spilling.

"I think these federal guys aren't playing," John Coolin said. "In fact, I think they got you by the nuts is what I think: they were asking after me about you and your big deals and your property, they wanted to know if you had a joint in Wisconsin, they were asking if you had some buildings in a trust. Listen, when they start nickel and diming you that way, they are after your ass. That's the way they get the big guys. One day you're doing business with some turkey contractor from Brighton Park and the next day you're looking in the *Trib* and you're watching the guy march through the federal building to post bond. That's just the way it works. You see what I'm telling you, Frankie?"

Frankie saw; for a minute, he didn't speak.

"Hey, Joey, look at the big shot," John Coolin said. And Joey Coolin looked at Frankie.

Frankie did not look at him. He stared at his glass of beer, wet and waiting on the bar.

"See, Joey, the way it is?" John Coolin said.

"What's going on, Uncle Frank?"

"Hey, tell him, Uncle Frank. Tell him what's going on." John Coolin made an imitation laugh. "Sure. Big shot Frankie Coolin. You're so fucking dumb sometimes, Joey, you make me wonder if you were somebody else's kid. Frankie gives you a job and you think it's shit out of a golden goose when he's paying you under scale and you ain't getting no workmen's comp out of it. What happens if you get hurt on the job? You think you're covered now? You think I got you covered?"

"I ain't gonna get hurt. What's going on, Uncle Frank?"

"Yeah. Tell him, Frankie, what's going on with the feds, you tell him good for a change. You work like a nigger in heat, Joey, and Frankie, Frankie just keeps making his deals and cons and hustles and he keeps moaning about how nobody wants to work, how he's got to get the jobs for everyone in the family, that if he wasn't around, nobody would be around to see us all get fed. You know what, Joey? I'm sorry about this for Frankie but it's a good thing too, if only you see the truth about your uncle. Listen, Joey—" He grabbed his son by the arm because Joey started to edge away from him. "Joey, I could of told those FBI guys a million things about Frankie Coolin if I had to because there's nobody knows him better than I do."

"But you didn't," Frankie Coolin said finally. His voice was very low and hard.

"Hey, don't pull that shit on me."

"But you didn't," Frankie Coolin said.

"Hey, if I didn't, it's because I got loyalty in this family even when I know some don't have it," John Coolin said. "Talk's cheap when it comes down to talking about sticking up for your family. But not with me it ain't. I don't want to see your Irish ass in the joint, Frankie. I think about the way Brian was when he come out and when I had to go get him."

"You weren't anywhere near him. I had to go get him out of the joint."

"Sure, sure, make yourself the big man again. You always got to come out on top. Well, Joey, I can tell you and you were there, you seen the way Brian was when he come out of the joint and when I think about it, when I think about what it would do to Rose and the kids if Frankie went inside, then I can't stand it and I ain't saying nothing to a couple of coppers because that's all they are when you come down to it. They carry them federal cards and they dress like undertakers but when it comes down to it, they ain't nothing more than a couple of dicks on the pad in the city; and I seen those guys all my fucking life. I got loyalty, Joey, that's what; I know what you're supposed to do when trouble comes down. You got to close in with your family because your family is the only thing you got going for you."

Frankie stared at his older brother for a moment. He realized he wasn't seeing John's face as it was now. He never did anymore. John wasn't sick and John wasn't a drunk and John didn't have dead eyes and pasty skin and the smell of a corpse. John was just the kid he had been. It was as though Frankie had blanked out John's real face for the past ten years. He saw the kid who had played with him after summer rains in the flooded viaducts under the railroad tracks. He wondered if John only saw him as a kid too.

"Christ, Uncle Frank. What the hell is going on? Are you in real trouble?"

"Nothing I can't handle. I wish your father would keep his fucking mouth shut in this place."

"Christ, Uncle Frank. Christ. Feds? Feds coming around?"

"It don't mean nothing."

"Christ," Joey said again. He stared at his uncle and then at his father. "Christ," he said again. He reached for his beer. "Christ."

"Ah, Frankie," John Coolin said. "I shouldn't've blown my stack like that. Forget it. I just got pissed off with these federal bums coming around and with my wife running off to Goldblatt's. You know what she came home with? She came home with some of those mirror tiles, she wants me to put up some mirror tiles in our bedroom. Maybe she wants to turn it into a cathouse, for Christ's sake. I wish t'hell she'd go through the change in private."

Joey said, "Why d'ya talk about her like that?"

"Because she's my fucking wife is why," John Coolin said.

"Christ."

"Yeah, Christ is right, Joey. Christ and double Christ. Listen, Joey, I get sad when I think about it, when I think about Brian and those federal bums coming around trying to get Frankie in trouble. Sad." In fact, he was becoming sad in the face. His eyes were filling with tears. "We're getting older, Frankie, but we got to stick together."

"You're getting older, John, not me."

John Coolin did not hear. The tears flowed down the familiar paths in his cheeks.

"Ah, Frankie," John said.

Joey looked at Frankie; they knew the mood.

"Ah," John Coolin said again. "It comes with being Irish, you see the tears in everything. Irish, Joey, we're all Irish and when it comes down to it, all we got is each other because it was all we ever had. That and the Catholic Faith too. We got that. You never forget it, do you, Frankie, it's built into your blood. For a thousand years the bloody fucking English kept us down under their heel but they couldn't finish us off because we stuck together, because we kept the Faith, and when the time came, we threw the bastards out, didn't we? Joey, yer grandfather was one of them, threw them out. Didn't he tell us stories, Frankie? Didn't he tell us about making those black-and-tans dance to the tune of a Thompson gun? Didn't he?"

Frankie grabbed his glass and drank deep.

"Well, the same keeps going here, Joey, just you remember that. You gotta stick together, the Irish for the Irish. I know lots of people, I know Polacks and dagoes and slants and towel-heads and some ain't bad and some are but they ain't Irish and that's what you got to stick loyal to. I never understood why Two married that Polack."

"That ain't none of your business, John," Frankie said. The glass was empty. He knew he wouldn't fight John, not now; he hadn't touched John since that long ago day when he and Heinie had tied him up and thrown him in the boxcar.

"He ain't a bad guy for a Polack, don't get me wrong,

Frankie, Two could've done worse than him, but he ain't one of us and he never will be. Remember that, Joey, when you start fucking around with the skirts, remember you can fuck anyone you want but you only get married once. Remember that. They killed John Kennedy and Bobby but they won't kill us, not the Irish. They can't kill all of us."

Joey blushed. "Look, I'm going home. You want to go home, Dad?"

"Ah, shit, let's have one more. Emil? Let's have one more, one more time, OK?"

Frankie took the new glass of beer and said nothing. For a moment, no one said anything.

Joey said, "What's up, Uncle Frank? What's going down?"

"Nothing I can't handle."

"What do they want?"

"They're asking questions."

"They're asking about your Uncle Frank's income is what. You didn't file any tax last year or what?"

"I'm only two quarters behind," Frankie said and then stopped. He was getting loose, he thought. He never told anyone anything. "Sam and I are OK. I mean, you never get caught up but we're close."

"That ain't bad, Frankie," John said. "I was six quarters behind that time I fell off the roof. It was a good thing I was working for Signolli then and he had comp. I was out six months. That helped the taxes a lot, cut them back."

"Yeah. Too bad you fell on your head," Frankie said. For the first time, he was smiling again. He remembered how silly it had sounded, when John fell off the roof on his head. John had started drinking hard after that. Maybe he had gone a little screwy after that.

"Don't worry about my head," John Coolin said. "You got troubles enough of your own, you don't have to go around talking about me falling on my head."

"It was a good thing it wasn't your ass, you would of bounced right back up on the roof and then you would of still been six quarters behind on your tax. You couldn't of picked a better time to fall on your head."

"I don't need this shit about falling on my head," said John.

"It's a sensitive point," Frankie said to Joey, making the young man smile. "Not his head, I mean."

"Hey, fuck this shit," said John. "I try to tell you about being loyal when you got trouble and you want to make fun of me in front of my own kid."

"I don't want to hear about me having trouble in the taverns, John. I guess I should of said that from the start. I don't want to come back in here and hear some shit from Concrete Ben or Radio or MacLean that I got trouble. OK? You want to be loyal, be quiet then. That's loyal, not telling stuff about your family in the bars."

"Hey, take it easy, Frankie," John said. "You can lighten up too, you know."

Frankie said nothing. He held the cold beer in his left hand.

"Frankie," John said, touching his brother's face with the rough edge of his palm. He dropped his hand. His voice was sentimental. "I swear to God I wouldn't do nothing to hurt you. You know that." Tears again.

Frankie waited.

"Ah, Frankie, why do we fight? I guess we're just Irish, that's all." John put down his glass and sloshed beer on the bar. "You know I love you, you know that. You're my fucking brother, for Christ's sake, I love you just like I love my only sister, little Kate. You know that. We're all the family we got, just us now and the old man and mom out there in Queen of Heaven, God rest her soul. Joey, I want you to know something; I want you to know that no matter what happens, no matter what happens or anyone says, that your uncle is a fine man. I love you, Frankie. Just like I love Rose and Two and Peg and Mick and even the Polack Two married. We all got to stick together, no matter what happens, in bad times just like in good." He picked up his beer and suddenly set it down without drinking. "I really mean it. Frankie, I remember how you helped out when I was out with this thing with my ticker and you were by, not only in the hospital but getting work for Joey and all and helping out like the time you brought us that meat from Salvatori when you were driving the truck for them. I don't forget things like that. That was good meat, too, not the kind of shit now you get over at the grocery. I swear to God to you, Frankie, that if you need it, I'll go back on the roofs to help your family, they'll never miss a meal as long as I got a breath in my body left, and I want you to know that Rose is always going to have a home with us at our house, you know that, and that goes for Mick and Peg too and if it ever came down to it and the Polack died or got sick or threw her out, God forbid, but you got to expect anything, that I would take her in too, Two and Sean. You know that, you know that, Frankie."

Frankie stared.

"You know that."

Frankie touched his sleeve. John Coolin wanted him to do that. "Sure," Frankie said. "I know it, John." That was what John wanted him to say. But Frankie didn't know it at all.

7

When Frankie Coolin opened the side door of the house and walked into the kitchen, he saw the note on the table.

"Went to Two's. Sean is sick with flu says Dr. Back at ten. Frozen pizza in ice box. Rose."

Terrific, thought Frankie Coolin. He went to the refrigerator and took out a can of beer. He walked into the living room. Two side lamps by the couch were on, as well as the lamp next to the television set. The overhead lamp in the dining room was on, and the light in the hall. The lights in the bathroom were turned on. Frankie shut off the lights and the house sank into darkness, save for the kitchen.

He took a second can of beer and opened the door to the basement. As he went down the stairs, he could hear the radio in the old man's room.

"Hey," he said at the old man's door.

"Who is it? Who is it?" The old man always said that though he knew all the voices. It was as though, since his blindness, every unplanned contact was a threat to him.

"Me."

"Frankie. Is that you?"

"Me."

"Come in. You got a can of beer for me?"

"Sure."

The old man's room was clean because Rose saw to that. It was bare with an old easy chair they had picked up in a garage sale over in Broadview and a single bed and a lamp and a nightstand. A radio sat on a shelf above the bed. The old man sat in the darkness in the easy chair. Frankie turned on the lamp and walked over to him and handed him the can of beer. He went to the bed and sat down. It creaked with his weight.

"You got your clean clothes on? Rose changed the sheets

today, I don't want you sitting on the bed in your work clothes."

"I didn't do much work today," Frankie said. He held his can of beer in both hands and felt the coldness. He reached over and flicked off the light. The room was returned to gloom, objects made visible only by the small knife of light from the stairwell.

The old man let the radio keep humming. Neither man spoke for a moment.

"I was just thinking about going upstairs to get me a beer," the old man said at last.

"Yeah. I figured you would. Everyone's gone."

"Peace and quiet," the old man said. "Peg is on a date, I think."

"Yeah."

"She's young for the boys, I think."

"Yeah."

"Watcha working on now, Frank?"

"We're finishing up the new building. Joey and me. Did painting today."

"I hope you ain't got no dirt on your pants, I don't want to be sleeping in a dirty bed tonight."

"You should have another chair in here, I should get you another chair."

"What for, Frank? Company? Do I look as though I am on the entertainment committee in this room?"

"Well, I come down to talk to you. And you don't want me to sit on the bed."

"I can come upstairs and talk to you if you want me to. You're not doing me a favor coming here." The voice was high-pitched and the Irish accent was quite strong still, after fifty years in America.

"Jesus," Frankie Coolin said softly.

Neither spoke for a moment. They listened to the silence that hovered in the same space and time as the background noise of the radio.

"Ah," the old man said. "How's Joey working out, then?"

"Fine. He's a good worker, he ain't afraid to get dirty. I wish I had enough for him, I could keep him busy all the time. I was working on a deal with a contractor down to the federal building for a winter job." Frankie paused. "Maybe I can get Joey in there. Maybe I can keep him busy all winter."

"Winter's coming," the old man said. "I felt it today. I felt the cold in the walls, you know?"

"You can't feel cold in the walls. I put up one-by-three and insulation and drywall before I even put the paneling on."

"Ah, I still can feel it. In the spring, I can feel the damp beginning, even before the rains come. I can feel it in the walls. And the cold. In the fall, I can feel the cold settling in to the ground."

"You got good feelings."

"It's true, you know, Frank. What they say. When the eyes go, another sense takes over. I can feel the cold in the walls. I can hear things that other people can't hear, too. And smell. I can smell like I never did."

"When I gave up smoking a couple of years ago, I could smell better."

"D'ya have a cigarette on ya, Frank? I'm afraid I'm fresh out."

"Yeah." Frankie felt in his pocket but it was empty; he had forgotten to buy a pack at the tavern.

"Sorry," he said. "I guess I'm out too."

"Ah, well," the old man said, as though he were accustomed to such disappointments. "It's just as well, I suppose. I like a smoke in the evening, you know."

"I know. I'll get a pack later. I gotta go out again, Rose didn't leave me nothing to eat."

"Ah," said the old man. He did not eat at night anymore or even join the family upstairs. But he was up before dawn, when Frankie was up, and the two of them padded around the sleeping house on separate missions, Frankie getting ready for work, the old man making coffee. The old man would sit at the kitchen table in the darkness, drinking coffee alone, until the rest of the house came awake. And then he would tuck into an enormous breakfast, whatever Rose made for him. He would eat again at lunch, sometimes down at the Bo's tavern where he would walk alone, and then, at night, recede into the silences of his basement room, listening to the radio summer and winter.

Again, they kept the silence between them for a long time.

"Frank? I was wondering after you been to see your brother? How is John doing now?"

"He's OK. I saw him today."

"Ah, today?" He paused. "Down to the tavern, was it?"

"Yeah."

"Ah, John, John." The old man shook his head in the darkness but Frankie caught the gesture in the sliver of light.

"John's all right," Frankie Coolin said.

"John's not a well man, not at all. I suppose we have to be happy that Joey's grown to a man is all, he can help him out."

"John's all right."

"Ah, I never understood it, there hasn't been any heart problems at all in your family. Yer great-grandfather in the old country lived to ninety."

"Potatoes," Frankie said.

"There's something in that," the old man said. "A potato is a fine thing. And eggs, plenty of eggs as well."

"Gives you cholesterol."

"Ah, to hell with all that talk. They never talked about that in the old country and when we had to go to the doctor, we had to go up to Ennis because there was none to be had in Doonaha. Ennis was fifty miles up, that's how far. I tell you, it was less trouble just being sick and leaving it go than to go up to Ennis for the doctor."

"Especially with these towel-heads," Frankie Coolin said.

"Towel-heads?"

"The Iranians, Pakis, all these guys. You go to a doctor now, you need a translator just to get through to them."

"Ah." The old man clucked a sound and sipped his beer noisily. "When yer going out later, would you get me some candy bars? I want some of them Hershey bars but without the nuts."

"Sure," Frankie said. "Dad."

Silence. Waiting.

"Frank? What is it, Frank?"

"Nothing."

"Ah, nothing is nothing. I can hear you breathing, boyo. Come on now. What is it? What are you trying to tell me, nothing?"

"Nothing," Frankie said.

"Ah, nothing. You could fool me when I had me eyes but you can't fool me now. I got no eyes but I got me ears and I hear yer voice. It ain't the words, Frank, it's the sound of it. I know you want to talk to me."

"Dad."

"Ah, tell me, Frank. Is it Joey? Is it John? Is that it? Is something wrong with John again? With his heart? Is that it?"

"Nothing's wrong with John. I saw him a half hour ago."

"Ah, don't lie now to me, Frank. If it's me John, tell me like a man."

"Nothing about John," Frankie said.

"Joey then? Or one of yours? What is it, boy?"

"Nothing. There's nothing wrong, Dad."

"I can hear it in your voice that something's wrong."

Frankie closed his eyes to make the darkness deeper. He felt the cold, wet can in his hand. He heard John's voice, protesting his love for him. Stick together.

"Dad. I got some problems. In fact, I got one problem."

"You do?" Another pause. "What's wrong now, Frank, then?"

"I got involved in some trouble. I didn't exactly get into it but I got into it backwards. You know."

Silence. Darkness. Frankie's eyes were still closed. The silence of the house held them.

"What kind of trouble?"

"Federal."

"Jesus Christ, Frank, what the hell have you been doing? You ain't been paying your taxes?"

"It's a little more than that."

"I tole you to pay yer taxes, Jesus Christ, yer like a child with money." The old man's voice was angry. "When you were a kid, you never let a dime wear a hole in your pocket but you had it out to spend it."

"This is more than that," Frank said.

"Is it? And what could it be?"

"Ah. Nothing. Nothing I can't work out."

"Do you need money, is that it? You come down here to talk to me and you need money, is that it? I told you from the first day I came into your house, I told you, let me pay my way here. I told you I'd pay for me own light and gas but you wouldn't hear of it and now you need the money, is that it? Well, I've got it, Frank, and you just tell me how much it is and I got it for you."

"It isn't money—"

"Ah, sure it is," the old man said. "When John and Kate come around me, I know what it is before they open their gob. Money. They figure it ain't right that I should have the money and they ain't but I said, their time is coming and my time is short. In time they'll get the money. And now you need it too and I won't grudge you for it. It's yours, Frank, you took me in, you and Rose, and I can do right for you just as I do for Kate and John." Triumph colored the old voice.

"No," said Frankie Coolin.

"No? 'No' is it? Ah, don't let your pride get in the way of feeding your mouth or Rose or the kids, Frank. Yer always was too proud about yerself and you know where pride leads you. To the fall, Frank, pride is the way to hell. It's nothing to me, Frank, the money is nothing." He paused. "How much do you need for this trouble?"

"I don't need money."

"That's a lie, Frank. Everyone in the world needs money. What do you think if we give the colored the money they need now to live like the white people live? Our problems would be solved is what. The colored are the same as us, Frankie, I said it again and again except they ain't got no money. So tell me what you need, Frank, before Rose comes back and we can settle it now and shake on it."

"I don't want money, Dad," Frankie Coolin said. "I never asked you for a dime and I never will, I don't want your money or Mom's money. You like it when Kate and John come sucking up to you? Light bill? You want to pay the light bill for what you use? Is that it? You use about four cents of electricity a month. OK, you owe me a half a buck for the last year. You want to pay me or what? What the fuck makes you think that every time someone wanted to talk to you that they wanted something out of you? What did I ever ask you for?"

"You never asked me for nothing, Frankie," the old man said.

"That's right. Nothing."

"You should of, Frank," the old man said. "You never asked

when you were a kid. I seen you get a licking once when I was coming home on the streetcar. I seen you bleeding right on the street and I come down off that streetcar and them kids saw me and they run, the ones was beating on you, Frank. And what did you do, little boyo?" The voice broke suddenly, became deep, lost in that past moment. "You saw me coming across Madison Street and you with your little bloody nose and them boyos running to beat hell because if I'd laid me hands on them, they'd see some blood dancing on their faces too. You saw me and I knew you was going to run to me with tears in your little eyes. You wasn't even seven yet and some of them lads were working boys. You wasn't even seven yet."

Silence. Darkness. Frankie Coolin closed his eyes again. The can of beer was empty.

"But you." Softly. "You ran as well. You ran from me and I called to you. 'Frank, Frank, it's me, I'm not mad at you, come to yer Dad.' But you ran, Frank, from me. You never were going to ask me for nothing. Not you, not yer pride that made you run away from me when you was only seven. And now what are you doing but the same thing, running away from me?"

"I ain't seven any more, Dad." Quietly.

"Ah. But I'm still here, Frank. I'm waiting to hear what you want from me, Frank. I'm here, boyo."

Frankie Coolin got up from the bed and it made a creak. The old man knew he had risen.

"Nothing," Frankie said.

"All right." The voice turned away from him. "Have it yer way, yer own prideful way."

"I'll get your cigarettes and candy bars," Frankie said.

"You'll do as you wish," the old man said.

8

ose stumbled in the darkness of the bedroom and
Frankie groaned and turned in his sleep. The dream was holding him and he knew he could not wake up from it; yet he knew
he was dreaming.

"Sorry," she said. She turned on the closet light. The bedside Big Ben said 10:45 P.M. "I got back late." She unbuttoned
her blouse.

"Uh," he said; the dream would not let him go. He saw
Arthur Klein smiling like Buddha.

"Sean was sick and Two was worried," Rose said.

Frankie opened his eyes.

She took off her blouse and pulled it over a wire coat hanger,
then she reached behind her to unfasten her brassiere. Her
breasts were large. He remembered the smell of her as she had
been when she was young, when he had first kissed her naked,
when he had buried his face between her breasts and held
them and closed his eyes and been lost in her softness, in the
feeling of her hands behind him, holding his head against her.

She had removed her skirt and underpants and pulled on a
blue flannel nightgown with a flower print in rows on it. He
didn't like it but he said nothing.

He remembered when they would sleep naked beside each
other. Rose had been afraid of him just a little at first; as he
had been afraid of her, when she had suddenly wanted him
very much.

Later she wore the nightgowns that he bought her for her
birthday and her anniversary. He felt so awkward in the
women's department at Field's, asking for a black sleeping
gown, all ruffles and bits of satin and lace—as though he were
doing something illicit.

She turned off the closet light and found the edge of the bed

and sat down. The bed creaked towards her. His eyes were
open in the darkness; he saw the curve of her back beneath the
flannel gown. The curve of a naked young woman's back be-
neath his hand. His woman and he could make love to her.
Frankie touched her back.
Flannel.
"Did you set the clock?"
"Yeah. I got to get up early. I got a plastering job at that
woman's house."
"I thought you were going to get to that today."
"I wanted to but I couldn't get to it. Joey and me were
painting in the building, I think we'll get it finished up next
week. Willie is hustling some tenants for me."
"I don't understand why he does it. We don't pay him noth-
ing."
"He gets a flat."
"Well, that's true."
"I had some other guys to see. I had to go downtown."
She sank back on the bed and the mattresses creaked again.
She pulled the covers up to her chin and stared straight up at
the dark ceiling. Frankie turned in bed with his back to her and
stared at the clock. Ten fifty-two.
"So how's Sean?"
"He's sick."
"You said."
"He'll be all right. Two never had to go through that before.
You hate to see a little baby like that sick, they can't under-
stand why they're sick and they can't talk to you and they can't
understand why you don't do something to help them. They
look at you like you're punishing them. It breaks your heart,
even when you know it isn't anything. Just the flu. He has a
little diarrhea but that stopped tonight. I just wanted to talk
to Two, I think the baby is getting her down and with Andy
working two jobs."
"What two jobs?"
"He's doing night security over at the Sun Electric plant,
he's filling in on weekends, he says he wants to pick up some
property over by Carol Stream. I think they want to build out
there."

"This ain't no time to build. Besides, how's he going to get his money out of the place they're living in now? Why the hell do people always want to move away?"

"We moved away, Frank."

She touched his hand beneath the covers. Frank slept naked. She put her hand on his stomach. "Did you eat?"

"I ate down by Carm's. I had a sandwich."

"I had a pizza in the icebox."

"It's too much and I don't like that frozen pizza. Besides, the old man wanted me to get cigarettes for him. And candy bars."

"Peg home?"

"She came home at nine. I thought she had a date."

"I thought she had a date too. That's what she said."

"She was her usual talkative self. She said 'Hi' I think and then went into her room and closed the door. She didn't even play her records."

"Maybe I ought to check on her to see if she's all right."

"She's all right."

Rose let her hand drop away; Frankie realized that he did not want her to drop her hand. He touched her and felt flannel.

"I suppose Mick isn't home."

"You suppose right."

"Well, I suppose Andy knows what he's doing," Rose said, making another tangent.

They were silent in the darkness of the bedroom.

"He's a good worker but he doesn't know all the angles yet. Now isn't any time to move away. The economy stinks, you can't build a house any more."

"Well, she said she was thinking about it. She says she doesn't want to bus Sean to school with the coloreds."

"Sean is one year old, for Christ's sake. He's got time. Besides, what's wrong with the bus? I wish I had a bus when I was hoofing to school."

"We didn't have a bus, did we," Rose said in that dreamy voice she took on before falling asleep. It was as though her voice were already in another world.

"I wish I was back in the city now."

"Do you?"

"Sure. We came out here to get away from the shines but

the shines keep following us out. So if I got to live with them, I'd rather live with them back in the city. I like the city."

"You always liked the city. You were the only one didn't try to talk Dad into coming out here when the neighborhood went so bad and your mother died."

"I knew why he wanted to stay in the city. I wish I was in the city now."

"Where would we live?"

There, he thought. She was always ready. He once said he was going to try to get on the pipeline in Alaska and she went to the library and got a book about the state. He thought of her in all their years. He turned in bed again and touched her waist beneath the flannel. He pushed the flannel up over her behind and felt beneath for the flesh of her waist. He rested his arm over her.

She didn't move.

He touched her between her legs and she opened them.

"We could live back down on the West Side. Around Taylor Street. It's nice down there now again, just like it was. Maybe better. You should see it, I had a job down there. Maybe we could take a ride down there on Sunday, I got nothing to do Sunday."

"Mick says he wants the car Sunday, he's going up to Rosemont to see DePaul."

"Who they playing?"

"They're playing . . . well, he told me. I don't remember." Silence.

Alaska. He might have gone to Alaska. He might have still been living on the West Side.

"Rose," he said.

She held him. She reached for him between his legs. They were sounds in the darkness in a moment; they were touches and smells. They did not speak; they closed their eyes. They thought of each other. Frankie Coolin realized he loved her and the thought startled him, because he did not think about it very often and he had not thought about it at all in the past two weeks. What would she do if he—

He was over her and she took him and he sank into her lap and let her arms enfold him. He kissed her.

"Oh, Frankie," she said once. The voice was soft; it did not

speak in passion. It spoke as though it were already a part of
a dream.

The bed creaked and groaned beneath their bodies as it had
in the old apartment on the West Side. Nothing had changed
in all the years. Nothing had changed. He was lost in her.

"Rose," he said. He came and shuddered and did not know
if she had climaxed as well. For a moment, he lay atop her and
then slid to the side and held her in the crook of his right arm.
She was suddenly small against him. He felt his heart beating;
he felt his breath coming in shallow draughts.

"Frankie," she said, the voice going to sleep.

"I'll get a towel," he said.

"No," she said. "Lay here for a minute and hold me. I'll get
a towel."

"The sheets will get wet."

"I got to wash tomorrow anyway."

Silence. The Big Ben ticked. A plane from O'Hare, an unexpected late plane bound for Florida, boomed in the sky. In the
Proviso yards of the Northwestern a mile away, they were
banging freight cars back and forth.

"It wouldn't be bad," Frankie said. "Back in the city."

"What about Peg and Mick?"

"Mick goes to school, it would be closer. And Peg'll be in
college by year after next."

"Peg is so secret. She's like you. She keeps secrets. I can
read what's on Mick's mind the minute I see him. I know all
about Two. But Peg. She's like you."

"Is that right? I keep secrets?"

"You always kept secrets, Frankie," Rose said. "You never
told me."

"I told you everything."

"You never told me until it was all over. You never told me
when you got fired off that highway paving job. You never told
me. You went out to work every day with a lunch-box and you
never told me there wasn't any money coming in and I was
going along like a silly wife, just spending money, buying
steaks."

"Sh. That was a long time ago. I didn't want you to worry,
you were pregnant."

"That was with Mick. And all those days you went to work and there wasn't any work to go to."

"I had odd jobs. I was doing things. That's how I got with Salvatori. On the meat trucks."

"I wish you didn't have to go with Salvatori. They're crooks, I think."

He smiled in the darkness. "Rose. Everyone is a crook when it comes down to it. Salvatori was all right. It was bread and I could steal a little meat. That came in handy later when John was in trouble."

"You worried about everyone except yourself."

"I worry about myself too."

"No. You never do."

"Sure I do."

"Are you worried now?"

A silence.

"You see, Frankie." She pushed away and got up in the darkness and tripped over the same object at the foot of the bed she had tripped over coming into the room. She steadied herself on the bureau and went to the door of the bedroom. In a moment she returned from the bathroom with a towel. She threw it to him and he wiped himself.

She felt around the bed again in the darkness. She climbed on the bed and it creaked and the mattress bent to her weight for a moment. She slid down in the bed and pulled the covers to her chin.

"I'm worried," Frankie said softly.

"I know. I knew it yesterday."

"I'm worried about winter. I got to hustle a winter job."

"Yes." Softly. They lay apart from each other. The Big Ben ticked on.

"Saw a man downtown about a winter job," Frankie said. "Today."

"Yeah."

"Do you have it? Will the building be full this winter?"

"I think so. Willie's working some scam with the tenants. I don't know what it is but they've been paying on time and as long as no one beefs, I don't care.

"I don't trust him."

"That's all right. I don't trust him either."

"Why do you keep him around?"

"There's nothing to do with him. Willie hustles. If he can see his way clear, he doesn't make any trouble; if he can't, you can't control him. So I got to let him think he can see his way clear."

"Is that it? Is it the winter job you're worried about? Is that all it is?"

"Joey," Frankie said. "I'd like to line him up with something for the winter. I seen John today in the Bohemian's joint, God, he's back on the stuff heavy. He looks like he's dying."

"I feel so sorry for Marge."

"Marge has her problems but she's got a good kid. Joey's a good boy. Joey'll do right by her."

"John's a good man too. I just think from the time he fell off that roof on his head, he wasn't right."

"Well, that's a lot of beers ago. John does it to himself."

"You drink too much too."

"I told you it was for my white blood cells."

"I asked the doctor about that. He said that was crazy."

"That towel-head you went to? What does he know about it? You just go to doctors to make yourself feel bad."

"Frankie."

He waited and listened to her little voice lost in a dream.

9

In the morning Frankie finished the plastering job he had put off for weeks. When it was finished, he argued with the woman for a check. She said he charged too much, but after a few words, gave him a check. He put the tools in the steel box in the back of the pickup truck and began the drive home. It was just after eleven in the morning.

He liked to drive. He had once driven to California, before he and Rose got married, in an old Mercury. He had driven all day and then, after pulling to the side of the road for a couple of cans of beer and a little sleep, he had driven all night. He remembered dawn light flooding the cornfields on either side of Route 66 and the utter sense of freedom and exhaustion that had seized him at that moment. Rose did not like to take long driving trips with him because he didn't talk to her; he only dreamed as he watched the road and changing scenes and listened to the tires humming on the pavement. He could never say what he thought about as he drove along but his mind always felt refreshed and his body a little tired at the end of a day's drive, as though he had been swimming or working out in the gym.

He turned off Butterfield Road before he reached Mannheim Road and found a side street. He wanted to see if Toberman Construction was working Saturdays to finish the three-flats they were putting up on some vacant lots. Toberman Construction was Dan Toberman, a slow-witted and amiable bear of a man, who was extremely lazy. Once he had a contract, he never rushed to fulfill it. He had talked about putting up three-flats on those lots for five years. He had the money but he never got around to it. Frankie needled him about his work when they met in the bars but Dan never took offense. Coolin realized he wanted something to take his mind off the thought of the G; he realized he wanted some ammunition to use to lash out at Dan Toberman.

Before he reached the building site, he saw the red Chevy pickup and turned. Andy Korza was stripped to the waist, standing on the edge of the newly poured concrete driveway.

Frankie parked the old Ford behind Andy's new pickup and climbed out. Andy Korza was his son-in-law, married to Two. He was Polish and some in the family had resented him; once, when Frankie mentioned this to Andy after he had married Frankie's daughter, Andy laughed. "That's all right. My family didn't want me to marry a potato eater either. I told Rosie it was a good thing we didn't have to marry each other's family."

He was the only one who called her "Rose."

"You're working hard for a change," Frankie said, walking to the edge of the driveway. The concrete was still in the process of setting and Andy was coaxing it smooth with a long-handled flat rake.

"Like a Polack," Andy said. He was watching the concrete like a young father watching his baby walk. "This fucking cement. I got to get a new supplier. I been fucking with this for two hours. Look at it."

"It's the weather, it's too damp today." It had rained lightly during the night. The day was cloudy and looked like rain. The damp air was chilly.

"Fuck, I got to get this done today. I saw the streets were wet this morning, but what was I gonna do? If I don't get it done this morning, I got to put it off until a week from now and then what kind of weather we gonna get? Shit."

"You gonna pack it in pretty soon. Got a winter job lined up?" The cement finishers could only work in the season when the temperature was above freezing.

"That's why I been doing that security at Sun Electric. I talk to this guy about getting a regular security job during the winter. It only pays eight bucks an hour but I can get some double shifts, he said. And I can do basements again. I got a couple basements I gave estimates on. Who knows? It's a tough year, Frankie. Tough. This time last year, I was way ahead, I was even caught up on my quarterlies. But I ain't up this year. I got two behind. Fucking government."

"I know what you mean."

"Hey, take this string over to the other side. Long as you're here, make yourself useful."

Andy handed him the string. He was blond and tall, with a big chest and powerful sloping shoulders and arms. He had fine white teeth and a sun-blackened face. Sweat covered his body. His shirt and undershirt hung from a branch of a tree and a jar of water sat on the grass at its base.

Frankie took the string and carried it to the other side of the driveway. They held the string taut against the cement and then Andy popped it to leave a slight mark on the cement to act as a guide when he made a ridge.

"You get this poured two hours ago?"

"Yeah. Look at it, it's really watery. You know, these guys give you cement now, you know what their attitude is? Hey, you want the cement, take it or leave it. Nobody gives a shit any more about quality with this stuff. Everything is done so shitty."

"Well, that's the way it goes."

"Well, it pisses me." Andy reached for the jar of water and swallowed a lot of it.

"So. Frank. How come you're over by here?"

"I didn't know you were working today but I saw your truck. I was going by Toberman's buildings to see if he was working on them today."

"Toberman don't work on Saturday. Only Polacks work on Saturday."

"I had a plastering job. I picked up a check."

"Good. When I get through, you can buy me a beer."

"I'd like to but you know how it goes."

They smiled at each other.

"Rose says she was by your place last night. How's the kid?"

"Oh. He's all right this morning. I looked at him before I come out. He was breathing okay. We put that vaporizer in his room and put Vicks in it. I don't know if it does any good but he was breathing all right."

"Yeah. Rose said it was nothing but said Two was upset."

"Well, we both were. I mean, when it's a little baby, you feel dumb because you can't do nothing for it and he just cries at me."

"Yeah."

"Rosie has problems too." Andy bent forward, feathered the trowel over the concrete and drew it back. His boots were caked with concrete.

"Everyone's got problems. What problems does Two have?"

"Well, she's home all the time alone with the baby. I mean, I think it was more than she thought it was going to be. And when the baby came," he paused, "maybe it was faster than we thought."

"They got pills for things like that."

"She said she forgot."

"She always forgets. She'd forget her head when she was a kid if it wasn't screwed onto her shoulders."

"Well, that's all over anyway." He put down the trowel and picked up a brush and began taping a long, hollow aluminum handle to the brush. He studied the black electrical tape as he talked. "We like Sean fine."

"You're working nights over at Sun Electric, that's what's got her down." Frankie said it and pulled a cigarette out of his pocket. "You got a match?"

"In my shirt on the tree."

Frankie lit his cigarette and put the matchbook in his pocket.

"You know a lot of things, Frank," Andy said, beginning to brush the surface of the concrete. "Maybe you're right."

"You talk to her about it?"

"Sometimes it's hard to talk to your wife about things."

"Tell me about it. You want to build out in DuPage County, Rose said?"

"Well, I did at the start of the year. I figured with a little luck, I could get enough ahead and we could build next spring, pour the foundation now and just work on it in the winter a little at a time."

"Rose said you were working nights to get ahead to build."

"No. That's what Rosie told your wife. Rosie doesn't understand about the way it is." Andy was straining forward now, reaching to the edge of the concrete on the far side, and drawing the brush back across. "Rosie just thinks there's money and you spend it."

"Well, she's young," Frankie said.

"That doesn't mean nothing. Everyone is young some time.

Rosie doesn't see how bad it is. In summer, I ought to be working six, seven days a week. This year, I'm lucky to do five days. I had to work for Toberman on a house for two weeks. He just pays straight scale but I was lucky to get it. I thought I could back up my little jobs and get ahead. Shit, Frank. There was nothing to back up. How long is this recession going to last?"

"There's work if you look for it."

"Tell me." His face was hard, he was working his tongue against his teeth. His eyes, blue and intense, were building with anger. Frankie Coolin had seen Andy get mad.

"Tell me," Andy said again. He straightened up and dropped the brush on the grass. "I work anything. You want me to cut down a tree, I cut down a tree. You want a fence put up, I put up a fence. I do anything but it isn't there unless you're talking about some guys want to hire you for six bucks an hour. Fuck six bucks an hour, what the fuck am I going to do with six bucks an hour? I could do better on welfare. Shit, Frankie, I don't own no buildings, I'm just trying to build up a stake."

"Nobody says you don't work hard. It's tough times is all I said. I said there was work. I work. I did a plaster job this morning, got a hundred and a half off this old woman."

"I wish I could plaster. I can plaster but I got no skill. You can plaster, Frankie, you can always do work with a skill like that. But carpenters, cement finishers. Shit. You know what it takes for a guy to set himself up as a cement man? He's got to have a pickup truck with his name on the side of it, some business cards, and tools. And a pair of rubber boots." Andy grinned suddenly. "Look at me, I'm a contractor."

"The recession is going to shake them out, the guys who don't know what the fuck they're doing in the first place. I seen it before. In good times, you get all kinds of bums—guys like Archie by the tavern, you know, the carpenter, the only thing that guy knows about carpenter work is where the union hall is—you get these bums attach themselves on all kinds of jobs because the money in the trades is just laying around and everyone wants it. But you see who goes when the bad times come. Guys like you are always going to make it; you do nice work, Andy." Frankie smiled for the first time that day.

"Lighten up, you're getting yourself in a knot over nothing."

"I guess I got worried about the baby. Jesus Christ, how come they don't say in the book that you are going to feel like a fucking criminal when your baby gets sick the first time. It's like you done the wrong thing, gave it the wrong food, had his room too warm or too cold or something."

"When we moved out here, we kept having trouble with that old furnace was in the house when I bought it, and I was hustling around because I was breaking to make those payments on the house. So we didn't get the furnace fixed the first winter and Two came down with something like pneumonia but it wasn't pneumonia. I really felt guilty, especially when Rose wouldn't say nothing about it. We had to take her to the hospital."

"And you put in a new furnace."

"Fuck, no," Frankie Coolin said. "It was almost spring anyway. So I just felt bad, is all. That was the moral of the story."

Andy grinned then. "Son of a bitch, Frank. You're a hard man."

"I ain't hard. I was telling you about the way you feel about kids."

Andy went down on his knees and felt at the edge of the cement. "Look at that bitch," he said. "Hardened up in the last ten minutes. Cement is a bitch, like a goddam woman, never gives you time. It takes too long, it doesn't take long enough. Son of a bitch, it's tough now."

Frankie helped him carry the sawhorses to the front of the driveway and put up the pieces of rough framing lumber he used as a barrier so that no one would accidentally pull up on the driveway.

The aluminum storm door at the side of the brick Georgian opened and a man in a flannel shirt came out. He was wearing slippers.

"I seen in the window you were putting up the barriers. When can I drive on it?"

"A week. Not six days, a week."

"A week? I got to park in the street a week?"

"I don't know where you got to park, Mr. Hauser, but you got to stay off the driveway a week."

"Hey," said Frankie Coolin by way of greeting. He had seen

Hauser in the Dominick's grocery. Hauser stared at him with blank eyes for a moment and then looked back at Andy.

"You want your check now?" He said it like an accusation.

"Sure," Andy smiled.

Hauser pulled a green piece of paper out of his flannel shirt. It was folded in half.

Andy took it without looking and stuck it in the shirt pocket hanging on the tree. He took his rubber boots off and banged them on the side of the curb and carried them to the truck.

"You gonna leave that mess along the gutter or what?" Hauser said. He was about fifty-five years old and he had a big gut.

"I was getting my broom for sweeping," Andy said. He reached in the back of the red pickup and took out a broom and shovel. He also took out a towel.

He put the broom and shovel down on the gutter and wiped his face and arms and upper body with the towel before he put on his undershirt and shirt. He returned to the curb and began sweeping up the dust and shoveling the little bits of damp concrete clinging there.

"You want to turn on the water for the hose?" he said finally.

Hauser went into the house without a word. Andy looked at Frankie Coolin and smiled and shook his head. He went to the bushes near the base of the house and pulled out a green garden hose attached to a spigot on the brick wall.

"I love the old Germans and the old Bohemians the best," Andy said as he held the hose, waiting for the water. "This guy had me over twice to make an estimate. Did he think I was going to give him two prices? I think he got so many guys over here to make an estimate he called me twice."

"Look at the check and make sure he didn't stiff you."

"No," Andy said. "He wouldn't stiff me. You been dealing down in the city too long. With the niggers."

"Typical Polack," Frankie said. "You don't understand nothing. It's a lot easier when everyone deals with everyone else on the basis that nobody trusts nobody. So I get cash when I collect on the rent and I pay cash when I got to get the buildings taken care of. It's the easy way. Out here, you got to assume Mr. Hauser is a polite little kraut gentleman. He's civilized. He gives you a piece of paper that he says is money and you take it down to the bank and three days later, it does cartwheels down the street. Or he don't give you a piece of paper and he says he'll get you in thirty days and thirty days comes and then another thirty days and pretty soon, you're banging on his door twice a day and then he tells you he ain't got the money at all in the first place."

The water came out of the green hose.

Andy drank the water from the hose in great gulps for a moment and then let it play along the gutter, washing the debris and stains of white cement away. In five minutes, he had the brooms and shovels back on the pickup.

"So." He stood for a moment at the hood of the Chevy and pulled a cigarette out of his pocket. He looked at Frankie. "You got my matches?"

"Sure I got your matches. I needed them." Frankie grinned. "You got a smoke?"

Andy handed him one and Frankie lit both cigarettes. They stood in the damp air and let the smoke drift up from their lips and nostrils and hang in the air above them.

"I think Rosie wants a job," Andy said.

"Then she should get a job."

"That don't make sense. I told her that."

"Why? You're busting your balls on two jobs, why shouldn't she work?"

"We got a baby at home is why. I can't ask my mother to come over and babysit every day. Not for nothing. And I can't ask your wife, can I? I mean, if she wanted to work part-time for a couple of days a week, OK. But I can't ask someone in full time. Not without paying them and then what do I do? Rosie won't make the money to cover it, it won't be worth her while to work. I tried to explain that to her."

"You guys got trouble?"

Andy stared at him with narrowed eyes. "Everyone gets trouble once in a while."

"Two was always kind of crazy. I mean, flighty, that's what I mean. She gets a bee in her babushka," Frankie said.

"She gets down. Sometimes for days. She don't want to talk."

"She's finding out what married life is all about."

"Maybe so," Andy said. "That's the last of my work, Frankie.

I finish this job, I got one more job lined up for next week—this old guy wants stairs—and that's it. I never finished the season this early before; I really hate to see winter coming. I been thinking about Saudi Arabia."

"What about Saudi Arabia?"

"Oh, I know this contractor, they're building everything in Saudi Arabia except they got no people to do it. I could contract to go there for six months or so, make some real money and get ahead of the game."

"What's Two going to do when you're gone?"

"Two is all right. She gets everything she wants. Did I tell you, we got a Zenith last week? I picked it up in Melrose Park and I got a deal on it. A twenty-one with the Space Command thing so I don't have to get out of my chair to change the channel."

Frankie nodded.

"I want to put it down in the basement, I made that family room up down there, but she wants it upstairs because she says it's a nice piece of furniture. Son of a bitch. So I can't turn it on at night when I get home because you know the way our living room is right off the baby's room, so it will wake the baby up. So I got an old black and white still, the one we had, and I took that down in the basement."

"You shouldn't leave Two when she's got the kid so young."

"You mean for Saudi Arabia? I was just thinking about the job is all, I got to do something."

"You ought to be able to watch your color TV when you get home."

"That's what I said."

"But I see Two's point of view. I mean, a woman wants to have a nice house. Two always liked nice things. She made curtains for all the windows in our place."

"Is that right? She doesn't seem to like to do a lot around our house. When my mother comes over, she's always doing stuff for us."

"Well, you shouldn't have your wife compared to your mother. My mother was alive when we got married but I didn't let her come over and start running Rose ragged. You know, women got different ideas about houses."

"I know, I'm finding it out. I just wish to hell I could get ahead in the money department. It seems the harder I go, the farther behind I get."

"One winter I drove a cab when we were still in the city. I was working all night, from eight to eight. I'd try to get a run out to Midway Airport—this was before they had O'Hare opened—and then wait in the line for at least one, sometimes two back into the city. You don't know the South Side but they had all these motels on Cicero Avenue, they had some shit going on down along there. I got to know my way around; guy would come in, I could steer him to a couple of whores I knew were working out of this one place down near Sixty-fourth Street. About two in the morning, I got so fucking tired, I'd just lean against the back of the seat and conk out. But if I'd make it to four or five, I'd be awake again and by eight, when I had to turn the cab in to the Yellow garage, by eight I was ready to go. Sometimes I could go like that two or three days, doing some work in the day, working the night trick on the cabs. I was working at an inside job down on Clark Street then. Turn in the cab, go down to the job, work until three or so and then go back to the apartment and sack out. Get up around seven and have breakfast, for Christ's sake. I was eating breakfast at seven o'clock at night. But I made out that winter, two jobs, a lot of cash tips and I didn't report nothing to the G. By summer, I figured I had enough to pick up a house. I had the GI Bill but you got to have money on the side to do work. I wanted a lot of house and I figured I could fix it up."

"That's what I want," Andy said. "That's why I was working two jobs in the first place, to get ahead. Only there ain't no getting ahead, not this year. Shit. I'm running just to stay in place. Fucking government."

"You got a site picked out? In DuPage?"

"Right near Carol Stream. Guy's got ten sites but he needs a lot of paving work out there and we been talking about it. This is a bad time to build, the interest rates are killing you and nobody is looking for a new house. But things are going to clear up in another year or so. This guy wants to work a deal. He can sell me one of the lots less than four thousand dollars and I do the driveways on the other lots for my material only, I throw in the labor."

"That sounds like a good deal."

"It's a lot of work but I figure I get the lot for next to nothing. That's the first year. Second year, I build. We'd have the house we want to have. But I was figuring on it happening this year and now it can't. Besides, the guy can't start building yet either, he's got his problems."

"I know him?"

"Cantrowski. You know him?"

"No. One of your people, huh? I don't know him."

"He usually works up in McHenry but he picked this property up in DuPage County so he wants to see what he can do with it."

"Like you said, this is no time to build."

They were silent for a moment. Frankie Coolin felt the dampness of the day picking at him.

"I ran into Joey last night," Andy said at last.

Frankie puffed his cigarette. "When? After you came back from Sun Electric?"

"Yeah. He was at the L. C. Lounge over by Mannheim. I stopped by there for a beer on the way home."

"How come you didn't go by the Bohemian's?"

"I get tired of that place. So I stopped by and I seen Joey. He was with a couple of people. You know, I think one of them was Pat Salazar and a couple of girls. You know, Friday night. Just on the town."

"Friday night ain't no difference to me."

"Not to me either anymore. I wasn't even sure it was Friday night til I seen how crowded the joint was and I seen Joey. Joey was a little in the bag."

"Yeah. He worked for me yesterday."

"That's what he said. On your new building."

"Yeah." Frankie dropped the burning cigarette in the gutter at his feet and zipped up his jacket. He felt cold.

"He said you and he and his old man got into it at the Bo's after work yesterday."

"Is that what he said?"

"Hey, Frank." Andy stared at him with that plain, honest face and bright eyes. "You got problems with the government?"

"Nothing I can't handle," Frankie Coolin said.

"OK. I won't ask you then if that's what you want. Joey said something I thought I'd ask you when I saw you. I almost forgot about it."

"Yeah. Why don't you forget about it?"

"Sure. Is it bad?"

"What? You mean what you just forgot about?"

"Anything I can do?"

"Yeah. You can forget about it and you can tell Two nothing about it."

"I don't tell Rosie nothing."

"That's a good policy. I followed it all these years. Don't tell your wife nothing and you won't have her hanging around your neck with every word."

"Yeah."

"You just make trouble for yourself telling your wife about things."

"Yeah."

Silence.

"Frank. Everything going to be all right?"

Frankie Coolin stared at him and didn't speak.

"OK, Frank. You don't have to be hard with me. I ain't asking you so I can go out to the Bo's and start shooting my mouth around. I don't tell nobody nothing about my business and I see the way you want it. But I just don't like a surprise if I can see about it beforehand. You know, if you needed help or your wife or something."

"Yeah, I appreciate it."

"Look, we're in the family now."

Who had talked about family? John. John was crying in his beer.

"Don't worry, Andy. I can handle it," Frankie Coolin said. "I got a little problem is all. Income tax."

Andy stared at him. "I thought it was about that fire. In the warehouse on the West Side."

Frankie's face felt cold to him. He shivered and shoved his hands deeper in the pockets of his jacket. "Why did you think of that?"

"I know about it is why. I know about the television sets."

"Why? Why do you know all that? How come you didn't say anything?"

"I told you: I mind my own business."

"You ain't minding it now."

"Now it might be family business."

"How did you know about the warehouse?"

"Kostner. I know his kid. His kid was in a joint I used to go to in Lyons a couple of weeks ago and we hadn't seen each other in a long time. We was at Proviso together, but I haven't seen him in five years. He was in the Navy. He said his old man had this warehouse fire. Said the government found a bunch of television sets. I told him what I was doing in the meantime, that I married this Irish girl named Rosie Coolin and he said that was the name of the guy that was in on the television set job. Coolin. He didn't know what the guy's first name was. I thought about it and I thought you said something once about a fire in a warehouse but I didn't say nothing to nobody."

"Jesus Christ. Don't. Don't say nothing to nobody, especially don't say nothing to Two or Rose. For Christ's sake. Everyone's got a mouth. I never knew people talk so much about everyone else's business. Joey shooting his yap off in the L. C. Lounge and now you're telling me about some fucking kid I never even heard of and he's sitting in some bar in Lyons talking to you about me. For Christ's sake, can't anybody ever learn just to mind their own fucking business and keep their mouths shut?"

"Is that it then?"

"Is what it?"

"About that fire. Were those TVs hot? You aren't messing around with something like that. You never were fencing stuff."

"That's what I told the G."

"They want to get you on that? Is that it? On something like that?"

"Something like that," Frankie said. "It's getting cold. It was lucky you poured when you did. I bet it goes down under thirty-two tonight."

"It'll be warm enough for a couple of days," Andy said with a slow rasp in his voice. "As long as the ground don't freeze down. There's a lot of warmth in the ground."

"Don't talk about this," Frankie said.

"You want to talk to me about this?"

Yes, he thought. Yes, I want to tell someone. He stared at

Andy. Andy was nearly twenty-five years younger than he was but his manner was grave at times, courteous, solid. People thought he was older. He was an only child and he had played the piano when he was growing up. He went to college for a year. His father was a manager of a small plastics company in Summit. He was supposed to make something of himself. After a year in college—he had gone to Roosevelt downtown—he had come home and said he was going into the trades. He had broken his father's heart when he said that.

"There isn't a lot to say. Pat Kennedy wanted me to rent some space for him. I had my own stuff to store so I said OK. I put my shit there, there isn't room for all the stuff I can pick up. I never knew about the television sets."

"Well, they ought to see that. Why would they think you were stealing them? I mean, you don't look like a television dealer."

"Try to make them see it."

"They think you were working for Pat Kennedy."

"Maybe. I don't know what they think."

"Joey says they came by his old man yesterday to talk about you."

"Pricks."

"They want you, they got you. That's the way it works. They got more guys, they got more money, and when they say squat, you squat."

"I'm glad this isn't Russia."

"Maybe you can get a lawyer," Andy said.

"That's what Pat Kennedy said."

"Pat Kennedy knew about those television sets," Andy said.

"Wonderful. If only you and the G thought alike and left me alone."

"They know it. They must be working on you to get him."

"I ain't going to talk to them about nothing."

"I know," Andy said. "They must know that. You going to get a lawyer?"

"Maybe. This thing has been hanging over my head for four months. Four fucking months. I get up in the morning and it's there and I go to sleep at night and it's there, sitting right on the edge of the bed. This thing is just there. Every time I get a phone call or I see a piece of mail sitting on the television

set, I think about it. Every time I see those guys. Fucking G.
I tell you, when the indictment comes down, I think I'd be
relieved."

"Is it coming down?"

"Ask me three days ago, I might not know. But now they
come to see me again, and they're following me around. I
talked to Pat Kennedy, I think it was Thursday, yeah, Thursday
after the G talked to me, and they were out there at the practice
field, we were watching his kid Tommy play football, I mean,
and then they go over to John's house in the morning and they
start bugging him. John thinks it's about income tax but I know
John. The whole family is going to know about the G coming
around in a couple of days. John's big mouth and Joey too, for
Christ's sake. Telling you in a bar."

"It was OK that he told me. I won't tell nobody nothing, but
he's going to tell other people."

"Well, I don't want Rose to get worried before it happens,
if it happens."

"What's going to happen?"

"I don't know what they can do to me."

"They can do anything they want to you."

"Yeah. I thought about that and I thought about Brian. You
didn't know Brian, he was dead before you came into the
picture. Brian did two years in Sandstone and he took the two
pretty hard; he looked bad when he came out."

"You think you're going to do time?"

"What do you think I worry about, Andy? You think I worry
about getting a fine or something? You think I worry about
these morons going through my tax returns? Time, man, that's
the only thing to worry about. What if I went in for two years.
What happens to Rose for two years or to the kids? I think it
might kill Rose."

"What about you?"

"I can do time if I got to do it." He thought about it as he
had thought about it so many times in the past months. The
cell, the stink of urine, the pills, and sleeping and sleeping time
away. "But it would hurt because I didn't do nothing. I didn't
do nothing and to do a couple of years for nothing. God."

Leaves blew around them. Maple leaves collected along the
edge of the lawn. The clouds began to pick up speed again.

"Feels like rain," Frankie Coolin said.

"Shit," Andy said. "Help me get the plastic out."

Without words, the two men spread plastic clear sheets over the driveway and secured them at the edges with rocks.

"You ought to get a lawyer," Andy said at last. "You got to have someone give you advice."

"Advice from lawyers costs money."

"It's the only kind of advice that's worth anything, the kind that costs money. Free advice you can get from the Bohemian down at the tavern."

"You ain't as dumb as you look."

"Irish bastard," Andy said.

"I don't want you talking about this to Two."

"Don't worry, Two is in one of her moods when she doesn't talk to me."

"She doesn't talk to you sometimes?"

"Sometimes."

Frankie stared at him.

"Well, I suppose everyone goes through it."

They were finished and didn't want to part from each other. "How about a beer at the tavern?" Frankie said.

"No. I got to pick up Two and take Sean over by the doctor and then I got to get a little sleep for working the security job tonight."

Neither man made a move. They stood at the cab of Andy's red pickup.

"What kind of mileage you getting on this thing now?"

"Fifteen-sixteen," Andy said. "I can't complain."

"I'm gonna have to think about a new truck next year. I passed the inspection station the other day, I thought it was a miracle, I seen the clouds part and the sun coming down."

"You got a lot of good miles on that truck. Ford ain't a bad truck."

"I got a hundred thirty thousand. I can't complain but I wish to fuck I didn't have to think about picking up a new truck right now."

"Yeah, you got other things to think about." Andy stared at him. "Well," he said. "We'll see how it happens."

"Maybe nothing is going to happen."

As soon as he said it, Frankie Coolin thought about John,

about Joey, about the two G in the car by the football field.

"I tell you, Andy, I don't want to have you say anything to anyone but I wish to fuck I knew the way it was going to go, one way or another, you know what I mean?"

"I know. Waiting is the killer."

There was nothing more to say unless they wanted to say too much. They both knew it.

"Well, you sure you don't want to go down to the tavern with me and have a beer, Andy?"

"I have one with you, Frank, and the next thing I'd be sitting there for a couple of hours. I don't want Rosie to get pissed off more than she is; I tell you, when she doesn't talk to me like this, it drives me crazy. I mean, you can't do nothing about it when someone won't talk to you."

"Wait till you been married as long as I have. You'll find out you like it when they don't talk to you."

"I don't mean not talking to you like that. When things are good, they always want to talk to you too much. When things stink, that's when you could use some talk but that's when they decide they don't want to talk. That's women."

10

Hey, Frankie. Hey. I didn't expect to see you out here."

Pat Kennedy waved, his little pinkie ring glittering in the sunlight of early afternoon. It was three weeks later, a Saturday, and Coolin sat on a bleacher seat in the fourth row, on the Proviso West High School side of the field.

"I didn't expect to see you," Frankie said flatly, not turning in his seat. He stared hard at the players lining up on the twenty-two.

"I was going over by your house and my kid isn't playing today so I thought I come by and see the Proviso game." Pat Kennedy sat down heavily next to Frankie Coolin.

"Is that right? I never see you at Proviso games. I never see you at football games unless your kid is playing."

"What are you talking about, Frankie? I love watching football. I gave up my Bears tickets a couple of years ago because I wasn't going to freeze my balls off down at Soldiers' Field just to watch them fumble it away year after year."

"Sure."

"I come by lots of times to watch the games. Proviso's got a halfway team this year. Lots of shines, that's what you got to have now if you want a good football team, I guess, you got to have shines."

"How come I don't see you around, Pat?"

Quiet.

The red-jerseyed quarterback faded, pumping his right arm, turning to the right, telegraphing the throw. A player in black threw his body over the guard and pushed the quarterback down.

Frankie Coolin said, "They stare right at the receiver. They ought to teach them."

"You were looking for me?"

"I was looking for no one. I just didn't see you around."

"I been busy."

"Is that right?"

"Busy time for me."

"I'm glad to hear it."

"How's it going for you?"

"Never seen better days," said Frankie Coolin.

"Yeah, it ain't bad this year. Not if you hustle. Guys sit on their fat asses all year, now they're hurting. You keep hustling, a little bit every day, and you end with something at the end of the year, you know what I mean? Take you. You hustle, Frankie, you always did and now I bet you got some money stashed away."

Frankie Coolin felt cold; it was as though Pat Kennedy's voice was winter, suddenly coming in the middle of an autumn afternoon football game.

"Nobody's got money stashed away. If I had money, I wouldn't have to hustle."

"You're shitting me, Frankie, you always were a guy with a shabby appearance but you got yours, I know you got yours."

For the first time, Frankie Coolin turned to stare at the pasty face.

"What's on your mind, Kennedy?"

"Nothing. I was just talking. I know that a guy hustles the way you hustle, you got to have yours. You got those buildings on the West Side, for instance."

"What about the buildings?"

"Nothing. Nothing about them." Kennedy twisted the pinkie ring and stared at other features of his hands. "I was just talking, don't make a federal case out of this."

Frankie Coolin stared at him.

"Speaking of that," Pat Kennedy said. He tried to smile and then let it go. "Federal case, I mean. Those guys come around two more times to me."

"What guys?"

"You know what guys same as I do. The G is what guys, the same guys that was by to see you."

"Is that right?"

"Not only that but they were by to my brother-in-law's place out in Bloomingdale, that's Leo O'Connor, you know?"

"I seen him last year at the wedding."

"Yeah. So they were by his place, too, the G. They want to talk about me to him, to my brother-in-law. That frosted my nuts, I tell you. So I talked to my lawyer."

"So what did your lawyer say?"

"He says I should talk to them. To the G. So I talk to them. You know what they showed me?"

"No."

"Pictures. They were taking pictures all the time of us. Remember when we were by the high school that day, the day when you called me? Watching the kid play football? They were there, I never knew that."

Frankie swallowed. "Yeah. I saw them."

"You saw them? You never said nothing to me."

"There was nothing to say."

"Nothing to say? How can you say that?"

Frankie lit a cigarette. He always dropped by the game in autumn, it was part of his Saturday habit, and now Kennedy was lousing it up, talking about the feds. Maybe, instead of the football game, he should just go to Saudi Arabia with Andy and get away from the G and all of it.

"Look, Frankie, this thing just gets deeper and deeper with the G, you know."

"Is that right?"

"Why do you keep saying that? Yeah, that's right. Your fucking ass it's right. They aren't spending all this time and wasting those two guys to come out and take pictures of us out at a fucking high school field if it wasn't important. These G, I swear to God, they got everything. You think we were Communist spies or something. All about a fucking piddling load of Jap fucking television sets. I wish to fuck I never seen those sets."

Frankie did not speak, did not move. He had heard the words but Pat Kennedy's voice did not sound right. He couldn't understand what sounded wrong about it, but it did not sound right.

"You been talking to them?" Pat Kennedy said.

"I don't talk to no one."

"I wish to fuck I was out of all this."

"I don't know what you're in."

"Come on, Frankie, what have we been talking about?"

"We haven't been talking about anything."

"What were we talking about on that practice field that day we went to see my kid work out?"

"We were talking about the G," Frankie Coolin said.

"We were talking about those TV sets you kept in your space in the warehouse."

"No, fuckhead." Quietly. Frankie turned, his face drawn and hard. "No. I don't know nothing about TV sets. Not sets in my space, not any kind of TV sets, not Jap sets or any kind. I rented warehouse space for you. As a favor. And you let me use some of it to store my building materials. That was that. That's all I did and all I know."

"You're full of shit, Frankie," Pat Kennedy said. He shoved his hands into the pockets of his high school warm-up jacket. His belly bulged against the metal snaps.

"I may be full of shit but I don't know about TV sets."

"Listen, you're not fooling those guys and you're not fooling me."

"It sounds like you're trying to get me into something that I wasn't in and that I ain't getting into, Pat. I don't know about the warehouse TVs. I knew a guy who knew the guy who owned the warehouse and you said you were looking for some space and I said I could help you out and you said I could store some of my materials up there, especially because winter was coming on. So don't give me any of that shit, you sound like you're talking a speech to me about something that didn't happen."

"You ain't dumb, Frankie. You know what's going on."

"I don't know anything. If I did I could wear pinkie rings like you and drive a fucking Buick."

"They played tapes, the G. They played tapes of you talking to them."

"That's right. It was their dime," Frankie said. "They bothered me out at the buildings when I was working. If you listened to the tapes, you heard I didn't say anything to them because I didn't have anything to say."

Pat Kennedy stared at him as though he were staring at a dead man.

"Don't gimme that look, Pat."

"I ain't giving you a look."

"How come your lawyer tole you to talk to the G?"

"He said I should talk to them because I didn't have anything bad against me, I could talk to them. You know, you can talk to them."

"No, I don't know that. They're cops and when cops want to talk to you, they want to put you in jail. That's facts. Cops don't talk to you to pass the time of day; cops want to put you in the joint or they want you to buy your way out. There's no other reason."

"I didn't have anything to hide," Pat Kennedy said.

"Is that what your lawyer told you?"

"Look, Frankie, don't be such a hard guy."

"I don't understand what you're saying to me, Pat. It sounds like you're talking from the moon or something."

Unexpectedly, Pat pulled away from him. He seemed to flinch. He turned his body away from him.

"What's the matter with you, Pat?"

"Nothing. I got nothing wrong with me, it's you. You don't want to face facts." Pat turned back. "You're such a smart guy, you always were a smart guy. Nobody's going to give a fuck if you go down, you know that? You think anybody down at the Bohemian's place is going to give a shit when you go to the joint?"

"I ain't going anywhere."

"You're being a smartass, not a smart guy. A wise guy."

"That's G talk, Pat, you talk like a trainee in the FBI school."

Pat Kennedy flushed for a moment but he did not speak. The silence puzzled Frankie Coolin; Pat Kennedy was not the kind of guy who didn't speak when someone rapped him.

"How was the cheese?" Pat said at last.

"The cheese? Oh, you mean the cheese you got me? It was all right." He paused. "I liked it but it don't melt right, not like American cheese melts, and Rose don't like it. She says it's too strong. She says her stomach's upset or something."

"She all right?"

"She's all right as long as she can go to some towel-head doctor at least twice a month to fix her toenails or something. Rose wants to worry is all."

"She always was like that," Pat said.

"Yeah."

"I'm sorry she didn't like the cheese. I could get you some other kind of cheese."

"Why are we talking about cheese, Pat?"

"Look, Frankie; this is serious."

"What? You mean about the G coming around? You finally figured out this is serious?"

"That ain't gonna get us nowhere, you talking like that. We ought to talk about our problem."

"Our problem? I don't have no problem, Pat."

"You got a problem the same as me, you know that. If the G thinks you got a problem, you got one, and it won't go away by you being a wiseass."

Frankie Coolin flicked the cigarette butt end over end to the dead grass below the wooden stands. There were whistles on the field and flags were thrown by the two referees in white and black striped shirts.

Coolin said, "Tell me about it."

"I heard the G was talking to John a couple of weeks ago about you, same as they went out to my brother-in-law in Bloomingdale. John, your brother, I mean."

"I know who you mean. They talked to John and John couldn't take it. He went on a drinking jag and he had to go to the hospital for a couple of days, they thought his heart was screwing up again."

"Was it his heart?"

"Who knows? The towel-heads didn't want to mess with him at all. They just told him to take it easy, dry out, you know what they tell you. They gave him pills. When they can't think of nothing to do for you, they give you dope."

"Hospitals," said Pat. "Bunch of fucking pushers. I hate drug addicts."

"I hate snitches."

The three words lay flat between them, putting them in different worlds. The light changed in that moment; nothing would be the same again.

"Snitches," Pat said dreamily, as though he had never heard the word before. His voice caressed it. "I don't know why you'd say something like that. You want to rile me or what?"

"Are you riled, Pat?"

"You are just pissing me off in front."

"Is that right?"

"You think I'm snitching?"

"I see you a month ago, you come on like Bogart, tell me not to talk to the G, tell me to get a lawyer, you give me the name of a Jew lawyer that you got from your fucking cheese man. I don't say nothing to no one. And then out of the fucking blue today, you come by to see me while I'm watching a football game, I ain't seen you around for a month, and you want to talk to me about the G and how I ought to go to the G and cop a fucking plea or something for something I didn't do or have nothing to do with in the first place. You tell me your lawyer tells you to talk to the G. OK, Pat. What did you talk about?"

"I told them I didn't know nothing about what they were fucking me around about."

Coolin stared at him.

"That's it? A conversation like that must have taken four seconds."

"That's the gist of what I told them."

"Is that right? You didn't happen to mention me, did you? When you were doing your four-second spiel?"

"They mentioned you, Frankie."

"I'll bet."

"I told them you were family."

"I ain't no family to you, Pat, you're only my wife's cousin."

"Come on, Frankie; we go back. You don't want to talk like that."

"I don't want to talk to you at all, Pat, and that's the way it is." Frankie lit another cigarette. His face was hard, his gestures slow, his hands were steady. He sucked the cigarette and let the smoke out through his nose.

"You got nothing to worry about, Frankie."

"The only thing I worry about now is what a tough guy you are, Kennedy. That's my worry. If you were a little scared or a little soft, I wouldn't worry so much. It's the tough guys like you that I worry about because you're meat. You were down talking to the G and they put on a show-and-tell for you, showing you pictures of me and you and who knows who else."

"Jesus, Frankie, you don't have to come down hard on me."

Pat looked at him and touched his arm. Frankie stared at the field: the quarterback faded, threw, and the ball wobbled over the line to a receiver who was caught flat-footed the minute he touched the ball.

Pat Kennedy let his hand drop.

"Tommy," he said, invoking the name of his son. "That kid means everything to me. Kevin, the other one, he's a bookworm, I love him—don't get me wrong—but he's got it made by himself. He don't need me, we got nothing to talk about in common. Kevin's a good kid, don't get me wrong, I encourage him, I tell him whatever he wants to do is OK by me. But sometimes when Kevin is talking to me, he looks at me like I was a specimen, you know, the kind they put on a glass slide, like he's got in his room with the microscope and everything."

"I don't want to hear this, Pat. Listen to yourself. You don't make any sense."

"Kevin collected butterflies for a while and stuck them on pins. Put them on a board. It's kind of terrible when you think about it, even though butterflies got no feelings."

"Pat, you're talking screwy."

"Jesus, Frankie, listen to me. Tommy is a kid who needs me now, not like Kevin. Tommy is great, this kid is great, he's going to be a player like I never got a chance to be. I want him to go to Notre Dame even if he don't get a scholarship, but I think he will, I want him to go down there like I never had the chance to do."

Frankie stared at Pat. Pat's eyes filled with tears and made them soft. "I don't wanna do no time," Pat said. His voice was like a whisper. "I swear to God I don't wanna do no time."

Coolin looked at him.

"You know, Frankie, when they start talking about counts, about indictments, about what they can do to you, you know they gotcha when they gotcha. You know it. Man, they come down on you like a ton of bricks. They put it right in front, they tell you the way it's going to be."

"What are you telling me, Pat?"

"Man, I feel so sick inside all the time, you don't know what it's like. You don't know. I get knotted up so I can't eat or sleep or nothing. I haven't been able to throw a fuck in the old lady for a month, you know that? That ain't like me, I can tell you that. I'm scared all the time thinking about the G. Sick and scared. I throw up in the morning."

"Maybe you're pregnant."

"Funny, Frankie, that's funny, that's right: everything is a fucking joke. Sometimes I can't take a shit for a couple of days and then right all of a sudden, I get diarrhea. Man, I feel like I'm dying, you know?"

"Maybe you are, Pat."

"It couldn't be any worse. I see you acting cool and calm to me but you got nothing to be calm about."

"Is that right, Pat? You know something about me? Something I ought to know?"

"Frankie, it would be all right for you, your kids are nearly grown. Tommy is only fourteen and Brian is twelve and you know how it is. You got a big family, you got Andy could help out if it came down to it—"

"Andy is going to Saudi Arabia this winter."

"Why the fuck is he doing that?"

"That's what everyone says."

"Fucking Arabs, I wouldn't work for an Arab prick if he was the last man on earth."

"So what are you telling me that Andy is going to help me out in?"

"Inside. What the fuck you think I been talking about? I'm talking about doing time. I got no one to help me out if I got to do time. Who's going to see to my boys? Who's going to see to my old lady? I got my fucking brother-in-law in Bloomingdale, he told me after the G saw him that if I got into any trouble, not to come running to him. He's as worthless as tits on a boar. My brother, my older brother, he's out in California, he might as well be on the moon for all the good that's going to do me. So I'm alone, Frankie, and I got to hustle alone."

"Don't tell me your troubles, Pat. Please."

"Frankie. We go back, right?"

"We don't go back, we ain't pals or buddies. I don't want to hear that shit from you."

"Look, I got to tell you—"

"You got nothing to tell me."

"Frankie, please."

"Pat, be a man. They're working on you like they worked on me, probably like they worked on that guy Kostner at the warehouse. Everyone gets their turn. You just take it."

"You can take it."

"And you can't, is that what you want to tell me? Well, go ahead and snitch on your pals if you want but you got nothing to snitch on me because I didn't do anything."

"Come on, Frankie, you know what's going down—"

"How dumb do you think I am, Pat?"

"You're a smart guy. I always said that. I mean it, Frankie; you not only knew how to hustle but how to keep what you hustle. You never were a greedy guy or wanting to grab off too much to queer the deal—"

"What are you talking about? You talk like a fool. Shut the fuck up and get away from me. You're talking crazy."

"If you took anything, you always knew not to take too much."

"Fuck you, shut up. What kind of crazy shit are you talking about? I got no deals with you, I never had a deal with you."

"Look, Frankie, this is hard—hard on you and on me. It couldn't come up at a worse time in my life with Kevin and Tommy so young. This is like getting cancer the way they keep after you and telling you what they're going to do to you."

"Get away from me, Pat. Tough guy. You're so tough you look like Irish jelly right now."

"We got to stick together, Frankie; we're family."

"I ain't no kin to you."

"Frankie, honest to God, I want you to know I honestly was never involved in stealing those television sets in your space."

Frankie got up without a word and dropped four feet to the hard-packed ground next to the bleachers. He started away.

Pat leaped down and followed him to the cyclone fence. "Listen to me for a second."

"I don't want to hear your shit, not for one second."

"Look, when you rented that space for me—"

"Why are you talking like this, Pat? Are you crazy, they must have put your thumbs in the rack down at the federal building."

"Listen one second. When those guys were hijacking those TV sets, they said they wanted me to get some space for them to hold the stuff for a while and then we could send it out through—"

"I don't know nothing about this, I don't want to know nothing. You want to talk about your pals, go down to the G and talk to them, but don't you mention my name because I got nothing to do with this."

"Look, Frankie, I didn't mean to get you caught in the middle on this. I figure we could both be doing ourselves a favor and you knew what was coming down, you know that, you knew from day one when you rented the warehouse—"

Coolin pushed him away and turned but Pat Kennedy grabbed him. The grip was strong and desperate. Coolin turned.

"You knew, Frankie. All along, from day one, maybe you didn't exactly know they were TV sets until later, I grant you that, but you knew something was going down or why am I asking you to rent the space in the first place and then letting you keep your shit there for nothing."

Frankie's face was hard, his eyes were flat. "What are you talking to the G about, Pat? What are you saying to them?"

"I told them I didn't know anything."

"For a guy didn't know anything, you sure kept talking a lot. Like you're doing now to me."

"Sure I'm going screwy, this thing is driving me screwy. I got to talking to myself. I never woke up at night before, I always sleep like a baby. Now I wake up at three in the morning, always at the same time, I can hear the grandfather clock striking in the living room, the one we bought last Christmas; I wish to fuck I bought the kind you can turn off at night. I hear the clock and I know I ain't going back to sleep. Look at me, I'm forty-four years old and I got gray hair already, I feel like an old man. Jesus Christ, Frankie, I ain't an old man. I got two boys at home, I got responsibilities to them, to my family."

"Give those lines to your pals at the G."

"You're tough, that's what I was telling you in the first place. I heard you talking to the G, they played tapes, you're a tough guy. If the worst thing comes to happen, then you can handle it, I know you can. Frankie, I know you can handle time the way your uncle Brian couldn't handle it. You got balls, you're a stand-up guy."

"I ain't a sucker, Pat. Not for you, not for anyone."

"I could help out your kid, your wife. She's family to me—"

"Get away from me. I got nothing to say to you." Frankie pushed him away. "Shit," Frankie said. "Shit. Shit. Shit." He walked from the shadows of the bleachers and climbed into his green Ford pickup and slammed the door twice to make sure it caught on the lock. He sat and waited for his hands to stop trembling.

He watched Pat walk across the parking lot and disappear around the corner.

Frankie started the engine and pulled into traffic. He went a long block west and then turned south and came around the playing fields from the back.

He saw Pat Kennedy on the sidewalk. Standing next to a Pontiac sedan. Talking to two men inside.

"Shit," Frankie Coolin said again.

11

Frankie stopped at the Bohemian's after he left Pat Kennedy but the place was nearly empty and the beer didn't taste good. He finished his draft, bought a square in the football pool for Sunday and drove slowly to Andy's house to dump the load of studs. He hoped Andy was home; he wanted to talk to someone.

Two was at the kitchen door when he drove up.

"I got some more studs."

"Andy's gone, he's estimating a job, some guy wants him to build his basement."

"Oh."

"You all right, Dad?"

"I'll dump the wood in the garage."

"It's open. When you're done, come in and I'll give you a beer."

"About time," he said, trying to smile.

He worked hard enough to sweat. He tried to make the work blot out the picture of Kennedy talking to the G in the white Pontiac.

He entered the kitchen and shuffled his feet on the rug by the door. Two was at the stove and a pot of split-pea soup was bubbling on the gas range.

"Where's Number One?" Frankie said.

"Sleeping. He always takes a nap about now. It's the only time I get to myself, when he's sleeping. Andy was going out to Schiller Park with the estimate, he should have been home by now."

Coolin opened the refrigerator and took a can of Bud from the door. He popped the top.

"Tell him that's all the studs I can get right now."

"I'll tell him when I see him. I see him about two hours a week, it seems like. He's working nights and he's been putting in for all the overtime he can get. And now he's talking about Saudi Arabia. That'll be just perfect. Then I won't see him for two hours a year."

Frankie sat down in a yellow plastic-and-chrome kitchen chair. There were four chairs from the old kitchen set that Rose had wanted to throw out and which Andy and Two had taken. "I understand his point. He wants to make a little money to get ahead is all, there's nothing wrong with that."

Two was dark and tall. She wore jeans all the time, and sweaters. The sweaters made her look good and made her pale skin more pale. Her eyes were dark. She looked like Rose except there was something of Frankie in her too, in the curve of her jawline and in the set of her mouth when she was listening to someone else speak.

"You busy now?"

"Not too busy, but I'm still trying to line up that winter job. I don't know if it's coming through or not. I'm trying to get Joey on it."

"Saudi Arabia. You think we'd been married twenty years."

"Twenty years wouldn't make it any easier. I was over by Proviso High, watching the game."

"God, I hate football. Last Sunday, all Andy wanted to do on the one day I get to see him was park himself in the front room and watch the Bears game. On the new set. We get a new TV set and all he wants to do is watch football, football, football. One day a week we get together to see each other and he watches football."

"It's only three hours."

"It's all day, it seems like."

"Watch it with him."

"I'd rather be on a desert island." She wiped the top of the counter with a sponge and sprinkled Comet in the path of the sponge.

"It wasn't that good a game anyway last Sunday," Frankie said.

"I'd rather be on a desert island," Two said again. Her voice had taken on the stubborn tone she had adopted first as a little girl. "I said to Andy why didn't we get a babysitter and go see a movie. You know how long it's been since I saw a movie? Not since we were dating. You watch movies on television, they just chop them up; besides, they're all the same old movies anyway. I want to see something new."

"I don't know, I don't watch television."

"Sure, Dad. But you don't have to sit with a kid all day and all night. Sometimes I feel like I was locked up in a jail or something."

Frankie Coolin stared at her. He and Rose had tried and tried to have children from the first but nothing had happened. Rose went to a doctor and he said nothing was wrong with her. And then she made Frankie go to the same doctor and the doctor had said nothing was wrong with him; that it happened this way sometimes. Two had come as a miracle to them and they had hovered over her like angels.

"So how's Number One?" Frankie said.

"Sean keeps having these colds, one after another."

"Maybe you ought to see a doctor."

"A doctor? I see nothing but doctors. If I didn't see doctors, I wouldn't have anyone else to talk to."

"Come on, kid. Stop feeling sorry for yourself."

"Thanks, Dad, I needed that. You make my day complete. Just another nice Saturday, a nice day outside and maybe the last nice day we'll have before winter. And so Andy is out gallivanting around and Sean is crabby all morning until I finally put him down and now I got you coming over and giving me a hard time."

He thought of the angel child. He thought of the miracle. And then he felt Pat Kennedy's hand on his arm. It wouldn't be so bad for him, would it? His kids were practically grown.

"Hey, baby," he said. Frankie got up and went to the counter and gave her a hug. Unexpectedly, she yielded to it and buried her head against his jacket for a moment. And then they broke apart without a word.

"Rose could come over by your house tonight, she could sit for you. Or bring Sean over, you know we'd like to have him, and we got the room: Mick is going to be up at DePaul overnight, for basketball. That's what he says. Probably screwing one of his girlfriends."

"Mick has got girlfriends finally?"

"Yeah, Two. And he doesn't carry frogs in his pockets anymore."

She grinned. "They grow up fast."

"Wise girl," he said. "Whatever. Mick's going to be away,
you could leave Sean over so we didn't have to wake him up."

"I'll talk to Moneybags when he gets home."

"Andy is all right. He's had a tough year, he says."

"We haven't had a tough year, it just seems like it. I do the
checkbook, you know. We got money coming in, we aren't
rich, but we got money coming in. I'm not a complete dope,
you know, but Andy is turning into such a Polack, I never knew
it when we were going out with each other. When we were
going out, it was do this and that and go here and there, it was
like he had all the money in the world. But as soon as we get
married, he looks at every dollar for spots on it."

"Well, Two. I don't want to get between you two guys. Just
bring Sean over by our house if you want."

"And Saudi Arabia now. That's the last straw. Six months in
Saudi Arabia. He says it's for a house out in DuPage County.
Hell, I don't want a new house. I like this house."

"It's a nice house."

"Not for him. Not for his mother. His mother is over here
nearly every day, I'm surprised she hasn't been by today. She
looks around, you know? Just looks around all the time. She
stares at things. I never seen a woman do that. She stares at
the counter. I look at the counter and I don't see anything. Or
maybe there's a coffee stain on it. I don't see it until I stare at
it the way she stares at it. Then I see it. A stain. Oh, my God,
a stain in the kitchen. You think someone had crapped in
church."

"Don't talk like that, Two. I don't like that language. Sean
shouldn't hear his mother talk like that."

"Sometimes it drives me crazy."

"Well, baby, she's just a Polack is all, you got to allow for
it. You know the way Polacks are."

"I married one."

"Andy is all right. I like Polacks but the women drive me
crazy, they're always cleaning everything twice over, they make
a house look like an operating room."

"Not like we shanty Irish women."

"That's right. There's no point in overcleaning things."

"I wish I had married you."

He smiled. "But Andy isn't like his mother."

"Listen, Dad; Andy expects things his way too. This isn't all just one-sided, you know, when I complain. He wants his shirts ironed. I mean, for Christ's sake, Dad, who irons wash-and-wear work shirts from Sears? He says he likes the way they feel when they're ironed. I said he's crazy, they're work shirts, but he says his mom ironed his shirts. I bet she did. That woman probably irons underwear." Two threw the sponge in the sink and opened the soup pot. The green soup bubbled. She stirred the pot and lowered the flame until it barely flickered on the gas ring.

"So I wouldn't iron his shirts and you know what he did? He started ironing his own work shirts. Him. What the hell am I going to do then? So I iron his work shirts for him."

Frankie didn't know what to say. "Well, he looks neat. I never knew he ironed his work shirts. That doesn't seem right."

"You see, Dad? That's the way he gets his way. If you don't do something for him, he does it himself."

"Well."

"You know what I feel like doing sometimes? I feel like taking all my clothes off and sitting around all day and when he comes home at night, tell him to go out and get a pizza. That's what I feel like."

Not for the first time talking to Two, Frankie felt embarrassed.

"Well, baby, everyone's got troubles."

"Is that right? What troubles do you have, Dad?"

He searched her face. Her eyes were Rose's eyes. He couldn't tell Rose, he couldn't tell her. He felt trapped again, panicked as he had once panicked in cold water in the middle of the lake in Wisconsin. He was going to drown right before her eyes. She would be talking to him and he would be drowning. He wanted to speak but he could not.

"Nothing I can't handle," he said.

She grinned. "You always say that. You always said that, all your life."

"That's right."

"Tough guy," she said, smiling, her face clearing. She touched his sleeve.

"Maybe I'll talk to Andy when he comes home. It would be nice to go out. I'd like to go out on a Saturday night again and get dressed up. God, what a handsome hunk Andy can be when he is dressed up."

"It's the ironed shirts that does it for him," Frankie said. She grinned. "Maybe."

"They got a new rib place over on St. Charles Road in Villa Park you ought to go to. Rose and I went over there last week, we had to wait about twenty minutes to get in but it was nice. The ribs were just right. I had ribs and chicken."

"Maybe Moneybags will pop."

"Look, Two, you shouldn't be running down Andy to me. Andy is all right. If I was on a job, I'd rather be working with Andy than some other guys I got to work with. Andy holds up his end."

"He's a good worker, so what? That doesn't do anything for me."

"He wants to go to Arabia to get the money to get ahead. I see it even if you don't that kids can't get ahead no more. Look at me. When I was starting out, you didn't have to have anything going for you. Just a place to live, you go out and hustle a buck and you get ahead. Taxes weren't nothing like they are now. You could save. Andy wants to get a nice house—"

"This is a nice house, I like this house, it's close to you and Mom and the neighborhood is nice. I don't understand why I got to go live out in Carol Stream. I don't know nobody in Carol Stream. How come I don't get a say? It's different with Andy. He's got the wheels, he can get around as much as he wants. I got nothing."

"You got the Plymouth, I didn't see it in the garage."

"That junk? It's sitting at the gas station. There's trouble with the electrical something or other. It won't ever start but what does Andy care? If the truck goes bad, he's right in Jim's Standard station like that because he's got to have the truck. But I got to get around too, don't I? I'm not driving that truck. He says he can get the groceries. He doesn't understand that I got to get away sometimes, from him and from Sean, I got to have some time by myself. Do you see that?"

Frankie nodded because he couldn't talk to her anymore.

Everyone has troubles, he thought. Even Two. Even me. The voice and face and touch of Pat Kennedy lingered in memory and threatened to overwhelm him. He was drowning and the walls of the kitchen were collapsing. He thought he might scream and he was afraid of himself.

"Look, you talk to Andy today and if you're going out, you give Rose a call."

She laughed then but there was nothing funny in it. "I'll talk to him. We can have a couple of dates before he goes to Saudi Arabia. It's funny, Dad; this must be the way it was for the old-country Irish when they had to go to America to get work. Work, work, work. Nothing means anything except work. You can do anything if you say you're doing it for work. Andy abandons me eighteen hours a day and it's okay because it's for work. We need money, we got to get ahead, we got to buy a new house or a new car or a new television set—I heard everything and it doesn't make sense. I want Andy now, not when he's sixty and we're sitting in Florida. I want to see him now and talk to him now."

Frankie put the beer can in the garbage bag by the refrigerator and opened the kitchen door. Outside was fall, crisp winds, no walls.

"I got to go," he said softly.

"I'll tell Andy and maybe if he doesn't want to go out, maybe I'll just bring Sean by anyway and I'll go out on my own and go over to the L. C. Lounge by myself."

"Two," Frankie Coolin said.

"The hell with it," she said, suddenly and fiercely. "I feel like a widow already. Is that what you're supposed to feel like? Why would he want to go to Saudi Arabia and leave me?"

But Frankie Coolin had pushed open the storm door and was on the steps, descending to the walk, to his truck. He heard her voice behind him but he didn't turn.

12

Mick was raking the leaves on the lawn when Frankie pulled up to the house. He parked the truck on the street and shambled across the grass to Mick, who paused and leaned on the rake.

"How come you're working around the house? Don't you have a game tonight at DePaul?"

"I'm going later. Al Brescia is coming by to pick me up."

"Who are they playing?"

"Dayton. We'll take them."

"You're just going up to Rosemont for the game?"

"No. Afterwards we got a party."

"You need some money?"

"I could use some money."

"I'll see what I can do when I see how good you finish this raking job."

Mick smiled at his father. "You're a hard man but I wasn't raking because I wanted to make extra money. I got a paper route."

Frankie grinned. "Shit, you're coming up in the world. By the time you're a lawyer, we'll get you a job at a soda fountain."

"Nobody has soda fountains anymore."

"All right. A bar."

"I could make some money tending bar."

"Don't do it. That's a chump's job. You end up like the Bohemian."

"I was sort of waiting for you."

"Is that right? Where's your mother?"

"I wanted to talk to you."

"Here I am."

"That doesn't make it easy."

Frankie looked at his son. The second child. A second miracle, unexpected as the first. A boy at last, Frankie Coolin had thought when he was born. My son, my boy, he had thought. And then, when he was fifteen, the knee injury on the football field and all the guilt. Even Rose had blamed him: What did he expect from Mick? Did he want Mick to be the things he had not been?

Of course. Of course, it was just that: he wanted Mick to be an extension of him. Mick had tried and when it came down to it, it ended as a popped knee on a football field. He had felt guilt for weeks and the pain in the boy's face had haunted him. Finally, he had begun to leave Mick alone. So much so that they rarely talked any more, not out of hostility but because they each seemed afraid of the other. Frankie Coolin still thought of Mick as fifteen, as the boy who would fulfill those dreams Frankie had once had of his own future. And Mick—what did Mick think of him?

They walked around to the back of the house without a word and Mick hung the rake in the garage.

"You want a beer?" Mick said.

"I always want a beer," Frankie replied.

Mick went up the back steps into the house. A moment later he emerged, carrying two cans of beer. He passed one to his father.

They stood in the chill of the dying afternoon and sipped cold beer. Above, in the electric blue sky, planes boomed low on the approach to O'Hare Field to the north.

"What's on your mind?"

"You."

"What about me?"

"What's wrong?"

"Nothing's wrong."

"You got problems."

"Nothing I can't handle," Frankie Coolin said for the second time that day. "Why? Who you been talking to?"

"Joey."

"Is that right? What's Joey got to say?"

"About the FBI coming around. Was this about the warehouse fire last year?"

"What about it?"

Mick stared at him. "Dad. You're talking to me, not to someone else. You can talk to me."

"I got nothing to say."

They stared at each other.

"Hey, Mick." He yearned to speak now but he did not know
how to begin. "I got a few hassles, everyone gets hassled by
the G sooner or later. Like the time I got audited a couple of
years ago."

"This isn't an audit. Not with the FBI coming around to see
Uncle John."

"Fuck, they're just fucking him around, trying to fuck me
around. It don't mean nothing."

"This is about the warehouse fire. What happened?"

"Nothing happened. I lost some building supplies."

"Dad."

"Look, I don't want you worrying about something that ain't
nothing. Nothing is happening, nothing is going to happen."

"I'm twenty years old. I'm not twelve. You act like I'm
twelve."

"I don't act like you're twelve."

"Talk to me."

"How come you suddenly want me to talk to you?"

"Because you're in trouble. I've seen it in your face but I
didn't know what it was. I thought you were worried about
Mom."

The beer tasted flat, he thought. He was cold. *What about
Mom?*

"What about her?"

"She's got anemia, you know."

"She didn't say anything."

"Her doctor is doing some tests. She's run down all the
time."

"She wouldn't be run down if she didn't do laundry in the
middle of the night. That would run anyone down."

"I didn't even know what was wrong with you until I talked
to Joey. Why can you talk to Joey and you can't talk to me?"

"I don't talk to Joey. Joey is getting a big mouth, I got to talk
to him about that."

"You got a lawyer?"

The question startled Frankie. "Yeah."

"Not Flynn. You're not seeing Flynn on this." Flynn handled contracts and other small family business.

"You don't think I'd get an Irish lawyer for something involving the G, do you?"

Frankie smiled but Mick did not.

"Who?"

"You don't know him. A guy named Klein."

"What's going down?"

"I don't know, Mick. I honestly don't know." He tasted the beer. God, he thought suddenly, he had to talk to someone or he would burst. But Mick was just a kid.

"What was in the warehouse? Hot stuff?"

"You think I'm a thief."

"No more than anyone else in the trades," Mick said.

"You don't have a high opinion of me."

"I love you."

He sipped at the empty beer can to hide his embarrassment. He turned away from Mick and looked across the lawn, watched a 727 boom away over the treetops. He saw the clothesline in the back of the house, the back fence that needed painting, Butorac's dog tied to the doghouse across the alley. He saw the rusting garbage can at the alley.

"Yeah," Frankie said when his voice returned to him. "There was some hot stuff. But it wasn't mine. That's the problem. I ain't involved in it but when the G starts messing around, they want to get everyone."

"Was it in your loft?"

"Well, they say it was."

"I'm not a lawyer yet, Dad."

"OK. Sure. I guess they know. But I didn't have anything to do with it. Here I am, pleading to my own kid."

"Dad, if you did or you didn't, you should have talked to me. You don't tell anyone anything."

"That's the best policy."

"Dad, what are you going to do?"

"There's nothing to do. It's the G's game, not mine. I got a lawyer, I keep my mouth shut."

"Who put the stolen goods in your space?"

"Beats me."

"Kennedy," Mick said.

"What are you, Sherlock Holmes?"

"You and Kennedy went into that loft together, didn't you? So it must have been Kennedy."

"I don't want you going around badmouthing people about things like that. If you think it's Kennedy, just keep it to yourself."

Frankie walked to the garbage can at the alley and dropped the beer can into it. I love you, he remembered. He stared at the garbage can and felt the closeness of Mick behind him.

"You getting hot at me?"

"No. Not you, not ever."

"Come on, Dad. What's going on, you can tell me."

"Look, Mick. All I want you to do is to get out of school with good grades and be a mouthpiece so that when I get into trouble the next time down the line, I won't have to hire a Jew attorney."

"You wouldn't want me; I'd still be Irish," Mick said.

Frankie laughed out loud. The laughter carried relief with it. For the first time in five years, he reached out to touch Mick. He touched his son on the shoulder and let his hand stay there for a minute. Neither moved, as though what passed between them was too fragile for movement. And then his hand dropped.

"Well, it would all be in the family so I suppose I could throw you the business."

"Dad, if you got a lawyer, you got to talk to him. And if Kennedy is involved, you shouldn't talk to Kennedy."

"I don't go out of my way to talk to Kennedy in the first place."

Mick looked into his face. "Yeah, but does Kennedy go out of his way to talk to you?"

"What do you mean?"

"Does he go out of his way to talk to you? I mean, if the G has been talking to him, talking to you, maybe he's talking to them back."

Coolin saw Kennedy on the street, leaning into the car, talking to two men.

"You're going to make a good lawyer."

13

"You got a nice house," Frankie Coolin said.

"Yes."

Arthur Klein made a little face as though the remark displeased him. He pursed his lips together. He wore a stretch denim jump suit that neatly fitted over his immense body. Frankie Coolin thought he looked like a blue tank.

Arthur Klein led him down a hall decorated in a red and black Mediterranean style past a heavy chest topped with silver candelabra. The hall was dark, rich and gloomy.

It opened on a living room with white walls, full of white furniture and glass cocktail tables with chrome supports. There were two such tables planted in the center of two groups of furniture at either end of the white rug. The grand piano was white as well and on the far wall was a Picasso black and white drawing.

Arthur Klein went to a white chair, turned, and slowly fell into it. Frankie Coolin stood on the white rug near the hall entry.

"Sit down," Klein said.

Frankie brushed a hand against his jeans. He had not expected a white room. And then he thought about the fee and he went to the couch and sat down on it.

For a moment, the two dots of color in the white sea faced each other without words.

"Look. I appreciate your seeing me on Sunday in your house."

"Yes."

"I had to see you. I thought about it all night. I had to call you up."

"Yes. I can understand your gratitude just as you can understand my annoyance. I attempt, albeit unsuccessfully, to keep my private life apart from my public life. You are part of my public life; you have now crossed to the portals of my private life." Klein paused. "On the other hand, I am extremely fond of this matter that has arisen between us. Fond. Yes, that is the word for it."

"I'm glad," Frankie Coolin said.

"What happened?"

"What happened was that I hadn't heard from the G for three weeks and I began to think everything was going to blow over. Especially after they went after John and John didn't tell them anything because he didn't know anything to tell."

A woman in a plain white dress appeared at the door; she was small and looked Spanish.

"Mr. Coolin. Would you have a refreshment?"

"I'll have a beer if you got one. You got an ashtray?" He pulled a cigarette out of his pocket.

"No, sir. The rules of my private life differ from my public life and I cannot permit you to smoke in my house, not for the sake of my wife or my children."

Coolin stared at him. "They're sick?"

Arthur Klein turned his head a quarter of an inch and said, *"Cerveza fría, por favor."*

The woman nodded, turned and disappeared into a dark hall.

"You told her you wanted cold beer."

"Do you speak Spanish, Mr. Coolin?"

"I do work down in Pilsen neighborhood in the city, down by Eighteen and Blue Island? I like it down there. Lot of spics but they're Mexicans. I can't handle Puerto Ricans but I like Mexicans."

The woman appeared with a bottle of Heineken and a frosted glass on a tray. She poured from the green bottle into the glass for Coolin and then walked away without a word.

"Gracias," said Frankie Coolin.

For just a moment, the woman stopped, turned. A ghost of a smile crossed her face. *"De nada,"* she said, and disappeared into the hall again.

"Good beer," Frankie Coolin said.

"What happened?"

"The G were leaning on Pat Kennedy pretty hard. He says."

"Your cousin."

"My wife's cousin, I told you. Not a cousin to me."

"And? When did you see Mr. Kennedy?"

"Yesterday. I was over by Proviso West, watching the high-school game. Sometimes I stop over there when I'm passing. Well, Pat Kennedy stops by too and that is strange because Pat Kennedy doesn't go to no football game unless his kid is playing."

"His kid wasn't playing."

"Bingo. That part was peculiar and the way he started talking to me. He's talking about the G and how heavy they're coming down."

Arthur Klein did not move or speak.

Coolin sipped the beer again. "He said his lawyer told him to go talk to them when they started hassling his brother-in-law."

"Who is his attorney?"

"I don't know."

"And did he? Talk to them?"

"That's what he said he did."

"And what did he say to them?"

"He said he said nothing. That is bullshit."

"Of course."

"He started telling me about how he's got two young kids and my kids are mostly grown. About how he don't want to do any time."

Arthur Klein sighed. The sigh made the silence of the room more profound. Both men waited for a moment and let the silence sink into their consciousness.

"And then he starts on about how he didn't know nothing about what was going on. Except he keeps edging around that I knew something about what was going on."

"And you, Mr. Coolin. What did you do?"

"He scared me."

"An insight. A wise insight, Mr. Coolin."

"I blew him off. I got out of the bleachers and started walking away from him. I told him I didn't know what he was talking about."

"And what happened then?"

"He splits and I got in the truck. I go around the corner. I took Wolf to Harrison and around through the new section and down to Roosevelt and back over, sort of going around the field."

Klein waited.

"He was talking to the G."

"You're positive."

"Yeah. I guess I am. I knew it from the minute he started going weepy on me in the grandstands."

"Mr. Kennedy. The tough guy." The words were sharp and brittle, like glass broken from a window. Klein leaned forward. "Your wife's cousin. Not family to you. You don't trust him."

"I should never of rented that space for him."

"No. You should not have but that is in the past. You rented the space for him in the warehouse. He was a stand-up type, wasn't he? He told you not to talk to the federal officers, didn't he?"

"Tough guy," Frankie Coolin said.

"This is not a pleasant development," Arthur Klein said. "You have to tell me everything now, everything real and unreal, the dirt and the clean parts, from the beginning. Without covering up."

"I never tell anyone everything."

"I am not anyone."

"Look, I know about confidential communication and all that and I believe you as far as it goes. But it's like that diploma on the wall in your office; when it comes down to it, it's just a piece of paper that doesn't mean shit."

"I appreciate your caution, Mr. Coolin. You have not paid me a red cent yet and I appreciate everything you say. Reach in your pocket now and hand me a dollar bill."

"I don't have change."

"A ten or twenty then."

"How about a five?"

Arthur Klein took the five-dollar bill and put it in the single pocket of his jump suit. He reached in a drawer of the stand next to his table, got a pen and paper, and wrote a note.

"There. A receipt. You are my client now. I have received payment from you and acknowledged it."

"And now you only want forty-nine hundred and ninety-five dollars when the time comes."

"Precisely."

"I was by the bank and they were talking about nineteen percent interest rate on a second mortgage. Nineteen. This guy is sitting there talking like that; I know juice men never charged nineteen percent."

"I told you before that the way you get the five thousand dollars is not of interest to me. And I think you must consider carefully now where you will get the money because danger is close at hand. Very close."

"You say it just like death."

"Yes. Like death. I am certain of two things: death and your indictment. Would that your wife's cousin could have been as stand-up as you were."

"You think he snitched on me."

"I will put money on it. Or, rather, you will."

"I should have decked the prick when I saw him yesterday."

"Perhaps. But do not see him any more." Arthur Klein made a tent with his fingers. "The question is this: What did he tell the federal officers and the United States Attorney? And how much of it was the truth? And what can we offer in mitigation of what he told them? You see why you must be honest with me, direct and straightforward, without reservations."

Coolin looked at the ice sliding along the stein of cold beer. Mick had been right. He had had to talk to Klein right away. It was like going to the dentist first thing in the morning and getting it over with, even if you had to live with the pain all day. At least it was done. Mick had been up when he rose. They had not talked to each other in the kitchen because the old man was there. The old man had said something about not being able to sleep.

Did you sleep? Mick had asked his father.

I always sleep, Frankie Coolin had said. I got the conscience of a baby. . . . But it wasn't true anymore.

"OK," Frankie Coolin said to Arthur Klein. "Here it is." And he told him everything. It took a long time because the story had side roads to travel and relationships to explain. At the end, Frankie Coolin said, "You see, I'm not a virgin but I'm not a crook. Not in this. Not in what they're trying to hang on me."

Arthur Klein stared at him. "Mr. Coolin. You obviously knew your cousin was dealing in stolen goods."

Quickly, without hesitation, Frankie Coolin shook his head and said, "I didn't know anything."

"That is what you can say to the federal officers and to the United States Attorney in good time; but it is not what you will say to me. Not now on Sunday morning in my own house as you presume to intrude upon my private time and private space."

"Look. What do you want me to say to you?"

"The truth, Mr. Coolin, that most elusive of elements in your life. The lies will be constructed later for other ears but for me, for now, the absolute truth."

"I told you the truth."

"You did not. I am your priest or rabbi, your confessor. If you cannot tell me the truth, if you cannot trust the only human being who can possibly extricate you from this mess—then we waste our time. Do you see what I am saying?"

Frankie Coolin did not speak for a moment. And then he said yes.

"Well?"

"OK. I knew that Pat Kennedy must have been scamming something or someone. Nobody does nothing for nobody. But I did know about this warehouse space and it was logical for him to ask me to rent the space for him."

"Did you know about this interstate theft business? Did you know the items stolen were television sets? Do you know the other principals in the ring?"

"No, I didn't know any of that stuff. What do you take me for? I thought Pat was stealing material from his company, I thought it was innocent stuff, I didn't know he was actually stealing. I mean, interstate theft isn't a laughing matter. I figured he was skimming off the top at his company like everyone does."

"I am astounded continually by the odd ethical stance I run across. Your wife's cousin, if he were engaged in stealing from his employer, is no less a thief than if he steals from strangers at truck stops. The theft of a television set or a thousand sets differs only in the gravity of the offense, not in the type. A thief is a thief. Mr. Kennedy is one and you knew it; further, you aided in his thieving by setting up the coffer in this warehouse.

You are the accomplice of a thief and therefore, in the eyes of justice, you are a thief yourself."

"Hey, I'm glad I didn't go to mass this morning but came here. I like your sermons much better. Understand this: I didn't steal nothing."

"But you knew Mr. Kennedy stole TV sets."

"I didn't know nothing about those sets."

"And I say you knew a great deal."

"Look. You think you know what I am or where I'm coming from." Frankie Coolin pulled a cigarette out of his pocket and found a match. "Fuck your sick kids." He lit the cigarette and threw the match in the empty beer bottle on the table.

"Mr. Coolin," Klein began.

"No, you listen to me, you want me to talk. You want to get me hot with your bullshit but I know what I am a lot more than you think I do. I talk bad and I don't know all the words but I ain't stupid, Jack. I know what I do and I know what I got to do. I got in a jam because I trusted a little bucket of sleaze like Kennedy not to fuck me up. It isn't the first time. You think you understand me and you don't understand dip shit."

Coolin got up and pointed his finger at him. "Look at you. You're a fucking lawyer. I happen to think lawyers are the scum of the earth. I'd rather be digging ditches with a gang of niggers on the West Side with my ass in muck and it raining cats and dogs than spend ten minutes with a bunch of lawyers. Or those towel-head doctors that Rose goes to because all the other doctors went to the North Shore because they don't want to deal with people like me anymore. You guys drive Mercedes or what but you still ain't shit to me. I know what I am which is more than you know. I know I'm a hustler and I'm not proud about it or what I got to do—"

"Sit down."

"Fuck you with sit down, I'm getting ready to pull outta this joint, I just got to say a few things." Frankie Coolin's face was red and his eyes seemed to catch fire in the muted light of the room.

"My kid wants to be a lawyer and I'm busting my balls not because I think that being a lawyer is so fucking great but because I know what I do is worse. I get a fire job at three in the morning and I go out in the cold and I'm boarding up

windows in the stinking mess of the building, with the floors
all wet and the walls wet and I get so fucking wet and cold that
I can't even feel my hands. I got buildings on the West Side
with rats down in the basement bigger than horses and when
I get called out at midnight because the toilet's overflowing
because some blue-gummed nigger from Alabama don't know
you ain't supposed to throw hairbrushes down the toilet, well,
I go over to the building and fix the fucking thing and go down
the basement and clean up the sewer lines that backed up. I
ain't saying this for pity or honor or anything. I know what I
am and I don't want my kid to be it and I don't want no one
I know to have to do what I have to do. Which doesn't make
me ashamed either. I ain't ashamed of myself but I wouldn't
wish what I do on anyone. But at least I'm honest. So don't
give me your two-dollar words about ethics and right and
wrong and the rest of it; I know what wrong is and right but
I know what I gotta do to make a buck and that's what it comes
down to in the end. The guy with the mortgage won't take
right or wrong every month or the guy at the grocery don't
care where the money comes from. If they did, they'd be looking a lot closer at your money than they would at mine."

More silence lay between them.

"Sit down, Mr. Coolin."

Frankie stood.

"Sit down."

He sat.

"I apologize for my remarks." Arthur Klein nodded slightly.
"As you say, we all do what we can. Even Mr. Kennedy who
thought he was doing his little bit to get ahead. And now he
is doing more. He is putting you in the way of harm to save
himself. Is that part of your code as well?"

"To be a snitch? I don't snitch. No one snitches."

"Ah. Some do, however; otherwise, the federal machinery
for criminal prosecution would come to a standstill. If there
were no talebearers, there would be no indictments."

"When am I going to get it?"

"Soon. I will make inquiries. I will see the federal people.
In the meantime, stay away from Mr. Kennedy. I think that
should be obvious to you."

"It was yesterday."

"Nothing . . . er . . . nothing you said in your conversation with Mr. Kennedy could be used against you?"

"I said I didn't know what he was talking about."

"I see."

"You think he was wired?"

Klein's eyes widened. "Do you, Mr. Coolin?"

"It never crossed my mind until now."

"Well, let it cross your mind."

"I didn't say nothing to him. I don't think I did."

"Say nothing now in any case. If Mr. Kennedy approaches you again, treat him as though he had the plague."

"I'd like to pound that little prick."

"Restrain yourself."

"How could he do this to me? We were the same family."

"So were Cain and Abel," Arthur Klein said.

Coolin dropped the cigarette in the beer bottle and stared at the smoke curling up the green glass.

"As you said," Klein continued, "he was only your wife's cousin after all."

14

The telephone rang for a long time in the darkness of the silent house. And then Mick was at the door of the bedroom.

"Dad?"

The whisper was harsh and urgent. Frankie Coolin turned under the covers and felt the form of Rose's body next to him. He opened his eyes in the darkness as though he were dreaming.

"Dad."

"What? What is it?"

"Telephone."

"What time is it?"

"It's from the buildings." The property on the West Side they all called "the buildings."

"OK. I got it."

"What is it, Frank?"

"Go to sleep, Rose. It's nothing."

"You got to go out?"

"I don't know."

Bare feet on the floor. He went to the hallway. Mick was in a tee shirt and pajama bottoms, his hair tousled by sleep.

"Who is it?"

"I don't know."

Frankie pulled his green robe around him. He stumbled in the hall. A nightlight plugged into the dining-room outlet near the kitchen cast sinister, large shadows throughout the house. All the familiar objects took on the appearances of monsters.

The phone was on a wall in the kitchen.

"What?" Coolin said into the receiver. He closed his eyes and waited for the voice.

"Hey? Frankie, is that you?"

"Who else would it be, Willie?"

"You gotta come down now."

"What's wrong?"

"The new building burned down."

He felt sick; he said nothing. He kept his eyes closed. Maybe it was only a dream. Maybe there had been no phone call, no voice from the West Side.

He opened his eyes. "What happened?"

"Man, that building went down. Two-alarm fire, they tole me. Firemen is still here now."

"Christ."

"Some cat must of got himself in that first-floor apartment because that was where the fire started."

"Is it all gone?"

"That building is gone, man."

"Anybody hurt?"

"Naw, not anyone I know. Except the cat who was broke into that apartment on the first floor, he dead."

"Christ."

"Ain't nothing to you, Frankie; I tole the firemens that you didn't rent that apartment. Must of been a bum is what they say."

"Yeah."

Silence.

"Ain't nothing on you, Frankie. Not you fault."

"The whole building."

"Whole thing. Man, I mean that building is a thing of the past."

"They take the stiff out?"

"Oh, yeah. There was a fireman, he got a smoke insulation. But he all right."

"Smoke inhalation?"

"Yeah."

"OK. Where you, Willie?"

"I be here. You coming down?"

"Yeah. I'm coming down."

"I be by Tort's now to use the phone but I meet you at the building."

Frankie replaced the receiver in the darkness of the kitchen. Mick opened the refrigerator and took out a can of beer and brought it to the table. Frankie Coolin opened it and sat down without a word.

"What happened?"

"The new building burned down."

"What happened?"

"A bum must of broke into one of the apartments and let his cigarette burn down or something. But it's burned down."

"Who was that?"

"Willie Oboe."

"What are you going to do?"

"Go over to the West Side."

"I'll go with you."

"You got school tomorrow."

"I can cut a class."

"Don't cut no classes, please. I got enough to think about."

"Dad. I want to help you."

"I don't need no help because I ain't doing anything. I'm just going to look at the building." He looked at Mick. "Don't give me a hard time, OK? There's nothing to do over there, I just got to go see what's going on."

"You need my help," Mick said.

"Look, Mick, I don't and I ain't got time to argue it right now. Just leave me alone, will you?"

"Sure. I can do that all right."

Mick went into his bedroom and closed the door. Frankie sat at the kitchen table for a moment and thought about the building, about the work of a summer, about wrestling radiators down the stairs and about the G waiting for him on the landing.

"What happened?" Rose said when he went into the bedroom. He didn't answer, but opened the dresser and took out a clean pair of jeans, underclothes and white cotton socks. He pulled a flannel shirt off the hanger in the closet.

"I got a problem in the buildings."

"Frank? What's wrong? What happened?"

Rose sat up straight in bed. He could see her in the darkness, in the flannel nightgown. Her eyes caught the yellow light from the closet.

"The new building burned down."

"Oh, God, Frankie, was anyone hurt?"

"No, just the asshole who started the fire in the first place."

"Oh, Frankie. All that work."

"Tell me about it." He picked up his wallet from the dresser and shoved it in his back pocket. He thought of Klein and Pat Kennedy; of the buildings and the summer that had fled without work being finished on the new building; and Joey painting the apartments with him. And the G. He felt nauseated.

"Frankie."

He went into the bathroom and closed the door and pulled up the toilet seat. He stood over the toilet for a moment, staring at the water in the bowl, then retched into the bowl at last. When he was finished, he flushed the toilet, wiped his mouth and gargled with Listerine. When he opened the door of the bathroom, Rose was standing in the darkened hall.

"It's all right. Go back to bed."

"Are you all right? Do you have to go down to the building now?"

"What am I going to do? Go back to sleep? The building just burned down. Either I lay in bed and stay awake all night or I go down to the West Side."

"It's dangerous down there."

"Tell me."

"Frankie, are you all right? You seem so strange yesterday and today. Where did you go this morning?"

"I had to see a man. Go back to bed, Rose."

He went into the kitchen and opened the cabinet near the refrigerator. It was the only cabinet he locked and he was the only one who had a key to it. He took out the gun and shoved it in his jacket and closed the cabinet. Rose knew he had a gun but she pretended that she didn't; no one else knew, not even the kids.

He went out the side door and climbed into the truck parked in the driveway. It was cold and the wind blew hard and wet with the smell of rain or snow.

The truck turned over and he let it idle for a moment, then pushed it into gear. He went down the sleeping suburban side streets until he reached Butterfield Road and then turned west. At Wolf Road, he made a left turn and went past the Hillside shopping center and then left again on Harrison Street to the entrance ramp of the Eisenhower Expressway. The expressway was brilliantly lit and empty. It was just past one in the morning.

He did not listen to the radio; as usual, he lost himself in the driving. He pulled off at Western and went north into the heart of the ghetto.

The streets around the building glistened with standing water. The fire trucks were gone, the police were gone, the crowds were gone. He parked the truck and got out with a flashlight in his hand. He walked up the stoop. The front door was smashed. He walked through the charred entry. The smell of burned wood filled his lungs. He was familiar with the smell; he had worked on enough fire wrecking jobs.

He played the light around the shadows. The stairs were gone, burned away. A gaping hole inside the building pointed to the apartments that had been on the second and third floors.

He played his light across the blackened flooring of the first-floor apartment. The windows were all smashed. Nothing to show there had been a death.

"Shit," Frankie said.

He went out of the building and down the stoop and around to the side. The brick walls stood but the building was gutted. He had picked it up in a tax sale for fifteen hundred dollars. How much work had he put into it over the past two months?

"Hey, Frankie."

Frankie played the light down the dark gangway and saw the figure.

"Willie."

Willie came up the gangway, his feet sloshing the standing water. He looked down at the ground and made a face. "This is a mess."

"What happened to the people?" Three families had moved into the still unfinished building in the past three weeks.

"They be all right. Salvation Army took them to the shelter."

"Who torched this?"

"Never gonna find that out, that boy was frizzled, he musta been living in that empty flat downstairs. That boy was fried, he look like a hot dog been on the grill too long."

Willie handed Frankie a pint of J&B Scotch.

"I don't drink whiskey."

"Everybody do something he don't do when he got to do it."

Frankie tasted the light Scotch; it burned his tongue and he felt a pain in his belly when the Scotch reached it.

"Should of seen that fire, Frankie, that was a fire. I'm talking about flames, my man. Jump right up out of the roof."

"Why do you sound so happy, Willie?"

"I be philosophical."

"Shit, Willie. Double shit."

"Hey, man, don't be laying heavy on me. I was the one that calls you, I could of just waited till you come down again for your rent. Then you be surprised."

"Nothing surprises me. That family we put in on the third floor on this side—"

"Gowan."

"Yeah. They look solid, got a daddy around. No welfare, right?"

"He work for the post office."

"Let's get some space for them. I think I'm gonna give them Galliger's apartment."

"Yeah. I be thinking about Galliger myself," Willie said. "That dude ain't been around a couple of weeks anyway, I check around and some dudes say he's on the inside right now. You want Gowan to have his place."

"I got to paint it. I can paint it next week. You can put them in tomorrow. Galliger never was worth a shit, he was three months behind." Frankie made a face and kicked at the wall of the burned-out building. "Do a midnight eviction on him. Dump his shit in the alley unless he's got something there you can give to Gowans."

"I can handle that. You should of seen it, Frankie. She went up like *that.* The firemens had a snorkel out and everything. They be taking people right out of the window. That fire department, they be dudes; dude on the roof, ventilating. Ventilating your building."

His eyes glittered in the light of the street lamps.

"If they hadn't found a body in there, I would of thought you torched the place yourself."

"Shit, you crazy. You crazy, Frankie. Shit. You talk jive shit again. Why I want to torch your building?"

"Take it easy."

"No man, I ain't gonna take it easy. I be your man here, your main man. I be calling you, watching out for you down here. You white dude sitting out there in the suburbs, shit, man; what you think is going on down here if I wasn't down here for you?"

"Hey, fuck you, Willie. I had a building before I met you and I'll have one long after you're gone. I don't need you, man."

"You do. You needs me. You just like to talk that jive that you be so cool, you don't need no one. Well, man, you needs me."

"Whatever turns you on, Willie."

"What turns me on is this. We be here and we got three building when we had four. That ain't no good. It ain't no good for you and it ain't no good for me and for the thing I was going to lay on you."

"What thing is that?"

"Well, we could still do it with three buildings but we got to get another building soon. Maybe this winter."

Frankie stared at him for a moment. "Willie, this is not we. This is me. You is you and me is me. These are not your buildings."

"Frankie, I know you upset because of that fire."

"Tell me."

"Look here. You got sixteen apartments left now, same as you had before you bought this building and started fixing it up. Now, I dig what's happening and I know you been seeing the Man about this and that. Now, dig, listen to me: what's going to happen to these buildings you got left if you had to go away for a little while? I mean, you see where I'm coming from."

"No. I don't see it at all."

"Shit now, Frankie, you dig what I'm saying, I know you do. I seen those mens from the government. They is federal dudes and they be out here talking to you, I know they ain't coming into the neighborhood to see if you discriminating on your housing."

"You see a lot of things, Willie."

"That's right. Man, what is going to happen if you had to go inside for a while? I mean, I seen that white cat you got down here, you think that boy is coming down here in the middle of the winter when some nigger fucks up the toilet in your buildings?"

"What do you want to talk about, Willie?"

"I want to talk about what you want. We all talking about the same thing."

"Is that right?"

"We talking the green, Frankie, we talking money. When money talks, the bullshit walks, you know that. You hitting your head on a wall in these buildings, Frankie. You be coming around every month, you be pushing for the rent money, you be out in the middle of the night because some nigger fucked up your toilet, you be all the time living and breathing with these buildings and then what happens? Say the Man comes down on you. You got to do some time for a crime or what—"

"That ain't none of your business."

"Dig, listen to me: You got to do your time and you ain't around the buildings and then what are you gonna do? You got shit all of a sudden, Frankie, brown in the ground."

Frankie stared. Willie was glittering, weaving and selling. He held the bottle in his hand like a baton, leading an orchestra of words.

"Dig, this is the time, now. We got to talk, you and me. We got to set some shit straight."

"What shit is that, Willie?"

"Look here. You know what's happening in real estate?"

Frankie stared at him as though Willie had started to speak French.

"Dig, I get around and I studies it. You know what we need in this ghet-to, Frankie? You know? We need sta-bil-lit-tee. That's it. That means we got to get out the transients and get in the stickers. We don't need lickers, we need stickers. People that sticks and builds." Willie's voice had risen; there was a rhythm to it as if he were seizing the words and making them play in tune.

"Now, dig: We gets the stickers if we gives them something to stick for. I figures it out that you be taking about eighteen-fifty a month out of these buildings. Now, you putting back in about four a month so between the difference, you clear about fourteen. That's cool, I mean, I wish I was clearing fourteen."

"Yeah. But the difference between us is that I still pay taxes."

"Yeah. I dig that too. Dig: How'd you like to make some real change for a change on these apartments? And fix it so you don't have no trouble. And fix it so that you still getting a good dollar out of it on top of the money you be getting in front?"

"You're on dope, Willie; I don't got time for this. I got to go."

"Don't go, man, listen to me. Have some JB."

"I don't want no fucking whiskey."

"Shit, we go by Tort's, you can have a beer."

"I don't want no beer. I want to go home."

"Listen, Frankie, because this be important."

"All right. What is it?"

"Condominiums."

Frankie Coolin stared at him. Willie Oboe smiled and his eyes glittered still. He danced around Frankie and laughed.

"Condos, man."

"What are you talking about?"

"Dig. I been looking and checking up and reading up and talking up and getting my shit together on this. Condo. That's what the white people do. They got a building, they put paint in it and they sell apartments."

Frankie stared at Willie in amazement because he understood. Every word.

"What have you got in mind?"

"Contract, man. Ain't no bank gonna give niggers money to buy a house but condos, man. You give them a contract and they be paying you like rent. But you carry the paper and they be coming through. Onliest thing is, they gots to put money down. They got to get a piece of the rock. They got to believe they gonna own it. Can't be like rent."

"What have you got in mind?"

"Five hundred."

"Where they gonna get five hundred in front?"

"That ain't your problem. There's people can get five hundred dollars."

Frankie thought he sounded like Klein.

"They put five down and what do I set the price at?"

"Well, we can work that out. In five years, they be owning the apartment, dig?"

"So I don't have nothing after five years?"

"Shit, Frankie, you got everything. You make your money on the buildings in five years, you can buy some more buildings you want to. But what you got is what always stays with you: you and me, Frankie. We sets up the maintenance agreement. In front."

"What maintenance?"

"Shit, just what you been doing now, Frankie, only you gets paid regular. We gets paid regular. Oboe and Coolin Maintenance. We fix up the toilets just like you doing now but that's on the side. You see, when they own the apartments, you don't got to do nothing more for them."

"Willie. This sounds all right. I don't like it."

"I know you don't like it." Willie Oboe smiled. "You think you should of thought of it. But dig this, Frankie. We get five down from sixteen apartments. That's eight grand and I take just one grand as my commission fee."

"You take shit, Willie."

"Eight hundred."

"Why the fuck are you in this at all? I mean, I bought the buildings, I fixed them up, I collected the rent, and I give you your apartment rent-free. So where do you come into this at all?"

"Frankie, I come in the front door."

"That's shit."

"That ain't shit, what you saying now is shit, Frankie. I figured this out a long time, this be perfect for you and perfect for me. Look, you got a house be full of jive-ass people, they give a fuck about taking care of it. You think anybody pays mind to something they got no say in? Look here. You get your money out of those buildings in five years and the people, they be getting their own home and everything. Shit, if they pay taxes, they even can write them off."

"Half those people on welfare, they can't afford to buy no apartment, they sure don't pay taxes. Besides, the welfare won't let them buy."

"No, my man. You got four peoples in four apartments on welfare. You don't count too good. All the rest working or hustling. You got the white problem, you know? You think we all niggers down here. This neighborhood is going, Frankie. This be the first fire in two months down here. Man, we are not into burning, we are into sticking, you dig? Shit, man, we be getting together, we be buying these places and making a com-munity."

"I'll think about it."

"Yeah, right, you think about it."

"I'll see you around."

"Hey, Frankie. I want you to think about it now."

"I told you I would think about it."

"No, man. You told me you would think about it like a cat ain't going to think about it; I want you to say you going to think about it like a cat is going to do just that. Don't jive me."

"And don't jive me. If this is such a great deal for me, why are you so happy about it?"

"Because I get mine. I gets a commission and I take a per-cent from the monthly mortgage for collection service and making sure everything is cool in the buildings. I be your man, dig?"

Frankie stared at him. "Why do I trust you exactly?"

"Because you got to. You gonna get that little white cat what was your nephew to live down here with the brothers to watch the buildings? What you gonna do when you gone, when the federal comes down to you? Shit, Frankie. You got me because you got nobody else."

"Willie, you're hustling me."

"You right. You know what I'm doing because you be doing it all the time. Listen here, Frankie." Willie Oboe came close and put his arm on Frankie's sleeve. "Listen here." His breath smelled of Scotch. His eyes were bright, bright even in the shadows.

"Frankie, you white but you cool. You a dude. I watch you. You hustle, you got a streak in you to hustle and I see it. I see it in me, Frankie. I be like you inside me. I see the main chance and I grab it. I ain't no shuffle, I don't sing and dance like a shine. Four years since we talk over at Tort's pig, Frankie, and that be a long time. I didn't never do you wrong in four years."

"And I didn't do you wrong, Willie."

"That's right. That's all we gotta do, don't fuck each other.

I ain't asking you to love me, I ain't asking you to be my momma or my brother. But I be telling you that I am here and I am coming through like a truck. I am coming through, Frankie. Now, dig, stand aside and let me come through."

"I'll see you, Willie."

"Frankie, you think about what I'm saying. You be thinking tonight."

Frankie knew he would.

15

The green pickup truck turned down the familiar side street, headed south a block and then rolled to a stop in front of the house in the middle of the block. Frankie Coolin sat behind the wheel, his eyes bloodshot, his hands cupped over the top of the wheel.

Dawn light in the east over the lake, gray and moody, poured across the lawns on the suburbs. He fished in his pocket for a cigarette and thought about a hundred things. Each was clear for a moment, then swept into a corner of memory, jumbled like rags in a basement rag pile. He thought of Willie and the buildings and of the burned building; of Joey; of the G; of Rose and Mick and Peg at home. After a while, he was not even aware that he was home, sitting in his truck at the curb, still alone. Mick opened the door of the truck.

"Hey," Frankie said softly, by way of greeting.

"Hey."

"Early for you."

"It's eight o'clock. I'm going down to the train. Got a class at ten."

"Eight o'clock," Frankie Coolin said, as though he had never heard the phrase. "It's eight o'clock already."

"You were gone all night."

"I talked to Willie Oboe. The building's gone."

"Tough."

"Yeah. Tough."

"What did Willie have to say?"

"Some shit."

The two of them watched a rabbit parade across their front lawn. The rabbit moved rather slowly, as though it were an old rabbit.

"I wish we still had the cat," Frankie said, watching the brown rabbit.

"The cat couldn't catch a rabbit."

"He could've caught that rabbit, look at that fucking rabbit," Frankie Coolin said.

"Slow. Old. Gonna die this winter," Mick said.

"You got a lot of sympathy for rabbits."

"What d'you want from me? I'm looking at a slow rabbit."

"Doesn't mean he's going to die."

"No. He might get lucky. Drive me to the train."

"Sure."

Mick got in and slammed his door as Frankie pulled the truck away from the curb slowly.

"I wish you let me go down with you to the building."

"No you don't. Nothing to see, just standing and listening to jive-ass from a shine."

"What did he want to tell you?"

"About condos. He says he wants to condo those buildings."

Mick stared at the road. They were heading north on Mannheim towards the Northwestern station. A plane pulled into the sky at O'Hare Field seven miles north and pulled up in a straight line down Mannheim Road, trailing smoke, flattening sound waves behind it.

"I wish your mother flew," Frankie said. "Sometimes I'd like to take off on the first flight outta O'Hare. I don't give a shit where it was going."

"Cleveland," Mick said.

Frankie smiled. "Well, maybe the second flight outta O'-Hare."

"After you left, Ma came into my room and talked to me," Mick said.

"What a convention. We get one call after midnight and everyone has got to talk about it."

"I told her. About the FBI and the other stuff I heard from Joey."

Without a word, Frankie slapped him. He uncoiled his right hand from the wheel and shot it blindly to his right and connected with the side of Mick's face.

"You little shit," he said. "What did you do that for?"

Mick stared at him. His face was red. His eyes were hard and hurt. Frankie pulled to the side of Mannheim Road. He looked at Mick: his face was unyielding but his eyes already showed retreat from the blow his father had just dealt him.

"Why did you do a thing like that?"

"I can't remember when you hit me."

"I can't remember when you did a dumb thing like that."

"If a guy hit me like that, I'd hit him back."

Frankie said nothing.

"I told her because that's the thing about you guys, it was always the thing about you. It was like living in two different worlds growing up. You don't tell her anything and she doesn't tell you anything."

"You don't tell her a thing like that. She's just going to worry and what good does that do her?"

"She's gonna worry anyway," Mick said. "You think you fool her so much? She knows something's wrong, she's known that for weeks. So have I. Even Peg knows that and Peg doesn't pay attention to anything."

"Is that right? Did I come home at night crying to all of you about my troubles?"

"You don't have to. Everyone knows when something's wrong. The trouble is you can't tell anyone and Mom can't ask you. And she can't tell you her own troubles."

"You mean that anemia thing. Yeah. That's all I need."

Mick flushed. "You got to have the ego of the world. What do you need? Who is having the tests? Who's worried about getting cancer? You? When I hurt my knee, you think you were the one that it happened to; it was as though I wasn't there."

Traffic rumbled past them. The morning had begun. Trucks followed each other like elephants in a circus line. More planes boomed up overhead, following the straight line of Mannheim Road.

"You never said that before. You're just pissed off." But Frankie said it softly.

"I'm pissed off is right. I ain't a little kid any more."

"Ain't? You learn to talk like a fucking monkey up at De-Paul? Is that the way they talk there?"

"Fuck school," Mick said. "We aren't talking about school right now. We're talking about you and about whatever is going to happen to us."

"Nothing's going to happen; nothing ever happened before and it won't happen now."

"Dad."

"What?"

"Oh, shit. I can't say anything."

"It looks like you can't say anything without saying shit or fuck or something. Jesus Christ, you get a chance to get a leg up on the game and you talk like a fucking cement finisher working with a nigger gang. Don't you know you talk like that, those people at school mark you down as another West Side dope that ain't never going anywhere and ain't going to be nothing?"

"I don't mind what I am. Your trouble is that you want to make me feel ashamed of what you do for a living."

"You know what I do for a living, Mick? Hustle. I do what I can. I got into the trades when I was your age. I remember the day I got my card in the plasterer's union. Fuck. I was set for life. Plasterer's union, there was fifteen thousand fucking guys in the union, we had it made. Pension. Benefits. The whole thing."

Frankie held the steering wheel with both hands and watched the heavy traffic thundering down Mannheim Road. Cars and tractor-trailer rigs and panel vans and pickup trucks crammed with tool cases and studs and wheelbarrows and cement bags and aluminum ladders.

"I had it made for life except in ten years, there wasn't a plasterer's union. You know how many guys are in now? Two twenty. Fuck pension, fuck benefits, there aren't any plaster walls any more or plaster ceilings and even where there are, no one needs us. So I hustle along, wondering if I'm going to make it tomorrow or not. That's what this is all about: you got a chance to get out, get out of this bullshit, get an education that is going to make you a buck you can count on, not bullshit like I got."

"You're doing all right."

"Tell me about it. I got a three-story six-flat that just burned down. What do I lose on it besides what I paid for it at the tax sale, besides what I give Joey, besides my own time all summer, besides paying off the electrical inspector when he came around three weeks ago? Three weeks ago I dropped him half.

Half. So you tell me how I'm doing all right because I don't see it this morning."

"Dad, you're not the only one in this. We're all in it."

"I know that, that's what I'm trying to tell you. I'm fifty years old next year and I'm running flat out just the same as I did when I was twenty, except I was better off when I was twenty because I didn't get winded. You know all about it, right? I got the fucking G on my case, I got three buildings when I had four yesterday, and I still don't have that winter job lined up. Tell me about how I'm doing. I know we're all in it but I want you to get out. You're at the top of the pot now; crawl out. Ten years from now when you're living in Winnetka with three cars and three kids, then maybe I can come up to see you and you can help me out. Ten years, Mick. I'm forty-nine now and in ten years, I'm sixty years old. What the fuck am I going to be doing when I'm sixty?"

Mick stared at him.

Frankie Coolin said, "The same fucking thing, Mick. The same fucking thing. It never changes, it never gets better."

Mick didn't speak.

"I'm worried now about your mother," Frankie said, his voice becoming soft. "I shouldn't have said what I said. You know I'm worried now about her, I'm worried about this exam she's going to do. Listen, I'm not that much of an asshole. I'm sorry I clipped you."

"Don't," Mick said. "It didn't hurt."

"Yeah. Well, that's because I'm losing my punch with old age."

Mick tried a smile but it didn't work.

"And Two," Frankie said. "Andy is bound and determined he's going to Arabia for that construction job. Two sees it but she don't want to see it."

"Work isn't everything," Mick said.

"It's the only thing. If you ain't got work, you ain't got nothing else."

"It isn't living. It isn't health or having fun or your life. It's just as bad as if Andy was making a religion out of working."

"He's trying to get ahead."

"You just said there ain't no getting ahead."

"That isn't what I said, Mick. There's me and you and Andy.

Andy ain't dumb; he sees where I am and where he's going to be in twenty years if he doesn't hustle a stake and jump ahead of the game. There's you: two or three years, you get a degree and you're a lawyer. You have a couple of bad years but you move ahead. In ten years, you're ten times better off than I'm ever going to be on my best day."

"If you didn't think you were going to get ahead of the game someday, you wouldn't keep hustling."

"Sure I would. I never learned any other way."

"You get it from Grandpa?"

"The old man." Frankie shook his head and managed half a smile. "What a ballbuster he was. He knew how to count funny on the trolley lines, believe it. He hustled ahead of the game."

"Uncle John never learned anything from him."

"That's John." The smile faded. "John's another case. But Joey has got it, Joey can see the game. Maybe it's like genes, it skips around from generations."

"No, Dad." Mick was thoughtful. "You got Joey wrong."

"Is that right?"

"Joey's not dumb. He knows the work and the hustle, but knowing isn't doing. Joey wants life on a platter, he don't want trouble."

"Nobody wants trouble."

"You really hustle, you got to take trouble with the rest of the chances."

"Now you're going to tell me about it."

Mick looked at him sadly. Frankie caught the look and turned away. He put the truck in gear. "You're gonna miss the train. I'll drive you over to Oak Park, you can catch the El."

Mick didn't speak. The truck joined the line of semis pouring over the Proviso freight yards bridge on Mannheim Road.

"I don't want to fight with you, Mick," Frankie said suddenly. "I just got to think a few things straight."

But Mick didn't answer and they both settled into the familiar, uneasy silence.

16

The Bohemian was at the far end of the bar, washing glasses. On the television screen above the bar, a man and a woman were in bed and they were talking to each other in the slow, exaggerated way of soap operas.

Three older men—retired and with nothing to do in the mornings—were sitting near each other in the middle of the bar. An electronics salesman who lived in Westchester and made ninety-five thousand dollars a year—or so he said—was at the near end of the bar, next to the front door and the coat rack. He was wearing a gray suit and he was sipping a martini on the rocks. It was just after nine-thirty A.M.

"I knew you were going to come in early. I never see you at this hour but I figure someone told you about the pool," the Bohemian said to Frankie Coolin. "You want a beer?"

"Is the Pope Catholic?" Frankie sat down. He had driven Mick to the El and then gone home and tried to talk to Rose. Maybe Mick was right and Rose lied as much to him as he lied to her. No, nothing was wrong with her, Rose said, Mick was exaggerating and he shouldn't have worried Frank in the first place. No, nothing was wrong with the G, Frankie said, it was just some stuff about last year's income tax and the fire loss. It would get straightened out. When they had finished their lies to each other, they had parted. Rose went to the doctor in Elmhurst and Frankie, who could not sleep and could not stand to be in the house alone with the old man, went to the tavern.

The beer tasted too bitter.

"I won the pool?" Frankie said.

"As if you didn't know. A guy wins a pool and I guarantee I see him the next morning, first thing. You won all four quarters, you lucky fucking son of a bitch. All four quarters."

The Bohemian looked down at the salesman. "Can you believe
it?"

"Hey, Emil, if you don't want no one to win the pool, why
do you have it?" Frankie said.

"Four quarters," said the salesman. "I haven't won that pool
for two years."

"Four quarters," said one of the old men. "You're lucky,
Frankie."

"You got that right," he said.

"You want your money now, huh?" the Bohemian said.

"No, I want you to keep it in your sock for a couple of weeks
in case you run short," Frankie said.

The Bohemian put five twenty-dollar bills on the bar top.

"You gonna buy a round or what?" the Bohemian asked
with a sour face.

"You're a joy, Emil. I come in here because you're more fun
than cancer." Frankie picked up the money and shoved it in
his pocket. "I don't buy rounds."

"Jesus Christ, you win a hundred bucks on the football pool
and you don't even buy a round."

"I learned from you, Emil."

Emil shuffled down the boards away from Frankie Coolin.

"I haven't won the pool in two years," said the salesman
loudly. "Hey, Emil, let me have another bullet."

Emil looked up, annoyed.

"Hey, Frank."

Frankie turned around. In the open doorway stood Pat
Kennedy. He looked frail, even more than he had just two days
before. "Hey, Frank," he repeated and shuffled into the bar-
room.

Frankie Coolin turned back to his drink.

"Hey, Frank, how's it going?" Pat Kennedy said. He sat
down heavily next to Coolin at the bar. He waited for his beer.
Coolin did not speak.

"Funny to see you in here at this hour," Pat said.

"Is that right?"

"He won the football pool, all four quarters, that's why he
came in," said Emil.

"Is that right?" But Pat's voice was dull, his eyes without
sheen.

Emil brought a glass of beer to Pat and put it down.

"Buy Frankie a drink," Pat Kennedy said, shoving his money on the bar.

"No thanks."

"Come on. Have one."

"No," said Frankie Coolin. Emil stared at Coolin and then shook his head and picked up a dollar bill from the pile in front of Pat.

"How about another, Emil?" the salesman asked again.

"Just a minute, will ya?" Emil said. "Jesus Christ, I never seen so many morning drinkers. Ain't you guys got jobs?"

Coolin looked at himself in the mirror behind the bar, framed by two whiskey bottles.

"What's wrong, Frankie?" Pat said.

"Nothing I can't handle."

"Frank."

"I got nothing to say to you, Pat."

"Hey, what's happening all of a sudden?"

"You tell me, Pat."

"Hey."

"Hey yourself."

"I took the day off work. I don't feel so hot."

"You don't look so hot, Pat. You look like you're real sick."

"I feel sick. I don't feel good in my gut. I been taking days off."

"Everyone's got problems."

"Frankie."

Coolin said nothing. Next to his image in the dusty glass was the image of Pat Kennedy, hunched at the bar. Pat Kennedy picked up his glass of beer and sipped and put it down. He hardly tasted it.

"I wish this whole thing was over," Pat Kennedy said. "It's driving me crazy."

"Is that right?"

"Jesus, Frankie. I'm shitting, thinking about it, about—"

"Hey, Pat. Don't talk to me, will you?"

"What's wrong, Frankie?"

"I don't talk to the G, I don't talk to the friends of the G."

Pat Kennedy became even more pale. He closed his eyes for a moment and looked like a corpse. He opened his eyes. He stared at the glass of beer and started to reach for it and then let his hand lie on the bar.

"Frankie, I honestly wasn't—"

"Get away from me," Coolin said quietly.

"This is so terrible, I never wanted to do this," Pat Kennedy said softly. Emil was making a martini at the far end of the bar. The three old-timers were talking to each other.

"Four quarters is pretty lucky," the salesman said loudly at the bar.

"You're telling me," Emil said from the other end. "Cheap guy like Frankie don't even buy a round."

"I didn't, Frankie," Pat said. "You got to know that. But they came down so hard on me, I can't tell you what they told me, they came down on me like a ton of bricks and all I could think of was the boys and my wife. My God, what was I gonna do, it wasn't as though I was stealing all this time, that I had some money put away some place. They came down so hard on me that I had to do something. I talked to my lawyer, he said I had to do something. I mean, you don't know what they were saying to me. . . ."

Coolin stared at him.

"Look, Frankie, I would never hurt Rose, you know—"

"What are you talking about, Kennedy?"

"Please, Frank, listen to me—"

"You got nothing to say, do you?"

"Please, Frank—"

Coolin got up without a word. He zipped his jacket and walked to the front door and opened it. The door slammed behind him. The day was cloudy and cold. Leaves were blowing down the gutter, across the parking lot in front of the tavern. He stood for a moment and looked at the lighted Old Style sign on the pole at the edge of the lot: Old Style on Tap. Emil's Happy Hour Inn.

Happy Hours.

He couldn't even feel sick now; he felt empty, drained of anger and pity and any feeling that might have made him feel sick.

"Frankie, Frankie," Pat Kennedy said, coming out of the tavern. "It was never my idea."

Frankie Coolin turned. "If you were going to steal, why did you get me involved in it? Why the fuck get me involved in it? I wasn't stealing, you were stealing and now you're fucking me some more. Why are you doing this to me?" Quiet and even.

"Frankie, Jesus Christ, I could see why you want to hate me—"

"I think I'd want to kill you except I wouldn't want to do no time for it."

"They were so hard, they had me downtown five days in a row—"

"Get away from me, you dirty son of a bitch."

Pat Kennedy touched his sleeve and Frankie shook it off. Pat touched him again and pain and anger returned to Frankie Coolin. He felt sick and hard and full of rage. He hit Pat Kennedy in the middle of his pasty face. Blood appeared on the lips as Kennedy backed away.

Frankie Coolin hit him a second time. The blow hurt his hand and the pain felt good, final, as though something had been decided.

Pat Kennedy put up his hands. "Frankie," he said.

Frankie took a step and chopped again with his right hand and the blow fell on Pat's left ear and this time he went down, to one knee, in the gravel of the parking lot. Frankie kicked him then, aiming for his belly.

He hit something hard.

The shirt opened and he saw the transmitter.

"You dirty bastard," he said. He kicked Pat Kennedy and pulled him up. The transmitter was strapped to his belly. He pulled the straps and it came loose.

The white Pontiac wheeled into the lot.

Gribbs and Garwood at the doors. "All right, Coolin." It was Gribbs.

"Get the fuck away from me," Coolin said.

"All right, Coolin, just back off."

"Get the fuck away from me." Frankie Coolin thought his voice sounded like a cry, the sound an animal makes when it feels the bite of the trap for the first time.

"Frankie, I had to do it," Pat Kennedy said.

"Get the fuck away from me." The wounded cry again; he

didn't want to cry, he didn't want tears. "You dirty mother-fuckers." He took the transmitter and slammed it to the ground.

"Hey, man, what are you doing?" Garwood said.

"That's government property," said Gribbs. "Back off of it."

Pat Kennedy was on his knees. Blood streaked his face and filled his mouth. There was blood on his left ear but the color had returned to the pale skin.

"Frankie," Pat said.

"Come on, Garwood, you want to go, let's go, mother-fucker," Frankie Coolin said.

It was stupid and everyone knew it.

Emil came to the door.

"What are you guys doing to my parking lot?" Emil said.

"Just go inside," Garwood said.

"Fuck you, mister. You're on my property, get the fuck off of here or I call the cops."

Gribbs said, "This is stupid."

Frankie reached down. "Radio. You know what this fucking radio said? Nothing. I didn't do nothing, I still ain't done nothing. You want to fuck with me, Gribbs? Come on over and fuck with me, you motherfucker."

"Don't talk like that, that isn't doing you any good," said Garwood in a reasonable voice. "Come on, Frankie, don't make it harder on yourself than it has to be."

"I'm gonna call the cops," said Emil. "I give you one minute to get out of here and then I call the cops."

"We are the goddam cops," Garwood said. "Just go inside."

"You're cops, I want to see your badge," said Emil.

"It's OK, Emil," Pat Kennedy said. "I know these guys."

"Jesus Christ," said Gribbs. "This is getting stupid. We ought to get out of here."

"Are you all right, Kennedy?" Garwood said.

"Yeah. He hit me in the mouth," Pat Kennedy said. He wiped his face. "Look at it, I'm bleeding."

"You want to come with us, go to the hospital?" Gribbs said.

"I don't need no hospital," Pat Kennedy said. "I want to go home." He got up slowly and staggered to the Buick parked near Coolin's truck. He fumbled in his pocket. "I can't find my keys, my fucking keys," Pat Kennedy said. His voice was muffled with embarrassment now. Emil stood on the stoop of his tavern entrance.

Coolin stared at the two FBI men.

"You'll hear from us again," Gribbs said.

"That's a promise, Coolin," Garwood said.

17

Thursday afternoon, eleven days after the fire, clouds, sullen and low, crowded the sky. The wind had turned harsh; the weather forecasts on the radio said it would snow that night. November: trees were bare and the grass was brown and dead. Dusk was creeping in at four-thirty.

The job on the North Side had taken six days and now it was over. Frankie Coolin had knocked off at two and driven west and south through the thick, snarling city traffic, until he reached the boundaries of the western suburbs.

He had not seen Kennedy since the fight in the parking lot; he had not talked to Klein. Rose was waiting for the results of her test and he didn't want to talk to her about it. He didn't want to talk to anyone; he had lost himself in work, in mind-numbing hours on the job, in making his body feel the pain of too-heavy burdens carried and too many hours holding plaster in a trowel above his head while he finished ceilings. Work and work and work: it had made the past eleven days bearable.

Each night he awoke at precisely three. He always saw the bedside Big Ben first, the illuminated hands pointing to the hour. And then he would lie in bed, his eyes open, watching the still shadows of the room gradually become more distinct. Closet door. Dresser. Rocking chair. Lamp. Sometimes he fell back asleep; other times, he had to get up and go to the kitchen and sit alone in the darkness to wait for morning.

He had gone to the bank and taken out the papers on a second mortgage. He could get ten thousand dollars at seventeen percent. It was all arranged. They had a single T-bill which came up for renewal in two days. Frankie wanted to leave it alone for another six months. It was all that stood between Mick and having to quit college.

What money did he really have? The house was worth sixty-five grand and he still carried less than a two thousand mortgage. The truck was worthless and so was the car. A T-bill, a paid-up house. Nothing else: no life insurance, no pension.

More than the fear in him was the feeling that he had failed, that all the years of hustling, of being the wise guy, of keeping the balancing act up in the air had amounted to nothing.

He stopped at the Bohemian's for a beer before going home. The place was subdued. A few people had heard about his fight with Pat Kennedy but no one asked him about it. No one had seen Pat Kennedy around.

"Joey was in looking for you," the Bo said.

"Yeah? Give me the football card, I feel lucky."

"You got nothing but luck."

"You got that right. Did he say where he was working now? I ain't seen him around for two weeks."

"In DuPage. He got on a siding job for a development they're throwing up in Wheaton."

"Helluva time of year to put up siding."

"Better than when it's snowing."

"I'm glad he got something. I got zilch for him. I really thought I had a winter job lined up for him and me but it was federal and they're cutting back on the funding. I guess I just keep hustling this winter. Maybe I'll sell Christmas trees again, like I did that time."

"Times are hard all over. My business is way down."

"You never made more money in your life. Look at what you're charging for beer now."

The Bo made a face. "Frankie, my Miller man came in this morning and he says the beer goes up a buck a case next week. What do I do? Do I just absorb it or what? You know what the liquor salesman gets now for J&B?"

"You don't sell much Scotch here anyway."

"So, I sell brandy. You know what Christian Brothers goes a bottle? I remember when you could charge less for brandy than you charge for whiskey. Can't do that any more. Shit, fucking brandy is more than some of the whiskey I got."

"Yeah. Well, prices ain't never going down."

"I'm holding on to the end of the year and then I got to up the price. First of the year. Beer's gotta go up a dime."

"I guess I'll have to start drinking at home."

"Shit." The Bo stared at him and then walked away as though he had not seen him.

Frankie had two beers but no one seemed interested in talking. It was getting dark outside. He finished and left.

They were parked at the curb when he got home and he knew what it was, he knew what it was all about. For a moment, he sat behind the wheel of the truck and thought about the time he had driven to California. He thought about the endless miles and the face of the mountains as he approached them across the wide plain.

Garwood and Gribbs. Gribbs was behind the wheel. It was a different car, not the white Pontiac. This one was a yellow Chevrolet.

He realized his hands were trembling so he sat in the cab of the pickup for a moment. He thought of Rose and the kids.

Just like they said they would do it.

He opened the door of the cab and slammed it shut. And then he thought about it and opened it again and locked it. He walked around the truck and was on the driveway.

Gribbs and Garwood had opened the doors of the yellow car. They came at him ten feet apart, calm and careful. They had their jackets open but their hands were at their sides. Garwood had a piece of paper in one hand.

Frankie Coolin waited without a word. He thought of Arthur Klein and the ten thousand in the savings account. He would have to explain all this to Rose in a minute. He wondered why he hadn't told her before.

Because it wasn't going to happen.

"Francis Joseph Coolin," Gribbs said.

"Yeah." He held out his hand and took the piece of paper and did not look at it. His face was pale and he felt terribly tired. He was glad he had finished up the job on the North Side; then he remembered he was supposed to pick up the check for it on Saturday. He'd have to tell Joey to go for him.

Saturday. All the days ahead. He thought he would never be able to speak.

"Look, can I change my clothes? I just came in from a job."

"We were looking for you," Gribbs said.

"Sure," Garwood said. His voice was easy. "We got to go in with you."

"Sure. Sure. I appreciate it. I just got to change my clothes, these got dirt and shit on them."

"Go ahead of us."

"Sure, sure," Frankie said. He made his feet move. He went up the stairs. "Look," he said, turning. "My wife. She might start crying and all that but just give me a second. I'll get her calm."

Garwood said, "Sure, Frankie, it's all right. We got all the time in the world now."

Gribbs grinned.

Frankie opened the front door. Rose was in the kitchen. Peg was not home and Mick, he knew, was staying over at school again.

"Rose."

"Frankie? I got some lasagna tonight, Peg is staying over by her girlfriend's house."

The three men filled the hallway. Rose came out of the kitchen smiling, wiping her hands on her apron. She looked at Frankie and at the two men.

"Rose," he began.

"Oh my God," she said softly, still wiping her hands, staring at them.

"Look, could I talk to her alone for a minute—"

Gribbs said, "Frankie. You know we can't do that. You know we got to be with you."

"Yeah. I know, I'm sorry." He looked at Rose, at all the years between them. He wanted to touch her. He could not move.

"Frankie," Rose said and said nothing else. Tears formed in her eyes. She tried again: "Frankie."

"Look. These guys are from—"

"My God, Frankie."

The four of them waited for a moment. They listened to Rose's tears.

"Rose, I got to go with them."

"They're arresting you," she said.

"Yes."

"My God, Frankie."

"Don't cry. I got to tell you what to do. I got to change my clothes and go down with them. Rose, listen to me, for Christ's sake." He touched her arm.

She listened and cried as she listened.

"You got to get this lawyer." He took a pencil from the stand in the hall and wrote a name down on a piece of paper. "And we got money in the savings account now. These guys are going to take me down to the federal building. Klein, that's this lawyer, is going to know what they're going to do. I don't want you to worry."

"Frankie," she said.

Garwood and Gribbs stared at her. The hall was too small for four people and the setting was uncomfortable. But no one knew what to say for a moment.

Then Gribbs said, "You gonna change your clothes?"

"Yeah," Frankie said. He led them back through the dining room and a second hall to the bedroom.

He looked at the bed, neatly made. Today was the day she changed the sheets; clean, crisp sheets beneath the covers. He thought of her body next to him.

Garwood and Gribbs filled the doorway behind him. "You see, we got to stay with you," Garwood said.

"Yeah, I know." He started to unbutton his shirt. "I ain't going to do nothing. Oh, Jesus: You got to put handcuffs on? Do you got to?"

"You know we do," said Gribbs. "That's the way it is."

"Not in front of her," he said.

Frankie stared at Garwood. "Wait till we get in the car, please. Not in front of her."

"We got rules," Gribbs said. "That's the way we got to do things."

"Oh, Jesus," Frankie Coolin said.

Garwood said, "We can wait till we get in the car."

"We can't do that," Gribbs said.

"Sure we can," Garwood said. "What's the matter with you, you seen that woman, didn't you? Look, Frank, we'll do everything easy, just you take it easy, don't do anything crazy because then we'd have to cuff you now."

"Sure, sure. I won't do nothing crazy."

"OK. Just change your clothes and we'll cuff you in the car."

"We aren't supposed to do that," Gribbs said to Garwood.

Garwood did not speak. Frankie pulled on a clean pair of jeans and changed his wallet from the dirty pair. He shoved his car keys in his pocket and then pulled them out. Car keys. He dropped them on the dresser. He buttoned a clean flannel shirt over his undershirt.

"You gonna wear that baseball cap down?" Gribbs said. "You're just gonna lose it."

"No." He took the Sox cap off and put it on the dresser. Lucky cap.

"Okay? You ready?" Gribbs said.

"Yeah, sure. I appreciate it. Don't worry about anything." He said the words and they didn't mean anything.

"Sure," said Garwood.

Rose had not followed them to the bedroom. She stood in the hall and she had stopped crying. She stared at Frankie as they came back to the front door.

"What should I do?" she said to Frankie.

"Call that lawyer like I told you and then you can call up over to Two and get hold of Andy. When they set up the bail, you get the money. I took the T-bill out and it's in the saving account."

"We lose the interest if we cash it," she said.

"Jesus, Rose." Frankie looked at her.

She started to cry again. "I don't know what I'm saying. Oh, I'm sorry, Frankie."

"No, no. It's OK," he said with a soft voice. "Everything is OK, Rose. Everything is OK." He held his arms apart and she came between them and buried her damp face against his flannel shirt. He put his arms around her. He felt her sobs for a moment. He was aware of the two men behind him.

"It's OK," he said, over and over.

"No, no," she said. "Why do they—"

"It's OK," he said.

"We got to go, Frankie," Gribbs said at last.

"Yeah," said Garwood.

"Rose." He said it as though he would never say her name again. Gently, he pushed her away from him. She stared at him as though memorizing his face.

He disengaged himself and backed away. The three men

crowded the entry again. Frankie opened the front door and led them down the steps.

Across the street, the Heineman family—father, mother, daughter—stood on their stoop and watched the procession in the dusky light.

Frankie walked to the yellow car. It was locked. Garwood unlocked the side door and pulled the button for the back door. Frankie opened the door and climbed inside. Garwood sat next to him. Gribbs went around to the driver's side and climbed behind the wheel.

Doors slammed shut. Rose came down the steps and stood on the walk. Frankie smiled at her. Gribbs started the engine.

Rose put her hand to her mouth and did not move. He saw her tears.

Gribbs put the car in gear and edged slowly to the center of the street. Frankie felt the steel on his wrists. He heard the cuffs snap.

"All right, Frank," Garwood said. He recited his rights to him.

Frankie said nothing. He watched the scene pass out his side window. Butterfield Road and the turn at Mannheim. The familiar sights floated past his eyes. They went down the ramp and onto the Eisenhower Expressway. He thought of Rose.

"Oh," he said.

Garwood stared at him. "You gonna be sick, Frankie?"

Frankie nodded.

"You gonna throw up?"

Frankie nodded again.

"Jesus," said Gribbs, looking over his shoulder. He pulled violently to the side of the expressway, off the roadway. Garwood reached across Frankie and opened the door and pushed him out of the car. Frankie stood in his cuffs and then bent over and vomited on the pavement.

"You all right now?" Garwood said.

"Yeah. I'm sorry. I'm really sorry."

"It happens, Frankie. You aren't the first one."

It was awkward getting back into the car. They slammed the doors again.

Gribbs said, "Tough guy."

Frankie did not answer.

18

Frankie Coolin was a prisoner and the thought of it closed in on him all the way downtown. He felt his shoulders become heavy and the muscles tense in the small of his back. It was uncomfortable, sitting in the car with his hands cuffed behind him. Frankie felt cold and dark inside, the way it was that time when he was a child and had swum out too far into the cold of Lake Michigan in early June and then battled his way back, against the undertow dragging him out to sea. He had nearly drowned, they said, but he had not remembered it after a certain point—only felt the cold and dark inside.

He asked Garwood for a cigarette when they reached the entrance of the Everett McKinley Dirksen Federal Building on Dearborn Street but Garwood said no, that it would be too difficult to light him with his hands in cuffs and that Frankie would have to wait. He was a prisoner and prisoners had to ask, had to accept, had to depend on others.

He was processed at the United States Attorney's office and then Garwood and Gribbs took him by the special elevator back downstairs.

"What the hell," Gribbs said to Garwood. "Let's just leave the car and walk over. It's only a couple of blocks. I don't want to get tied up in that traffic again until the rush hour is over. We can take him in the M.C.C. and go across to the Irishman's and have a beer."

Garwood said, "Yeah. You aren't going to run away on us, are you, Frankie?"

"With my hands behind my back?" He tried to make his voice light but it sounded too heavy to him. Damn it, he thought. I'm not gonna be put down.

The Metropolitan Correctional Center on Van Buren Street was a triangular building that rose thirty-one stories above the El tracks outside the main entrance. A federal prison, it was designed to hold minimum-security offenders, work-release inmates, maximum-security prisoners awaiting court appearances, and people like Frankie Coolin who were going to be locked up overnight.

They walked in the front door and the ritual began. Garwood and Gribbs identified themselves to an unseen voice. A television camera monitored the three men. A box in the wall opened and Garwood and Gribbs deposited their pistols. They all went to an elevator and rode up to the ninth floor to a small, windowless room. Again, they were scrutinized by a television camera and an unseen voice asked them for their identification cards.

Into another room. This time, Garwood unfastened the handcuffs. Frankie Coolin's hands felt detached, numb.

"We got one for appearance in the morning," Garwood said and shoved the paperwork to the black man in the guard's uniform.

"What'd he do?"

"Interstate theft," said Gribbs.

"He gonna cause us trouble?"

Gribbs looked at Coolin. "No. I don't think so. He wasn't no trouble coming down. He even threw up once."

The black guard grinned. "Can't take it, huh?" The guard looked carefully at the sheets in front of him. "They be tough when they're out there but not so tough in here."

Frankie stared at him.

"Not so tough," the black guard said, grinning at him. "Is that right?"

"Tough as I have to be," Frankie said and knew he didn't want to say that."

"Say. I ain't the one that throwed up," the guard said. Gribbs grinned.

"Come on," Garwood said.

"We'll put him down at 819."

Doors. Locks. Down a corridor. Another door. An empty cell. The window was narrow, too narrow to squeeze out. Below, the lights of the Loop winked.

He sat on the bunk and stared at the wall in front of him, thinking of everything and nothing. He felt drained and beaten down. Once, he felt afraid but he pushed the fear back down his mind. He wouldn't be afraid. If it came to time, he'd do time. This was only one night, anyway.

He thought of two years of such nights. Or three years. Or five. How many years would there be of such nights?

The lights flicked out and he wondered what time it was. Outside the window, the lights of the city remained on and the traffic rumbled heavily beyond the building and everything was normal, one night like every other night. Except tonight Frankie was a prisoner.

Uncle Brian had gotten through it on dope but it had killed his health. It wasn't just that, though. Brian had told him, "They just take everything away from you and they give it back to you in dribs and drabs. They make you feel like a slave. They make you feel like such scum and it goes on so long that you think you really are scum."

They wouldn't make Frankie Coolin feel like scum. Not to-night. Not if it was two years of such nights. Not if it was five.

He heard someone coughing and he heard someone shout out in the darkness. Who was coughing? Who shouted? He felt a terrible restlessness. He wanted to go down to the tavern for a beer, to pick up Hershey bars for the old man, or just get in the truck and drive down to the West Side to see Willie. He wanted to be out in the world.

Christ, he thought, it was only one night.

He lay on the bunk with his eyes closed and awoke a few minutes later, thinking of Rose next to him. Where was he? Then he remembered. Take it easy, he thought. It's just one night.

"You do time," Brian had said, "you can get the dope. You just take it and you buzz out and that makes it work. At least for the nights. The days you get through."

When was it going to be morning? The night never seemed to end. He slept and woke, slept and woke, the cycle of sleep tiring him all the more.

And then, the first gray light, the purple shades in the build-ings as the sun rose over the lake. At full day, there were the first stirrings in the streets as commuters poured out of the elevated stations to their jobs. He could see the streets beyond the thin window filling with cars. Everything was normal, today was the same as yesterday, except Frankie Coolin was a prisoner.

Morning seemed to go on and on. Had there been a delay? When was he going to get his appearance in court? What was going on? Had Rose forgotten about him?

Take it easy, he told himself at last, pushing the rising panic back down inside him. He wouldn't be afraid, he wouldn't panic. They wouldn't make him feel like a slave.

They came for him at last and put his hands back into the cuffs. He shuffled forward with the others into a line, down the elevator, into a van which slowly rolled the two blocks to the federal building basement. Then the prisoners were taken in the elevator up to the cages behind the courtrooms.

Rose looked grim-faced when he entered the courtroom. Klein was shuffling papers at a table in front of him. They removed the handcuffs and Frankie rubbed his wrists and sat down. He did not speak to anyone. Prisoners did not speak to anyone.

They set bail at fifteen thousand dollars and Rose paid the required fifteen-hundred-dollar cash bond. Frankie was taken away again and given his wallet and money and told to sign a cash receipt.

It was all a dream in a way—the judge, the prosecutor, the bored guards, the other, sullen prisoners staring at him or at each other, the sounds of the courtroom. The dream only ended when he realized he was standing next to Rose, that she was holding his arm, that Klein was talking to him and that he was free again, on the street, in front of the federal building.

". . . and await developments," Klein said.

"Pat Kennedy," Frankie said with sudden vehemence, snapping out of the bad dream. "He was wired. I busted him in the parking lot at the Bohemian's and he was wired."

Klein stared at him. "What are you talking about?"

"Kennedy, that little prick."

"Frank," Rose said.

"Kennedy was wired. He was in the lot. He was trying to get me to say something."

"How do you know?"

"I popped him, I saw the transmitter and then the G came running up."

"Mr. Kennedy approached you?"

"Yeah, what do you think, I want to talk to the little creep? He talked to me like when he met me by accident on purpose at the football game that Saturday, because he knew I always stop by that game."

"What did you say to Mr. Kennedy?"

"When I popped him?"

"Yes."

"If you mean, did I say shit to him, I didn't. I didn't say anything."

"This is interesting. Are you certain you said nothing to incriminate yourself?"

"Interesting? That's a good word, interesting. I thought it was interesting in the joint last night. And this morning."

"We will have to make motions to have the transcript—"

"—Yeah, do that, make motions. Listen, I don't want to do time, Klein."

"Yes." The lawyer stared at Frankie and seemed to consider the silence between them. "Time is never pleasant, and it's worse in Sandstone."

Rose made a little noise and held Frankie's arm in a tight grip.

"I don't want to do time."

"We will certainly try to make sure you do not do time. You think that Mr. Kennedy was wired on both occasions, then? Do you think he was wired before?"

"What do you mean?"

"At other times. What about his phone? Do you think he was tapped?"

"Sure. I think everyone was tapped. I never said nothing on the phones."

"Wise. Well, there is something to explore here."

"Yeah. Explore. For five grand, you ought to explore a lot."

"Mr. Coolin. You must be patient. The law moves with slow gravity."

"Gravity is something that makes you fall. I don't want to fall. Seven counts in that fucking indictment and I didn't do nothing."

"An indictment is merely an accusation."

"The G don't indict unless they're gonna get you."

"A wise rule. But like all rules, it has exceptions to prove it."

"I don't know how my own cousin could have done this to Frankie," Rose said for the first time.

"Mrs. Coolin. We all do what we feel we have to do." Klein glanced at Frankie. "What do you have to do, Mr. Coolin? Your cousin has a single count in his indictment. A deal has obviously been cooked. But what about you? Are you willing to deal?"

"Deal for what?"

"For time off. For a lighter sentence."

"You mean plead guilty, right? You mean, say I done it, right? What have I been trying to tell you for the past weeks? I got nothing to say because I don't know nothing. I know Pat Kennedy asks me for some space to rent for him. The G says it found TV sets in the space. The G also found my insulation and twelve squares of roofing material there just like I said but they don't bring that up now. Everything is like I said."

"Then we fight this without deals," Klein said.

"Look, don't give me that civics lecture stuff. I want to get off and I will do what I got to do to get off. If you say I gotta make a deal, I'll make a deal. Except I don't know what to make a deal on. I don't know nothing. I don't know about this interstate theft racket, I'm just a guy hustling along."

"Then we fight it and await justice."

"Fuck justice. Justice is something you hang on your wall. I want to get off. This thing is over my head for seven months now. It never stops."

"It will stop," Klein said.

"How long?"

"A trial? Or the whole thing? Motions, discovery . . . it could go on and on. Maybe a year more."

"A year."

Frankie thought of a year and he remembered how long it seemed to him when he was a kid. Everything had seemed longer. Days went on and on. A week was an eternity. A summer stretched endlessly. And now a year seemed so short. Christmas to Christmas was all. How many Christmases left? How many summers?

"Hope for the best," Klein said. "I must find out about these alleged tape transmissions. There might be a key in all this."

"What key?"

"Perhaps the government became too greedy. . . ."

"That guy on the West Side," Frankie said, suddenly changing the direction of the conversation. "He kills that grocer and he gets two years. Two fucking years and he killed someone. Even if I was guilty, I ought to get two days compared to him."

"That's state," Klein said. "This is federal, a very different game."

"This isn't fair," Rose said. "When we were kids, there were guys who went into the Outfit, there were guys who made it big in the rackets. When I think all the years Frankie has worked and sweated—when I think of all those years—"

"Rose—"

"No, Frank. I'll talk now, I'll talk to the lawyer and I'll tell him a thing: Frankie had nothing and anything he got, he got the hard way. He's a plasterer but when there wasn't any work, he did anything he could. He was a carpenter and a plumber and he did roofing and he would come home at night so exhausted he couldn't even talk to me but the next day he'd be up again, seven days a week, summer and winter, working for us, and when one of those niggers called in the middle of the night, he had to get up, summer or winter, and go out to the buildings or else they'd call one of those crooks down at city hall to inspect the buildings and Frankie would have to pay them off out of his own money. Bums, crooks, dirty politicians and payrollers . . . I'm from the old neighborhood too, Mr. Klein. I know what Frankie could have done if he had wanted to—he could of been a crook like those bums we grew up with. But he just hustled, he worked his ass off all his life and now, he's going to be fifty years old and what's he got? He gets thrown in jail and I got to pay you five thousand dollars to hear you tell him that there is a good chance, just a good chance, that he might be allowed to be free. That's really terrific, Mr. Klein, this is such a great country. Well, they're not going to get Frankie; not on a bet. You're going to make them listen, Mr. Klein, for that five thousand dollars, you're going to take the sweat that Frankie had to have to get that five thousand dollars and you're going to make them listen, those dirty bastards up there in this courthouse and you're going to make sure they don't push Frankie around no more."

"Mrs. Coolin."

They both stared at her.

Her face was red and her fists were doubled. Frankie thought she looked like a girl again, as she had been, as he had loved her first in the old apartment building on the West Side.

"Mrs. Coolin. I appreciate everything you say and I understand you. Now understand me: I have to speak truly to both of you. I cannot tell you little sugarplum lies because the day will come when you see they are lies. This is not a good thing, a federal indictment. Not good at all. It is a difficult matter and I will do the best that I can; and my best is formidable. I appreciate your loyalty to your husband. When the time comes, I will find the words to speak of the things you have spoken of. Believe me."

Frankie stood apart from them. For a moment, he imagined they had forgotten he was there. Klein's eyes were shining. He had never seen emotion in the fat man. Klein touched Rose's arm.

"We are all the same after all," he said to her, in a rising voice.

Yes, Frankie thought, they forgot me.

"My father," Klein began. He held her arm. "An immigrant from Germany before the war, without language or contacts, only his skills. . . ."

Rose stared at him.

Klein faltered. He looked around as though looking for escape. He saw Coolin, the lobby, the pamphlet counter and the clerks and the Great Seal of the United States carved in marble. He realized where he was.

"Everything," he said in his normal voice. "Will be done. What can be done." He dropped his arm. "Believe me."

Without words, after another pause, they parted and Klein shuffled through the revolving door at the far end of the lobby.

Rose stared after him as she spoke: "I talked too much. I got mad. I didn't mean to."

"It was all right."

"I feel like a fool anyway."

"Where's the car?" Frankie Coolin said, trying to say something else to break the mood.

"I parked on Van Buren in a garage, I hope you feel like driving home. I was so nervous coming down here—"

"Mick should of drove down," Frankie Coolin said.

"No. He was coming and I told him no. He was aggravating me on top of everything else." She looked at him. "He said he'd finish up in school this morning. I don't know what he's talking about."

"He ain't getting out of school, is he?"

"No. But he was so strange. He just said he'd finish up this morning."

"It must be some kind of an exam or something."

"Oh, Frank, Frank. I thought about you all night, in jail, I didn't know what to do, I couldn't sleep."

"That makes two of us."

They passed through the side door onto Dearborn Street, walked to Sherman Street and then down to Van Buren. Above their heads, the rusting ironwork of the El blotted out the sky. A train screeched around the white building at the corner of the El and the pigeons roosting in the ironwork fluttered up.

"Pat Kennedy," she said. "Never in a million years would you think a member of your own family—"

"It's going to be all right," he said to say something. They walked into the dirty entrance of the indoor parking garage, paid for the car and waited while one of the attendants sauntered up the winding ramp to get it. In a moment, tires squealing, the Pinto appeared. The attendant jumped out of the front seat as though he had just finished the Indianapolis 500 and Frankie Coolin gave him a quarter, to the surprise of both men. He fitted himself behind the wheel. Rose pushed down the door lock on her side.

"I hate this fucking traffic," he said. He thought she was on the verge of tears.

"Frank, drive down by the old neighborhood," she said.

"Why? Why do you want to do that? It's just full of shines."

"Drive down by it."

"No, Rose. You'll just make yourself feel bad."

"I want to see it. I want to see where we lived in that apartment."

"That building's down. It was burned out a couple of years ago and they tore it down."

"I didn't know that."

"I thought you knew that."

"You never told me. I want to see it."

"There's nothing to see. There's rocks and bricks there in a vacant lot, that's all. That's all there is to see. You don't want to go there."

They were under the El ironwork, on Van Buren, following a slow-moving stream of buses and taxicabs.

"I can't believe it burned down."

"Buildings burn down sometimes."

"There's nothing left that we had then."

He said nothing. He turned at Franklin and followed the sign to the expressway entrance.

"Everything is gone," she said.

"Stop it, Rose," he said. But it was too late. She was crying now and the tears were making her eyes shine. The tears fell down her cheeks. She didn't wipe them away; she was like a child crying in pain, letting the tears testify to her pain.

"My God. All our lives. I kept thinking about the first time I saw you in the old neighborhood. God, I loved you from the first time I saw you."

"I love you," he said but he saw that the words did not penetrate through the tears and the pain. He didn't know what to do.

Traffic boomed around them. Tractor-trailers pushed each other along like elephants in a circus line.

"I want to go back," she said, still crying. "What's going to happen?"

"Nothing. It's all going to work out," he said. He felt dirty and tired. "Rose, you can't go back so forget it. There's no old neighborhood no more. There's just us, just our house, just the kids. It's going to be okay."

"No," she said, like a child who will not be comforted.

19

It was as though someone had died. All the rest of the day, into evening, relatives and friends dropped by the house to look at the corpse and to console the widow. Rose made sandwiches for them and Mick had to go to the liquor store to get beer. Whiskey was poured into milk tumblers. When Andy and Two came, they brought Sean who sat on Frankie Coolin's lap.

No one talked about it, of course.

"I go to Saudi Arabia first of the year," Andy said, taking a deep swallow of his beer. Frankie sat at the table across from him. The kitchen was full of bodies—Rose and Two were talking at the sink, the old man was in his chair at the table, Mick and Peg were hovering at the counter.

"You won't get no beer in Saudi Arabia," Frankie said.

"I can live without it for six months. When I get back, it'll just be June, I can go back into cement and still get almost a whole season in. Next year, Frankie, I'm getting ahead of the game."

"I hope you do," Frankie said, holding Sean and bouncing him gently on his leg. Sean smiled at his father but seemed content in Frankie's light grip.

"Six months," Two said, breaking in. "At least I get to drive the truck for six months."

"She doesn't like the truck," Andy said.

"No power steering and he's got that stick shift and I can't even remember how to drive with a stick shift," she said. "He got a stick shift so I wouldn't drive the truck."

"I never thought of that," said Frankie. "I'd never have stick again, not after that time I was coming over the Mannheim Road bridge and I was going from second up to third and the son of a bitch stuck right in the middle and I couldn't make it to the top of the hill. Stuck right in neutral and I couldn't get the stick out, up or down, and I'm sitting there blocking traffic . . . Christ."

"Ah, yer gone soft is all, Frankie," the old man said. "Yer want yer comforts too much is all. Automatic and power this and that, I'm surprised yer don't have air conditioning in yer truck."

"That's right," Frankie said. "Next truck I get I'm gonna have a chauffeur."

"When you gonna get a truck?" Andy said.

"Oh. Next year, maybe. One more winter on that truck and that's it."

They were all silent suddenly. They thought about next year in Frankie's life and Frankie understood what they were all thinking about. He bounced Sean and tickled him and Sean began to giggle. The sound of the child giggling broke the awkward silence.

"You want another beer, Dad?" Mick said.

"About time."

"What about you, Andy?"

"No. I had enough. I got to work tonight."

"At least you won't have to work two jobs in Saudi Arabia," Two said.

"They have these buildings with individual rooms in them," Andy said. "It looks all right. They got TVs and they play tapes of movies and TV shows."

"And women, don't forget about the women," Frankie said. Mick laughed.

Two said, "I don't want to hear about women. Those women wear veils on the streets still. If you get involved with one of those women, they'll stone you."

Andy grinned. "I thought they cut your hand off."

"That's for what you do when you don't have women," Frankie said and Mick laughed again and Two made a scolding sound and Rose smiled. It was a mild enough joke, risqué enough to make them all feel better.

John knocked at the kitchen door and Rose opened it to let him in. He looked very pale and coughed as soon as he crossed the threshold.

"John, is that you?" the old man said, his face brightening.

"It is, Dad," John said. "Hey, Andy. Hey, Two, how are you? Hey, Mick. Peg. Hey, Frankie."

"You want a beer, John?"

"First one of the day," John said.

"No wonder you look pale," Frankie said.

"Are ya pale, John?" the old man asked, turning his sightless eyes in the wrong direction.

"Just a cold, I picked up a cold, first one of the season but it won't be the last. It's going to turn cold tonight. Said on the radio we'll get down to the thirties."

"Winter's coming," the old man said.

"Ah, they get harder," John said.

"Harder," Rose said.

"I hate to think of winter," Two said.

"The last couple of winters we had, God, I hate to think of another winter like that," John said.

They sat talking quietly for a few more minutes. John finished his beer and took another out of the refrigerator. The old man sipped his whiskey.

"Well," said Andy, "I gotta be going, I got to work tonight. You can stay, Rosie."

"No. I got things to do and Sean is getting tired."

Sean looked at his mother and smiled.

"What a kid," Frankie Coolin said, hugging Sean suddenly and fiercely. "What a kid."

Slowly, awkwardly, they parted.

"If there's anything I can do," Andy said at the door, looking at Frankie.

Frankie smiled. "So long, Number One," he said to Sean, who giggled again.

Rose asked, "Do you want something to eat, John?"

"No. Just the beer."

"Do you want a glass of whiskey for yer cold?" the old man said.

"Yeah. I think I will. Have a shot. Mick, hand me a shot glass."

He poured and drank and made a face. Color came back to his cheeks.

"So how are you, Frankie?" John said.

"Same," Frankie said.

"And Dad? How are you?"

"Ah, all right for an old man."

John looked at his whiskey in silence for a moment.

"So what's going to happen?" he said at last.

"I don't know," Frankie said.

"What does it look like?"

"It looks like there's going to be a lot of time tied up in this."

"Well, does it look like you're going to make it?"

Frankie looked at Rose. "Sure," he said. "You know I'm going to make it."

"A federal indictment, that isn't a small thing," John said.

"Tell me about it."

"I thought I could drop by to see if there was anything I could do. Ask Rose, I came by last night to see if there was anything I could do."

"That's right, Frank," Rose said.

"No, John. There's nothing to do. But tell Joey I need him tomorrow early, I'll be coming by for him, I got to go into the city."

"I'll tell him," John said. "I hope you don't intend to stick him in your buildings like you did before and go off."

"I never stuck him in my life," Frankie Coolin said.

"Frankie, I know you stuck him, you do it all the time. I don't care, Joey's a big boy and he's big enough to not be a sucker, but I don't like the idea for the sake of his mother that you leave him alone down in coon town."

"Like you said, he's a big boy."

"Frankie, I didn't come over to fight with you."

"Then don't fight with me."

"Boys," the old man said. "The two of you can't be together for more than five minutes without fighting over something. I never seen nothing like it. Frankie, for the sake of Rose and me own peace, I wish you'd learn to talk to your brother without always picking a fight with him."

Frankie Coolin said nothing. He emptied his can of beer and aimed it for the garbage can in the corner, near the refrigerator. "Two points," Mick said.

More silence. Then John said, "I'm sorry, Frankie, we shouldn't fight but it's just that Joey isn't that smart about things sometimes, especially about the city. I mean, you been working in the city all your life but you got to understand that Joey grew up in the suburbs. It's a different generation."

"If you want to work in the trades, you got to learn the city," Frankie Coolin said.

"But you don't have to work with the niggers," the old man said.

"You work with anyone's got money," Frankie said.

"Frankie—"

"This is just bullshit, all of it," Frankie Coolin said suddenly, to them, to himself. He got up from the table. "I gotta go out back for a while," he said. He opened the kitchen door and went into the small back yard of the house. He stared at the mulberry tree and at the weeping willow near the alley.

"Bullshit," he said again.

The kitchen door opened again and closed softly. Mick sat down on the stoop. "Dad, I was gonna tell you. I made out some job applications today. I'm gonna withdraw out of De-Paul for a while and get a job."

"You need money or what?"

"I want to help you."

"That's all I need is for you to help me. Don't help me. If I get any more help, I'll go under for the third time."

"Dad."

"What kind of crap are you pulling all of a sudden? Withdrawing from school? What kind of crap is that? Did we pay all this money for you to withdraw from school?"

"I can't just keep going along, going to school, when you got problems and when Mom's got problems, I can't do it."

"I got no problems. What problem is your mother got?"

"She's got anemia. They want to run more tests on her. They think it could even be leukemia of some kind."

"Leukemia? She's got leukemia?"

"No. She's got anemia but they want to be sure."

"She didn't say nothing. Jesus, I gotta talk to her about this blood thing. Some towel-head doctor probably figured out a way to make her pay a little more—"

"Dad—"

"It just pisses me off, all of it. That bullshitter in the kitchen there, what the hell is the matter with him? Doesn't he want

Joey to make a living? Or doesn't he think Joey's grown up? I'll tell you one thing, Joey is twice the man already that his father ever was, I'll tell you that."

"Dad, don't get mad at John, John doesn't mean anything—"

"And what about you, what do you mean when you tell me you're going to drop outta DePaul? Yesterday you wanted to be a lawyer and we're talking about another three years of school and now you want to drop out? Who needs problems like that?"

Frankie looked at his son and wondered what he felt, what he wanted to think about him. He turned away and looked at the willow at the back of the yard, near the alley. "That tree, I like to cut that branch down, I think it's getting too close to the electrical line."

When Mick did not answer, Frankie went on. "Fucking tree, dirtiest fucking tree I ever seen. Branches and shit every time it rains. All over the yard."

Mick said, "You don't really get it."

"That tree. Your mother, when we first came out here, she wanted trees. She plants a fucking willow tree, the dirtiest tree there is. They grow faster, she told me. She got that right. Fucking tree has got to be forty feet tall. At least. How long ago was that? Twenty years? She could have planted something else. We had the time."

Mick said, "I want to help you."

"I got to get the ladder back from Hennessey. You lend him anything, you never see it again. Get that ladder tomorrow . . . no, not tomorrow, I got to go into the city . . . get that ladder next week early and cut that limb down, it's a good time to cut it down, in the fall, when the sap stops running."

"I'll take care of it," Mick said.

Frankie Coolin turned back to Mick. "OK. You take care of it. Now, don't say you want to take care of it then you don't do it."

"I told you I'd take care of it."

"Like you took care of cutting the grass this summer."

"I cut it."

"We got a lawn like niggers. You were going to take care of it."

"I'll do it tomorrow."

"OK." Frankie walked to the back of the yard and stared up at the willow as though he were considering cutting it down right then. "Fucking tree," he said at last, but Mick was still there in the yard, looking at him in the lingering half-light, as though there was something more to be said.

"The worst thing," Mick said finally. "The worst thing is going through all this alone. You aren't alone, you know."

"Alone? What are you talking about?"

"Everyone's with you. You know that. But I'm with you too. Me."

"Yeah." The tree swayed above Frankie's head. "Willows never drop their leaves. I don't like it when they get yellow like this."

"Me," Mick repeated.

Frankie looked at the tree and, after a while, the back door to the house slammed shut and he was alone in the yard.

20

Frankie Coolin slipped out of bed without a sound. The Big Ben pointed to five o'clock. He always set the alarm the night before and he always awoke before it rang. In the dingy darkness of the bedroom, he dressed: clean jeans, a gray sweatshirt. He carried fresh white cotton socks and his shoes with him to the kitchen.

When he was at the door of the bedroom, Rose turned in bed, groaned softly, and said, "Frank? Is it five already?"

"Go back to sleep," he said and closed the door behind him.

The house was in darkness; the November sky was black beyond the windows. Frankie pushed the thermostat from sixty-three back to seventy. The thermostat was part of the war of marriage: from the first, Rose had followed energy conservation hints from Washington; from the first, Frankie had stubbornly ignored conservation. Rose's Pinto was one of her victories; pushing the thermostat back to seventy before she awoke was one of his.

In the kitchen, Frankie turned on the fluorescent light over the stove. Then he sat down on a kitchen chair and pulled on his socks and his work shoes. They were over-the-ankle shoes, streaked with flecks of plaster.

Thump. Thump. Thump.

He heard the old man's step on the basement stairs. They had not talked much yesterday when he came home from court. The door of the basement creaked open. The old man entered the kitchen.

He went to the stove, put on a pot of water for tea, then reached in the cabinet above the stove for the bottle of Early Times whiskey. Surely, his hands moving as though eyes directed them instead of mere habit, he poured a small measure of the whiskey in a glass and then replaced the bottle in the cabinet. A shot every morning before tea, something for the blood, a habit borrowed from the old country; he had taken a shot of whiskey every morning for more than sixty years.

Frankie Coolin opened the refrigerator and took out a can of Old Style beer. He popped the top and threw it in the wastebasket. He sat down at the table and tasted the beer. The old man sat across from him.

"Well," the old man said, staring at him with sightless eyes.

Frankie did not speak.

"A mess."

"Nothing I can't handle."

"Big talk again, is it? I would have thought they took the wind out of your sails down to the prison you were in."

"It was just a lockup."

"Well, Frankie, where are you off to then this morning?"

"I got a job in Broadview for later; I got to go down to the buildings this morning."

"Frankie, Frankie, what the hell is gonna happen to your family with this mess?"

It was not as though he had not been thinking of it.

"Boy, I'll tell you, yer gonna lose those buildings is what. D'ya think Rose is gonna go over and collect the rents every month? Or Mick, do you think he'd stick it? Mick's a good kid now but he ain't the boy to be going to the buildings first of every month and shaking down the niggers for the rent."

"You ever think, Dad, maybe I ain't gonna go to jail?"

"Wish, Frankie," the old man said. He waved his hand as though wiping out a thought. "Give that talk to the women, don't give it to me. When the coppers come to yer house in daylight, it ain't to sell you tickets to the ball. I know coppers and seen them work all my life and they got you by the nuts, Frankie."

"Yeah. You're right. With your vast experience with law-breaking, I should have talked to you about this before I went down with them."

"You should have talked to me, Frankie. It's true, you should have. You never say a word to anyone, though, you never did. So now you're in a mess and you're alone in it and you still want to crack wise."

More silence between them. They were aware of the clock on the stove ticking. They listened to the gas jets hissing under the coffee pot and the clunk of the compressor in the refrigerator.

"Frankie. Think of someone other than yourself for once: what is Rose going to do?"

Frankie stared at the blind eyes.

"What is Mick going to do? I'll tell you, he's going to have to quit the college and get a job. And Rose is going to have to get a job."

"No she isn't. There's money. Besides." He paused because he was making it up. "I'm working on a deal on the buildings. She won't have to collect the rent."

"You going to sell them? Is that it? Who the hell would buy those firetraps? You going to sell them to the niggers? And where would they be getting money for them? Yer dreaming to yerself, Frankie. I thought by now you'd be talking sensible but you're still dreaming to yerself. Ah. The tea's up; I know you don't want a cup, you got your can of beer."

"Yeah."

The old man muttered something and shuffled to the stove.

Frankie got up and threw the empty beer can in the wastebasket by the back door. He went into the bathroom and took his baseball cap from the clothes post and put it on and then shrugged his shoulders into a heavy, wool shirt that acted as an outer jacket.

"It'll be cold out there," the old man said.

"That's the thing about November."

"Frankie. I can help Rose out with the money."

"I don't want no money from you."

"You can't be stubborn all your life."

"Sure I can," Frankie Coolin said. He took down the truck keys from the rack by the back door. The rack held keys present and past; there were keys to old cars they had long gotten rid of and keys even to the old apartment they had lived in on the West Side. After all these years, he thought. Keys to doors that weren't there.

"You never wanted a dime from me for yourself and I never pressed it on you," the old man said.

"Sure you did. From day one," Frankie said suddenly. "I don't want money from you, I don't want nothing from anyone. I can make it and if I can't make it, then I got no business being alive."

"So where the hell are you going to make money in prison?"

"I got money. I got money. I don't show you my bank account and I don't want to see yours. We're going to make out fine and I don't need a dime from you or anyone else. I'm going to be fifty years old next spring and I never asked you for a red cent and you're never going to see that day. Go give money to John or Kate if you got to give it away; they'd take it from you fast enough. But don't wave your pocketbook in front of me."

"Oh, no, not Frankie Coolin, he's better than anyone else. He doesn't need help, he doesn't need a thing from another man. Well, Frankie, I'll tell you this: you never were better than anyone else and now you're going to find out you're a whole lot less. You always were one to lord it over John or Kate, you thought you were so damned bloody different from them. Well, now it all comes out in the wash and there's John still struggling along with his infirmity and all, he's not going to jail; or Kate. Yer the one. You don't understand, Frankie, you never did; people don't want someone walking around with them thinks he's better than he is. Pride, Frankie; it goeth before the fall and now yer coming to harvest your fields and yer going to find out about it."

"Is that it, Dad? If I don't come sniveling to you for money, then I'm acting like a big shot? Is that it? I don't understand that at all."

"No, and you never will. You never understand how it kills John when you're after taking Joey away from him and filling his head with your big shot ideas about this and that. When you let me into this house, you even had to be the big shot with me, yer old man, building me that apartment down in the basement and not taking a dime from me for rent or nothing. Yer made me feel like a fucking pauper and me with more money in the bank sitting there than you've ever had in yer life, yer whole fucking life. But no, not a dime from me, never ask the old man for a thing because that would make you less a big shot and we can't have that happen."

"Hey, I'm sorry I fixed up the basement for you, I guess I

did the wrong thing again, right? I always did. When I come home from work today, I'll make sure to tear it all down so you can feel at home sleeping by the coal cellar. That'll make you feel more like a martyr which is what you want."

"I'm yer father, boy, and don't forget it."

"Don't worry. I'll never forget that."

"The trouble with you, Frankie, is you can't admit a fault and you can't admit you ever needed any help. Even when you was a kid, you never asked me for nothing, you never came home from school and asked for help, even when you had that trouble with your spelling . . . never asked anyone, always alone, always had to do it by yourself."

"That way it gets done and you don't kiss someone's ass to do it."

"Is that it, Frankie? Ass-kissing to ask me for help? Yer own Dad, that's ass-kissing? That's a twisted and sick thing for you to say to me, your Dad."

"Well, you get me going," Frankie said.

"You never understood a damned thing, Frankie."

"Sure." Fury bit the word out.

"Frankie. I want to help you," the old man said softly.

"You could of." He went to the kitchen door; he thought of himself as a child going to a kitchen door in an apartment building off Austin Boulevard a long time ago.

"Frankie—"

"You could of, when. . . ." But what was he going to do now, he thought. Was he going to dump the old man in the trick bag?

"Frankie, did I do something wrong then?"

Yes, Frankie thought. He wanted it. Guilt and the whole fucking trip.

He opened the kitchen door and felt November, raw and wet. He closed the door quietly behind him. He wouldn't slam the door. There was a smell of impending snow in the air.

The old man was right about the buildings, Frankie thought. Mick and Rose would never be able to control them if he had to do time. There had to be another way out of the mess.

The truck whirred and whirred and finally caught; the engine coughed and backfired. Slowly, he backed into the side street. For a moment, he waited in the street and thought of things he could have said to the old man. He looked at the house, at the single light illuminating the kitchen window.

A lot of things that could have been said, on both sides, a long time ago.

He realized he had left the house quickly because of the tears he knew were coming.

Dad.

21

Frankie sat in the pickup in front of Joey's house, reading the *Sun-Times* by the overhead light inside the cab. He finished a second can of beer.

Dawn made gray light: streets were dingy with it and charcoal shadows clung to the outlines of the bungalows on the block. The first planes of morning boomed overhead from O'Hare.

Joey appeared at the kitchen door and pulled it shut behind him. He walked across the frost-tinged brown lawn to the truck and climbed inside.

"Cold," he said, rubbing his hands.

"Want a beer?"

"God, no. I can't drink that stuff first thing."

"Let's go." Frankie pushed the truck into gear and it began grumbling down the quiet side street.

"What's the job in Broadview?" Joey asked.

"He got some water between the garage and the kitchen, in the entryway. Old Bohemian. So he wants it patched and then he wants me to spray a ceiling and fix up the flashing on the roof. I told him three hundred for the whole job, I know the guy from Terry who did some work for him last year. So he goes for it. We'll be in and out in three hours with two men."

"That's a job you could do yourself," Joey said.

"I'm getting lazy in my old age."

The truck was heading east down Madison Street, the broad old street that cuts a straight line through the West Side and the west suburbs, all the way down to the Loop.

"That's the last thing you're getting," Joey said.

"Well, I got to go down to the buildings too. I thought we could do that first, wait for the Bohemian to wake up and then do his job. We'll be in Broadview around noon, I'll take you over to this place I know on Roosevelt, they got the best chili out of the West Side."

"Hey, you didn't tell me we were going down to the buildings, Frankie."

"It was a surprise," Frankie Coolin said.

"What do you got to do there?"

"I got to see a man and I been getting a call on a leaky hot water heater in one of the buildings. I want to see if I can patch it."

"That's a one-man job too."

"I figured you didn't mind a little work," Frankie said.

"I never mind a little work, even on Saturday."

"Unless the Cubs are in town."

"It's November."

"So I figured I was safe."

"You were talking a couple of weeks ago about a winter job inside."

"That's downtown. That's from Grady, he's the general contractor on it. They're taking an old loft building on the south end of the Loop and converting it to condo apartments."

"That ought to look real sharp," Joey said.

"People'll buy anything. Anyway, there's about five hundred rooms when they're done and Grady is going to need all the painters and plasterers he can get. I figure the job is good for two months at least."

"You gonna get me in? It's getting cold out now."

"I haven't seen Grady for a week. He said he'd let me know right away. I'll give him a call later today. I'll get you in down there, don't worry about it."

"Money's running short. I only worked two days last week. I did a job on a roof of a garage over in Bellwood but it's getting too cold for roof work."

"Tell me about it. I thought you weren't going to do any roof work for John."

"Dad didn't have the job, I did. Besides, you got to hustle, you got to hustle."

"You got that right. God."

Joey looked at him but Frankie was looking out at the nearly deserted street. A bus lumbered away from the curb in a belch of diesel smoke. The bars and cleaners and groceries were all shuttered, some with steel gratings across the glass windows. The city looked shabby, barely awake on Saturday morning; the city looked hung over.

"You see all that, Joey?"

"See what?"

"I been in the trades thirty years. Thirty years. I bet I worked on a thousand buildings. A thousand buildings in the city. I drive into the city, it's like driving home. You know what I mean? I know it. I know it the way you can when it belongs to you."

"Yeah."

"See those buildings there? Over along that block? I worked in every one of those buildings, I remember it, it was a big job when I got it. Must have been in '56 or '57, I think Two was just born."

"Now it's all Puerto Ricans there."

"I don't mean about the people, Joey; I mean about the buildings. I know those buildings, I plastered in there, I did painting work in there—you see, I know every building in the city. I worked on a thousand. I was figuring it out the other night, I couldn't sleep."

"When you were in jail?"

Frankie glanced at Joey. "Yeah. When I was in jail."

"What was it like in jail?"

"Try it sometime, it's an experience. Nobody ever shuts up. Noise all the time and when there isn't noise, someone makes noise up."·

"You couldn't sleep."

"No. I was thinking about the city. About all the buildings I worked in. You know I'm going to be fifty next year. You know that?"

"Shit, you don't look like you're fifty. I guess that would be right because you're three years younger than my dad but you don't look like you're fifty. I mean, he looks like he's sixty or seventy."

"John's all right, he's got his problems."

"I know, I live with him."

"Don't you ever get a feeling for it, though, Joey? Don't you?"

"What? For my dad's problems?"

"For the city. You been working with me in the city. You know what they used to say? If you want to work, you can get work in Chicago. The old-timers used to say that. You could drift in here from the hick towns or from the east and if you wanted to hustle, you could hustle a living here. When I was a kid, my dad told me that. The immigrants all said that: if you wanted to work, you could find work in Chicago."

"I don't know. I only worked two days last week. Times are hard."

"Times are always hard."

"I work when I can find it."

"I know. You're a helluva worker, Joey, I told you that."

Joey didn't say anything.

"Joey."

"What?"

"Joey, you worked with me on the buildings, you're getting to know your way around."

"Yeah."

"You been down there by yourself."

"I been down there when you stuck me down there."

"Joey. Look. You know about this trouble I got in. With Pat Kennedy."

"Yeah. My dad told me about it. There was a story in the *Tribune* about the indictments."

"Is that right? I didn't see it. When was it in the paper?"

"Yesterday."

"I was in jail, that's why I didn't see it."

"They had your name."

"Is that right?"

"Yeah."

"OK. So you know about it."

"Yeah." Pause. "Did you do it?"

"No."

"Well, what's going on, then?"

"Nothing. I got caught up in something. I didn't do anything but that's the way it works."

"Well. You got to get a lawyer."

"Joey. I wasn't born yesterday. I got a lawyer. Look, Joey, I want to talk to you."

They both stared out the windshield. The streets unfolded in their neat grid patterns. The city hunched against itself, building against grimy building, thousands of buildings spreading out from lakefront to suburbs, reaching twenty miles north and south, the whole, sprawling low city with its flat-roof buildings and gaudy storefronts and steel gratings pulled across the plate-glass windows. In the silence of dawn, they could hear isolated noises: a squad car suddenly careening off with a piercing scream of sirens; a burglar alarm bell ringing forlornly on an empty street; an unexplained boom like an explosion. Silences and little noises breaking the silences into large bits.

"I might get some time out of this," Frankie said.

"What?"

"Time. I might get some time."

"Time? You mean, you might go to jail?"

"Yeah."

"Jesus. Is that right?"

"That's what it's all about," Frankie said. He braked slowly at a red light and saw no traffic. He drove through the red light and kept on.

"Joey. I got to have someone watch the buildings if I go inside."

Joey said nothing.

"The rent. I'm thinking about the rent. I got to have someone can collect the rent. Most of it comes easy and Willie's down there to help collect it. But I got to have someone watching everything."

"Shit."

"Joey, you been down with me on the West Side. You worked in the buildings. You been alone down there, you know it ain't nothing. If I had to go—if I had to go inside—maybe it won't happen for four or five or six months. But I got to start thinking about it now, while I got the chance. I can take you in on that winter job with Grady and we can go down to the buildings when we get a chance, fix them up, work on them so there's no problems for you and so that the tenants get to know you. We can go down together and collect rent and all; you'll see, it's an easy job, Joey. But I can't have Willie Oboe do it alone. You know, Willie and I got an arrangement: we don't trust each other and that makes it all right. But I got to have some family down there, watching over things. You don't have to do no stuff you don't know nothing about, you just got to be sort of general contractor on the thing. I mean, if there's repairs and stuff, I'll set up a bunch of guys for you to call, like Scottie the plumber and Harry the Spark, you know. But I got to have one guy in charge."

"Shit, Uncle Frank."

"Look, I'm taking about two thousand a month out of those buildings. I slip a hundred or so to Willie now and then and I know he's hustling on the side as it is. If you can clear Rose twelve hundred a month out of those buildings, you can keep the rest. Maybe a grand a month if you hustle it right and make sure those guys don't hustle you too much. I'll show you how to do it. That's a grand a month for as long as I'm in. That's for next to no work at all. Then every job you get on top of that is extra. If you hustle at all, you ought to be able to do thirty a year without working weekends while I'm inside."

"Shit, Uncle Frankie."

"You keep saying that and I don't know what it means."

"Man, I don't want to work down in the West Side."

"Joey, you been with me. What's ever happened to you on the West Side?"

"Nothing yet. But you were jumped on that meat truck."

"That was not in the buildings anyway. I mean, that could happen anywhere."

"I never hear about it happening in the suburbs."

"Look, Joey. Willie Oboe, he can't be trusted but he isn't a bad guy. I mean, he will mostly tell you the truth and what he hustles, he would be hustling if I was black. I mean, everyone hustles down the line. I'm talking about a grand a month. Some of my tenants, they been in the buildings for years. I got a woman been in there for four years. I mean, these are solid people, they aren't going to hassle you."

"How come you got to go down to collect their rent?"

"What are they going to do, go to the currency exchange and get a money order and send it to me?"

"Sure."

"Joey, you don't get it. These people can't be out carrying cash around on the streets. This is the ghet-to. I go down and they give me the cash."

"So you got the cash and it's still the ghetto. So why don't the shines jump you?"

"Because that would be a mistake on their part."

"That's you, Uncle Frankie; that ain't me. They don't know me."

"Look, Joey; I got to turn to someone I trust. I trust you. I worked with you, I know you can hustle, I know you play it on the square. I know that when you say you're going to show up for a job that you're going to show up for a job. Rose is going to need that money if I go inside."

"Jesus, Uncle Frankie; you're putting me in a spot. How come you don't have Mick go down to collect?"

"Mick? Mick is a kid."

"Mick is a year older than I am," Joey said.

Frankie realized it was true and yet he couldn't believe it; he had never thought of Mick as Joey's peer.

"Mick doesn't know anything about the trades."

"Uncle Frank, I don't want to be your rent collector."

"A grand a month, Joey. A grand. Twelve a year. You can't beat that."

"The money is all right, you know that. But I don't want to go down there alone."

They pulled up at the building on Arthington. Frankie turned off the ignition and opened the truck door and climbed down; Joey followed on his side.

They descended the stone steps of the gangway without a word. Frankie played his flashlight on the door to the basement, which was made of steel and secured by two large padlocks. He opened the locks and went inside and turned a switch. A single pale light illuminated the dark, damp walls. Joey followed.

The white water heater in the middle of the basement was near the silent gas boiler. Water leaked around the base of the heater and formed a little river that led to a drain in the floor.

"What's that?" Joey said.

Frankie looked up and played his light around the room.

They could both hear the sound. It was singing. It sounded like singing, like a chorus of boys.

"Horses," Frankie said.

Joey stared at him.

Frankie smiled. "Horses. The rats. Look, over there. See?" He played the light on the coal cellar, long abandoned in the back of the basement. On a ledge, a chorus of enormous gray rats watched them. They emitted a vibrant, whining sound that matched in pitch and harmony; it sounded as though they were singing.

"They sing all the time down here. I never knew rats sang until I got these buildings," Frankie said.

"God, I hate rats."

"They aren't too crazy about you either," Frankie said. "This fucking water heater, I'm going to have to replace it. I think the glass is shot. I'll leave it on and go over by Sears today. Maybe I can pick up a heater and we can hustle it in this afternoon, after we do the Broadview job."

Joey stared at the rats.

"OK, Joey?"

"Jesus, Uncle Frankie, they ever attack you?"

"Rats are bad, sure, but they don't bother me as much as the dogs. The German shepherds get all crazy, they run around in packs and they got nothing to eat. That's why you ought to carry a plasterer's hammer, got the hatchet on the other side. You hit a dog right, you can kill him with one shot. The rats don't bother you, though, unless you don't like their songs. They're sensitive about that."

"Uncle Frank. This is shit. I couldn't do this. I couldn't come out down in the basement here in the middle of the night."

"You don't have to. I'll make an arrangement with Willie Oboe, it'll be all set up. If you got to come out, Willie'll be with you."

"I don't see why being with a nigger is so much better than being alone."

"Willie knows the territory," Frankie said. "That fucking water heater must be twenty years old."

"Uncle Frankie, are we done here?"

"Look, Joey, there's nothing to be afraid of. Rats don't bother you."

"Rats bite people all the time."

"I don't get bit."

When they left the basement, Frankie slammed the door shut, pushed the two locks shut and pulled them to make certain they were secure. At the end of the block, a man in a security guard's uniform was walking along the sidewalk. He waved at Frankie.

"That's Tom Jefferson, works as a security guard in the Loop. He's one of my people, I think he's lived here for six years."

"Say, Frankie, what's happening."

"It's all happening."

"You come by to see about that water heater?"

"Yeah. I put a patch on it but I got to get a new one. I'll be by this afternoon or tomorrow and hook it up."

"Yeah, ole lady was talking to me about it and I tole Reverend Oboe to tell you, I was wondering if he tole you. That was Thursday."

"I was away," Frankie said.

Tom Jefferson broke into a grin. "I know that, Frankie. You was in the newspapers. I seen you was away."

"This is Joey, Joey's going to start working with me on the buildings. Tom, Joey. Joey is going to do some of the rent collection for me."

Tom Jefferson kept smiling, staring at Joey. "That's in case you go away, right, Frankie?"

"If I go away, no mice will play," Frankie said.

Tom Jefferson never changed the fix of his grin. "That right, Frankie? You been talking to Reverend Oboe about that scheme of his? He talking to you about it?"

"What scheme is that, Tom?"

"About the condominium plan?"

"I don't remember he talked to me about it."

"I *thought* he said he talked to you about it."

"Maybe he did and I forgot about it."

"That might be a good thing for us to talk about some time. I mean, soon, you know, in case you got to . . . go on vacation."

"I don't plan to be going nowhere. Besides, I got my main man here, he's going to be handling some shit for me."

"Is that right? You going to be the man?" He stared at Joey, the grin did not change, and he made Joey feel like raw meat. "Well, you been around here before?"

"He worked for me in the new building."

"That was a shame about that building burning down."

"That's all right. Uncle Sam is going to eat it for me on my taxes."

"Yeah, there's that. Well, I got to go up and get my breakfast and get me some sleep, I got to be hustling this afternoon, got me some things to be doing."

"You still working downtown?"

"Oh, yeah. That's my white job. I got some other job, though, you know." He turned the perpetual grin on Frankie.

"I know. I just wanted you to meet Joey, he'll be around."

"All right. All right, Joey. Ah see you, Frankie, and you see Reverend Oboe, he got a scheme to talk to you."

The black man went up the steps of the stoop and opened the downstairs door with a key.

"That guy makes me nervous," said Joey.

"Who? Tom? Shit, he ain't nothing, he's always jiving about getting schemes going. He was just giving you some shit, staring at you. When they stare at you, you stare back; when they smile, you don't smile. And when they frown, you laugh. You always got to keep everyone else thrown off balance."

"Uncle Frank, I can't do this thing for you."

Frankie looked at him. They walked back to the truck and got in. Joey rubbed his hands. "Cold," he said.

Frankie started the truck and it woke up. He pushed it into gear.

"We'll talk about it," Frankie said.

But he knew it was true; Joey couldn't do it for him.

22

The Chicago Bears, in their orange and blue jerseys, lined up along their own thirty-seven. Vince Evans took the snap from center and danced back four steps, pivoted on the fake, and shoved the ball into Walter Payton's flat belly. Payton charged head up over left tackle and shoved off two men before he was pulled down. Six yards.

The roar rose around them for a moment and then fell. The players on the field at the bottom of the bowl picked themselves up and trudged into their huddles.

Frankie Coolin smiled and reached into the small blue cooler at his feet. Mick sat next to him, hunched forward, hands together, arms on knees, watching the plays intently.

In the bowl of Soldier Field on the lakefront, the wind from the lake pushed icy breezes along the tiers of stands. Above the stands, the lights were on as they had been all during the game because of the gloomy weather. In the press box nestled in the base of the columns that marched across the lip of the bowl, little figures of reporters could be seen pressing against the glass. They were the only ones who were warm. The place was full, as usual.

The Bears lined up again, Evans took the snap, and this time he did not hand off but danced back into the pocket, searching down the field for receivers who sprouted from the line like violent flowers. A roar of expectation swelled in the stands. Both Mick and Frankie Coolin were part of it, climbing to their feet, shouts at their throats. The white jerseys of the Dallas Cowboys poured into the Bear line, it sagged, and the white shirts began to streak through the pit of the middle of the line.

And then Evans threw. The football cut through the air like a missile, high above the green field. The line of scrimmage dissolved before the ball fell. James Scott reached up and plucked the ball down with his fingertips; he was running. Dallas players streamed around him, reaching for him as he ran. Finally, a finger, an arm, a body thrown at him and he was pushed to earth at the ten, in Dallas territory.

Frankie Coolin felt the vibrations of the crowd through the soles of his work shoes.

Three plays later, the Bears—stopped cold at the ten—kicked a field goal to get on the board with points. The crowd subsided and the two teams trotted off the field for a moment before lining up for the new kickoff.

"They could play football twelve months a year," Frankie Coolin said. His face was open and relaxed; his eyes were bright. He seemed like a child.

"You'd get tired of it," Mick said. "It's like everything else."

"You got that wrong. Football is football. It ain't like nothing else, nothing."

"I didn't know you liked the game."

Frankie turned to Mick and smiled. Mick stared straight ahead of him but allowed a smile as well.

"Smart guy," said Frankie.

"If I was smart, I'd be home watching this dog on television with my feet up on the coffee table, not freezing out here."

"You want to stay indoors all your life? I love it here. I don't like it as much as when the Bears were still playing in Wrigley Field but I love it."

"I know," Mick said. He turned to his father. "When you die, they're going to bury your season pass with you."

"I ain't gonna die, that's first," Frankie Coolin said. "And when I do, I put the pass in my will. I give it to my first-born."

"Two, you mean."

"Fuck no. What would she do with the tickets?"

"Give them to Andy."

"Andy? That Polack would never find the time to come out to the games. They ain't got football in Saudi Arabia."

"He's only going for six months."

"Yeah. Maybe he'll be back in time."

Mick stared at him. "Time? Time for what?"

"Nothing."

"You mean the trial?"

"I don't want to talk about that now."

"Andy isn't going to do anything for you or for Mom or me that you aren't going to pay for one way or another."

"Andy's all right."

"Andy is all right, I know that. But that doesn't matter. If Andy does something for you, you're going to have to pay for it."

"What do you mean?"

The kick was high and booming and when it came down, Dallas could not move the ball beyond the fifteen. But it didn't matter. They were ahead by five points when the two-minute warning shot was fired; all they had to do to win was not lose the ball. In three plays, they made a first down and the clock was running. The stands started to empty.

Mick had not said what he meant about Andy.

The gun sounded.

"Another game down the tube," Mick said.

"Not really. The spread was six for Dallas going in so I bet the Bohemian ten on the side and took the points. I beat that asshole again."

"He doesn't care," Mick said. "He just waits for you to spend the money in his joint."

"But I drink ten dollars' worth for free now. I was gonna spend it anyway."

"Christ, it's cold. Let's get out of here," Mick said.

"What a pussy," Frankie said. "Me, I never want it to end. I could sit here all week and wait for the next game."

It was all ritual from the time Mick had been a little boy and accompanied his father to the games at Wrigley Field. Always, the last can of beer as though Frankie Coolin had a chauffeured limousine waiting for him; always letting the crowd surge to the exits first. Mick had been through it before and he still felt the little boy's impatience at wanting to be quit of the stadium and the game. He was always impatient to leave; perhaps that was part of the ritual as well.

They climbed down the stone steps at last. The interior, under the stands, was dark; the stadium smelled of age and dampness and cold, like a dungeon.

"How's the knee?" Frankie said, because Mick was limping down the steps.

"All right."

"No. Really. How is it?"

"I had some trouble the last couple of days with the damp. Fucking weather. It'll be all right when it dries up. I was thinking of going by the Y and taking a sauna, get a swim in. Work it out a little."

"Yeah. You got to work it out," Frankie said.

"Fucking knee," Mick said, wincing as they reached the street level and followed the funnel of people through the exit.

Soldier Field was on the lake, in Burnham Park south of the Loop. It was surrounded by acres of parking that stretched all the way to McCormick Place but Frankie Coolin always parked illegally, on Columbus Drive, across the parkway, so he could beat the traffic out of the parking lots. Most of the people heading towards Columbus Drive took the wooden footbridge over Lake Shore Drive but Frankie Coolin and Mick always ran across the expressway at a break in the traffic.

"Your knee hold up okay?" Frankie said when they reached the safety of the other side.

"Sure. What if it didn't hold up, were you gonna leave me in the middle of the Drive?"

"Every man for himself."

Mick smiled. They walked across the park in silence. Trees were bare, grass brown, there were edges of snow under the trees; the sounds of the Sunday city beyond the park were muted.

"I really hate it, you know," Frankie said.

"What?"

"When you're hurting."

"It isn't that bad. I get it sometimes is all."

"You're young, Mick." Frankie stared ahead at the trees, at the skyline of the city. "It won't get better. You got to work out more on it."

"Yeah, I know, but I was in a time jam this past week, I didn't have no time to work out on it. Trying to get stuff cleaned up."

"Don't talk to me about school now."

"All right. I won't. You don't want to talk about anything."

"That's right and you're getting like me. What'd you mean about Andy, before?"

"Nothing."

"Guy's going to Saudi Arabia for six months. I know why he's doing it, he's doing it to get ahead, I say God bless him. But you know what? Fuck it. I wouldn't go to no towel-head country if they were giving away gold bricks in the street."

"No beer. You'd die of thirst."

"You got that right. But that isn't the reason. You look at Two, look at the kid. How could you leave them now for six months or a year or whatever he goes over for? I mean, now is the fun of it. Give it ten or twenty years from now, shit, Two would be happy to see him go and so would he. But not now, not when you got that much youth between you."

"You talk like an old man."

"Don't give me that old man stuff, I can still knock you on your ass."

Mick smiled. "You sound like John."

"I ought to. John is my brother."

"I never seen brothers who weren't alike the way you guys aren't alike."

"No. We are. We're both the old man's kids. That's what Mom would say to us: 'Not so much me but the old man in you.' Even Kate my sister is more like the old man than she's like Mom. It's like the old man had a harder stamp on us or something."

"Genes."

"Yeah. Genes."

"Then whose kid am I?"

Frankie looked at him. "Rose, maybe."

"You. I'm like you."

"I never had no brains. You're gonna be a lawyer, even if I had the chance I couldn't of been a lawyer. Like Klein. I look at that guy in his blue overalls sitting home that day I went to see him."

"Overalls? You mean a jumpsuit."

"Yeah. He looked like a balloon."

"Yeah? What about him?"

"Christ. I just admired the shit out of him, you know? I mean, the guy had brains. No matter what he looked like, he had brains and you knew it."

"You just like guys using big words."

"That's wrong. He used big words on me the first time and I was going to cool it and then he came on with real talk, he talked the way we talk. Then I knew he could talk any way he wanted. I mean, Mick, the guy is like me. He's got to hustle for himself too. He puts it on the line, too. No bullshit about the money, no check is in the mail, no see you next week shit. Everything is down on the table. I figure a guy who can deal like that, make it cash on the line and tell you in front what the rules are going to be, a guy like that has got to have it all going for him or else someone would have told him a long time ago to go fuck himself."

"You make your own rules too."

Frankie glanced at Mick. "No, Mick. You got it wrong; I play by everyone else's rules."

"No. You don't know it but I know it. Every day of your life is your own day."

"That's too heavy for me. You know, I really do hate it when you hurt. You want to rest for a second?"

"No, I can make it all right. It's sitting for the whole game that does it. And I gotta pee. You can't find a rest room in that place."

"People didn't have to pee in the old days when they built Soldiers' Field."

"Yeah."

"I gotta pee too. Here, pee behind a tree."

They came on a grove of bare young maples and stood with their backs to the city and sprayed the base of the trees.

"Much better," Mick said, zipping up.

"Yeah. When you got to pee, there's nothing else on your mind."

"Yeah." They started again across the grass. "I'm sorry I hurt my knee but I'm not sorry I played. I liked the playing even if I wasn't too crazy about football."

"I thought you liked football."

"Not like you like it. I wanted to like it the way you did but I never could. Even when I played."

"Shit, you played better than I ever saw a kid play."

"Yeah. I was good. I knew I was good and that felt great. When I was out there, I knew I could do it all. But I never was crazy about the game. I kept thinking I was going to get hurt. That was always in the back of my mind; and when I got hurt, I was kind of glad it happened."

"Yeah?"

"Well, I wasn't glad to get hurt, no one is. But I was glad it was finished one way or another; if it hadn't been, I would have had to keep playing."

"You would have gotten a scholarship."

"Well. It worked out all right."

"Sure it did."

"But now, well, I don't really want to keep going on. I mean, I got a semester to finish and I think that's it, I'll just finish and get the degree and go out and get a job."

"What about being a lawyer?"

"No. I don't think I want to do that."

"Look, Mick, fuck the money. Fuck it. We can borrow it, we can steal it if it comes to it. The money don't mean shit. What means shit is being a lawyer. You're twenty years old and in three years, you'll be twenty-three. Twenty-three is shit when it comes to age. Nothing. I wish I was twenty-three every day of the week. But if you're twenty-three and you're a lawyer, then you got something."

"You know how many guys got law degrees? Millions. Look at the yellow pages some time under lawyers and see how many lawyers there are. When I got a law degree, I can use it and a buck and get a ride on the CTA."

"It means more than that," Frankie said but his voice was uncertain. "Look at a guy like Klein."

"For every guy like Klein, I can show you a hundred mopes just making it."

"You're looking at one now. What are you gonna do with just a college degree? Every guy in the world's got a degree now. You got to have a degree just to clean out the toilets."

"Right. So why push for it? That's what I was trying to tell you when you came out of . . . court that day. When we were home, in the back yard."

"Mick, I don't want you to be like me. I got to hustle every day of my life. The day I stop working, the money stops coming in. I didn't even have insurance when you were born. I had to pay the hospital bill outta pocket."

"You haven't done so bad."

"I haven't done so good."

"You got a house almost paid for, you got three kids raised."

"Peg ain't raised yet."

"You got your health, you got season tickets to the Bears games. Shit, what more can you want?"

"A son that's a lawyer."

"I don't want to do that."

"Then what the fuck do you want to do?"

"What you do."

"You're crazy."

"No."

"Mick, I told you once and now I tell you again, I don't want you to be like me."

"Genes," Mick said.

"What?"

"Maybe I got the genes. Maybe I got to be like you."

"Jeans is what I wear when I go to work. You want to be like me? What the fuck am I? I'm gonna be fifty next year and I got shit. I can't retire and I can't get enough work in the trades to put bread in my mouth. I gotta hustle until the day I die."

"You want me to run a tag day for you?" Mick said.

Frankie looked at him and was forced to smile. "Show me a little respect, will you?"

They reached the truck. Because Columbus Drive was a city parkway, no commercial vehicles were allowed. Frankie took the city parking ticket off the windshield and threw it away. He pulled onto the drive quickly and turned into Congress Parkway, which then led into the expressway. In a few minutes, they were legal again, driving on the expressway, heading out of the city to the western suburbs in the dying light of the gloomy day.

"Made it again," Frankie said.

"You do it just for a game, parking on Columbus."

"Sure. You got to keep life interesting."

"It does get boring," Mick said.

"You're too young to say that. You never know what's going to happen tomorrow. You got to keep moving, keep it interesting."

"What's going to happen, Dad?"

"I don't know."

"You been thinking about it, haven't you? All these months?"

"Sometimes."

"Jesus Christ. And I was just rolling along like there wasn't anything wrong."

"There wasn't anything wrong until those feds came to the house. I can't get that out of my head, how they came to the house. Somehow, when you think about things, you never think about them coming right to the house."

"Dad. I got to help you. You see that?"

"I don't see nothing. How're you gonna help me?"

"I can come in. I can help you down at the buildings."

"I don't need no help."

"You take Joey down there."

"Not any more." He paused and watched the traffic. "I don't think Joey likes going down there."

"You never took me down."

"There's nothing to see. It ain't Disneyland."

"I can help you down there."

"You don't know the trades."

"I can learn, like everything else."

"First, Mick, we don't need someone else in the trades. Every asshole in the world with a pickup truck and a wheelbarrow is in the trades. If you just say you're in the trades, you're in. The niggers tried to get in the trades for years and the government finally says we have to let them in. So what happens? It turns out there ain't nothing to do. There hasn't been anything to do since '73 really, when the Arabs started fucking us around. No buildings, no jobs, no overtime, no shit. So the shines get to eat the same thing we eat: nothing. Second, Mick, we don't need a rent collector in the family. We need a future, which is why I wanted to see you go to law school and in three years, you got a three-piece suit on and wing-tip shoes."

"Shit. I might go to law school and come out a public interest lawyer, suing the gas company or something for a group of Latinos."

Frankie Coolin smiled. "You would do something like that to me, wouldn't you, you son of a bitch? Peg can marry a spade for all I care, but I draw the line at you being a do-gooder."

"Is she gonna marry a black?"

"I tease Rose about it. Rose takes it all seriously."

"Not as much as you think."

"Yeah. I know. That's why I tease her. She likes it."

"You got to have someone down there. In the buildings."

Mick saw the set line of his father's jaw, saw his eyes dark and steady on the road. He loved Frankie so much in that moment that he was moved to tears.

Frankie Coolin never saw. He watched the road, he thought about prison again.

"I got to have someone but I'll get someone."

"Who?"

"I got Willie Oboe watching the buildings."

"Willie is a black."

"So what?" Frankie said.

"You aren't going to trust him, you don't want to tell me that."

"Willie is all right."

"Salt of the earth," Mick said. "But he isn't going to keep those buildings for you while you're gone."

"Who says I'm going?"

"If you go."

"Well, I'll work something out."

"I can help you."

"Mick, you don't know nothing about this stuff; I want you to get that law degree and start hustling some real bucks, not this nickel-and-dime shit like I do. Get into law, man, that's a growth industry. I ought to know."

"Dad, no one is going to help you except me. Not Andy, not John, not Joey, not Willie Oboe."

"What have you got against Andy?"

"Nothing. Andy is Andy, just like you're you. You're out for yourself and your family and Andy is out for himself. He'll help you if it's a matter of working for you some Saturday or getting you some cement or something. That's what a relative is for, like a friend. But Andy is for himself."

"Jesus Christ, you talk like you're a hundred years old."

"You don't have to be old to see things. I acted like a kid

with you because I thought that's the way you wanted it. Now things have got to change; we all got to pitch in on this. You got to trust me."

"I trust you."

Frankie Coolin reached across the cab and touched his son on the arm and then let it go.

"No, really," Mick said, returning the soft voice. "I thought about you last night, I dreamed about you in the kitchen with your can of beer in the morning, sitting at the kitchen table, the old man leaning on you—"

"He never leaned on me."

"The old man sees you the way you really are. You don't need anyone, that's the way you always wanted it. The old man wants to help you out but he can't do nothing, you don't let him. That's why he takes Uncle John's side."

"He don't take no sides," Frankie Coolin lied.

"Dad. I dreamed that you weren't there in the house. That you weren't in the kitchen in the morning and we weren't going to the Bears games together. It just hit me, it was a nightmare. I couldn't stand it; when I woke up, it was all I could think about."

"I ain't dead, Mick."

"Dad, I got to go down to the buildings with you."

"We can talk about it."

23

The last day of November. Frankie Coolin stopped by the house at one o'clock on the gray afternoon. He was working in Westchester, less than three miles from his home.

Rose was in the kitchen, staring at a piece of paper on the kitchen table. "You're home," she said.

"We sprayed the ceiling. I got to get out of these clothes, I got that shit all over me. Jesus Christ."

"What's wrong?"

"Nosebleed. Second time I got a nosebleed this morning."

"You get them. That comes and goes."

"I got plaster up there again in my Sinai Peninsula." Frankie went to the kitchen sink and turned on the cold water tap. He held his cupped hand under the water and filled it and sniffed the water up his nose. In a moment, the nosebleed slowed and then stopped. He felt as though he had been swimming.

"Are you all right now?" Rose asked, looking up from the table.

"Sure. What's that?"

"Lab report."

"Hey. Are you all right?"

Frankie sat down across from her and saw that her eyes were young again; they had been old for a few weeks, he thought, as though Rose had been looking at her life with the perspective of an old woman.

"I didn't want to tell you, with all you got on your mind. But now it's over, the real worry. I mean, I got anemia. A nonspecific anemia. They said I got to take some medicine, build myself up."

"You ain't got cancer."

Rose looked at him. Suddenly, she began to cry. "No. That's what I thought was wrong with me. I thought I had cancer. I just couldn't stand thinking about it."

"Rose. You ought to have a beer."

She took the can and drank from it and made a face.

"Rose, I didn't know you were thinking about that," Frankie said and realized he had known, that never in all their married lives did they tell each other their secrets. It was their bond.

She wiped her eyes awkwardly, like a child. "There was a call from your lawyer, he says for you to call him after two in the afternoon."

"What does he want?"

"It was his secretary."

"More bullshit. He calls me three or four times and he always asks me about Kennedy and when I saw him and what was he saying and what was I saying. . . . I don't know what's going on in his mind."

"You want something to eat?"

"I had a chili dog at Carm's."

"You ought to come home for lunch when you're working so close."

She touched his hand.

"I think I was thinking more about myself," he said at last.

"What?"

"Myself. I was thinking more about myself. When I heard about maybe that you were sick from Mick, I was thinking about how this was going to screw everything up even more. I just want to tell you that."

"It's OK, Frankie."

"No it's not. You're always thinking about me, about how it's going to affect me. And me? I just know you're there, that you're making supper, or washing the clothes. I didn't think about you being sick, that it would worry you; I just thought that you would be a problem too, along with the other problems."

"You're a good man, Frankie."

"No. I just told you I wasn't."

"Listen Frankie, I always knew the kind of man you are. That's why I loved you, from the first day, even before I met you. I knew what you were like. Full of secrets. Like surprises. You'd never tell me anything. Everything was going to be a surprise. Every day of our lives. All these years we've been married and I never got used to you, it was never dull."

"Dull it hasn't been," Frankie said. "Sometimes I wish it was a little duller. I'm getting tired of surprises all the time. I'm almost fifty."

"No," she said. "You're twenty and you got your card in the union yesterday and we're going to make it . . . you and me . . . whatever happens."

She got up and came around the table and sat in his lap.

"You'll get your dress dirty," he said. He held her, felt her weight against him, felt the firm flesh of her back dipping provocatively still to the top of her waist, down to her buttocks resting on his thighs. He thought of her as she had been the first morning of lovemaking when they were still too young to be married, when they held each other in the old Ford, glowing with what they'd just shared and with a whole life yet to come; they had watched the sun break on the rim of the lake horizon like an egg yolk, spreading a red stain across the sky, reaching over blue water to the car parked on the rocks, warming them.

He was as young as he was then.

"What will your father think?" Rose whispered, half in giggles, as he lay down beside her on the double bed. It was a girl's question.

"He'll think it's termites," Frankie Coolin said.

24

"Yes?"

"Frankie Coolin."

"Mr. Coolin. One more point, please. It wasn't worth bringing you downtown for. Did Mr. Kennedy talk to you about the warehouse fire at any time *before* the federal agents began their investigation?"

"What do you mean?"

"I mean, did you and Mr. Kennedy discuss the fire at any time before the federal investigation? That seems like a straightforward enough question."

"You know, Klein, you keep asking me about me and Kennedy talking about this thing and I don't get it: Kennedy and me had nothing to do with each other on those TV sets. If he stole them, then God bless him, but I didn't have nothing to do with it."

"I am not your accuser, Mr. Coolin; I am your lawyer."

"You sound like one in the same sometimes."

"Did you discuss the fire after it occurred?"

"Sure. What do you think."

"When?"

"What do you mean, when?"

"When did you discuss the fire?"

"Christ, I can't remember that. That happened two or three years ago. The fire was three years ago, we talked about it after the fire and that was it. Until the G started nosing in. But we didn't talk then."

"After the fire, then. Did Mr. Kennedy apprise you of the TV sets?"

"What?"

"Did you talk about the TV sets."

"It came up. Sure. I asked Pat what was going on. He said

I didn't want to know. Boy. He got that right. I wish to fuck
I didn't know."

"He said that to you? You asked him about the sets and he
said that you did not want to know about them? Incidentally,
I am taping this conversation."

"What? You too? Is there anyone in this country ain't taping
something? You can't take a shit without someone putting it
on tape."

"I am taping it for the simple reason that I wish an accurate
record of this conversation. Did Mr. Kennedy ever bring up
the subject of the fire in the warehouse before the G came
around?"

"What were we just talking about? Didn't I just tell you
that?"

"I mean, immediately before the first visit by the federal
investigators."

"No. I hadn't seen him around, I was busy, I had just bought
the new building, the one that burned down now, and I was
trying to see if I could get started on cleaning it out before my
busy season. That was in the spring, when the G started coming around."

"I see."

"Is that it?"

"Yes, Mr. Coolin. For now. I'll be in touch with you later in
the week perhaps."

"What's going on?"

"What do you mean?"

"When do we go to court again?"

"Preliminary hearing on the twentieth."

"Right before Christmas. Nice. Thanks."

Mick was sitting at the kitchen table the next morning when
Frankie came into the room. It was Friday, the day to collect
the rents.

"Why are you up?"

"I'm going with you."

"Fine. You're crazy, but fine."

While he was drinking his beer, Frankie reached for his
boots under the table and pulled them on.

"It's supposed to snow today," Mick said.

"Yeah, it always comes like a big surprise in December."

Mick smiled in the darkness. "Aren't you going to have nothing? Can of beer, cup of coffee?"

"Let's stop on the way in, I'll get a cup. You aren't going to knock on doors at six A.M."

"Sure. That way, you surprise them."

"They'll think you're cops."

"That's always a nice surprise too."

"You going to see Willie Oboe too?" Mick said.

"Always see Willie."

"Good. Then we can get that straight with him."

"Get what straight?"

"About me," Mick said. His face was set, his jaw was serious.

"Yeah. What about you exactly?"

"I'm going to be on the West Side," Mick said.

"No. That isn't the way I got it planned."

"You don't have a plan."

"I got nothing but plans," Frankie Coolin said.

"What's going to happen December twentieth?" Mick said suddenly.

"I don't know. I don't understand this law shit. I can't believe we're going to trial but Klein wants me down there anyway. I just as soon get this shit out of the way before Christmas. We got to get the tree out of the basement for Christmas."

"I wish we still had a real tree like when I was a kid."

"Your mother gets crazy reading those magazine articles about trees burning down all the time. She ought to see my buildings, they all got real trees and they got electricity a hundred years old." He paused. "I'm surprised the old man isn't up here."

"He went over by Two's house for the night," said Mick. "I think Andy and him are scheming each other."

"What?"

"Andy wants to do that Saudi job, you know, and Two is driving him crazy about it."

"I can see Two's point."

"Andy thinks maybe he can get the old man to stay in the house while he's gone."

"That's what Two needs, a kid and a blind old man. What's Andy gonna get her for Christmas? A parrot with TB?"

Mick laughed, short and harsh. God, Frankie thought, he didn't like that laugh. He was warming to Mick in the past few weeks, as though Mick was coming out of a phase of life or Frankie was going into one. But he still hated that laugh.

They left the house without a further word. It had snowed during the night and Frankie wiped it off the windshield before they climbed inside.

"Cold," Mick said, rubbing his hands.

"There's this place I stop at on Madison. They got chili."

"For breakfast?"

"Whenever you want it."

"Chili for breakfast?"

"Sometimes I have a bowl for breakfast, don't make me a bad person."

"God, I think I'd throw up eating chili for breakfast."

"The trouble with kids is they ain't got no good stomachs."

"Like you."

"Like me."

Mick said, "The city looks great, doesn't it? When it's all empty in the morning like this? Sometimes, when I'm going to class, I take the early train just to be in the Loop when it's still empty, when no one is on the street. You feel like the city is about to explode but you're in on it, from the beginning."

"Yeah."

"Do you ever feel like that?"

"I was born in the city," Frankie Coolin said. "I must have worked in a thousand buildings over the years. I know the city like I know my life. You never said nothing about the city."

"I never knew nothing about it until I started at DePaul. You get an education."

"That's a nice area, up by DePaul. I worked on some buildings there, on Seminary. Where they're rehabbing. You can't afford those buildings now. You ever go into a joint called Kelly's on Webster? I knew that joint from years ago, it was called the El tap. Right by the El?"

"Sure, I know it. They call it Kelly's Pub now."

"They call everything pub. That only means they want to raise the price of drinks."

Mick smiled. "I like it down here, don't you?"

"Tell me about it. I was talking to your Mom, I was talking

about moving back as soon as you kids get out of the house."

"I could move there tomorrow."

"Peg. We got Peg to think about. Where would she go to school? Some city school?"

"Peg finishes up this year."

"She's got her friends out here."

"Well, you got to make sacrifices."

Frankie smiled and parked the truck on Madison. The bright diner beckoned. They went inside and sat down and the waitress came up and smiled at Frankie Coolin.

"Who's the young guy?" she said.

"Too young for you, Mare," Frankie said. "Besides, guys don't know nothing until they get to be my age."

Mary smiled.

"This is my kid," Frankie said.

"Your kid? Honest? I didn't know you were that old, Frankie. I thought you were around forty."

"I am," Frankie lied.

"How are you," said Mary.

Mick smiled through it all.

"What'll it be?"

"Breakfast for him, I want a bowl of chili. I was telling him about the chili and I got hungry for it."

"Best chili on the West Side," Mary said.

"Which means it's the best in the world," Frankie Coolin said. "West Side is the best side."

Across the counter, a couple of Peoples Gas workers looked up from their eggs and smiled at Frankie. "You got that right," one of them said.

"Two chilis," Mick said.

25

ay, Willie," said Frankie Coolin.

"Say. Who the dude, Frankie?"

"That's my main man."

Willie opened the apartment door and then carefully locked it behind them. He led them into a kitchen with a yellow table covered with red oilcloth, three yellow chairs, a small stove, a refrigerator and an old-fashioned free-standing sink. Above the sink were two unpainted pine shelves that contained cans, bottles and pans.

"You want some coffee?" Willie said doubtfully.

"You got a beer?"

"I got Bud," Willie said and opened the refrigerator. He handed a can to Frankie Coolin, and offered one to Mick, who said, "No thanks."

"This is Mick, my kid."

"That right?" He said it without curiosity. The three of them did not sit down. Frankie popped the can and threw the top on the sink.

"You collecting?"

"You got that right. It's the third of the month, I give you three days grace."

"Amen," Willie Oboe said.

"I seen Tom Jefferson the other day."

Willie stared at him.

"You were talking that condo jive to him."

"We were talking about. Some of us in the association."

"Willie runs the Tenements Association," Frankie said.

Mick stared at the black man.

"What you thinking, Frankie?"

"I'm thinking ten grand," Frankie Coolin said.

Willie let the silence fall. Then he picked it up. "Ten grand what?"

"Twenty apartments. Ten grand on contract with eight hundred down. Each. We set up the contract, I got a lawyer, he holds the deeds. Twelve per cent interest over ten years."

"You jive," Willie said.

"You brought it up."

"For ten grand, you'd have to do some work in here."

"Like what?"

"Like new stove, new refrigerators, like that."

"Fuck that shit. For eight hundred down, I'm not putting all my money into stoves and refrigerators."

"You make that five hundred down because that be what we was talking about."

"You were talking about. I'm talking now."

"Eight hundred is heavy, when you want to do it?"

"I get a lawyer set up and we can start condoing now. We can finish this up by February, wouldn't you say? And, Willie, you be dealing with my man here. My son is an attorney."

"He setting up the deal?"

"No, we got another attorney for that. His partner. But he'll be handling the payments. Now, when we go condo, we got to have that money on the first with no hassles, no rent collecting. It has to be in up front, you understand, because the guy contracting loses out his deposit if he plays around. I mean, you dig what a condo is, don't you?"

"I ain't no fool," Willie Oboe said. "But you trying to rape the people."

"OK. Forget it. We leave it the way it was."

"You finally got that water heater fixed?"

"You hear complaints?"

"Man, I can't sell the people on this."

"I give you an incentive. You're my salesman. We do twenty apartments and sell twenty by February fifteenth and you get ten percent."

"Sixteen hundred bucks ain't that much."

"You figure as fast as I do," Frankie said. "Make it two grand then, but you got to sell them all."

"And then what?"

"You got another beer?"

Willie Oboe went to the refrigerator and pulled out a second can. His eyes never left Frankie Coolin.

"And then what?" Willie repeated.

"You need maintenance," Coolin said.

"So what you gonna do?"

"Twenty bucks a month, each apartment, and that's only for plumbing and electrical and roaches."

"Man, you don't want much."

"OK, Willie, let me give it to you. I own the buildings. I fixed them up. Now you think you're hustling me on this condo scheme because the way I figure it, you already figured out how you're going to buy the apartments yourself and stiff the suckers. I figure it through your association. You get some federal bullshit grant and you buy the apartments and resell them back or maybe rent them through the association. OK, I'm giving you the chance of a lifetime."

"You figure everyone be having an angle, Frankie."

"Not everyone, maybe, but I never met the man who didn't. And I know you, Willie, I know you in front. You got angles coming out of your nose."

"How long you hold the contract?"

"Ten years."

"What if we pay early?"

"That's fine too."

"Twelve percent is too much."

"Tell me about it. What do you think you're going to get from a bank, even if the bank was going to lend you the money in the first place, which it won't?"

"And what if I just wait on this and think about it? You got the time, Frankie?"

"You mean that federal case? Well, if you ain't got the dime, I still got the time."

Willie stared. Frankie laughed aloud and Mick smiled.

"I never seen a lawyer dress like that," Willie said.

"I didn't want to get my clothes dirty."

Willie frowned and Mick laughed aloud, the short, sharp snort.

Frankie said, "Let's cut the fucking around, Willie. I got all the time in the world but as long as you brought it up, I figure you ain't got the time."

"You keep renting these apartments," Willie said. "Who's

going to collect for you while you away? Your man here thinkin' to come round?"

"My man don't come round. My man is downtown. If I'm away, the road service stops. You send him your checks on the first."

Willie laughed now. "Are you jiving or what? You think you're going to get the rent that way?"

Mick spoke suddenly and quietly. "It's this way. I'm heavy at the Hall, you see? My partner is part of the fourteenth ward organization, you see? I don't really need shit to collect. All I need is a call and there will be furniture on the street and that is no shit, Oboe."

Willie stared at him for a moment. "Well, I got my own peoples to be talking to."

"We all got our clout," Frankie said.

"You saying that, Frankie."

"But Mick is got his clout too. Mick has got some heavy friends at the Hall. From DePaul to da Hall."

"Is that right?"

"That's right," Mick said. "We can cut the shit. Dad has got his business and I got mine but now we're talking family together. You see how it is?"

"No. Not exactly."

"Maybe when you brought up this condo idea, you figured Dad was in trouble, that he was going to have some problem coming around the first of the month."

"I didn't think nothing."

"Don't jive me now, Willie," Mick said.

Willie Oboe watched him carefully.

"You figured that Frankie Coolin might be detained and couldn't handle the buildings without you. So you figured you'd push your move. But we're family, like I said. When Dad told me the condo idea, I liked it. I still like it. But not to have anyone fucking anyone else. If the time is not right to condo we can wait. No matter what happens. You understand? No matter what happens."

"That right?"

"Look. Dad is an old-fashioned guy, he doesn't come around here with a lot of bullshit about clout or making threats. He runs decent buildings, you got to say that."

"They decent. I say that for him, they decent."

"So what are we all fighting about?" Mick said.

"Who fighting? I ain't fighting. You fighting, Frankie?"

"Not me. I like to get along."

"You want to get along," said Willie Oboe, "you goes along."

"You got that right," Frankie said.

"But you don't want to be messing around with no maintenance contract," Willie said at last, dispelling it.

"Why is that?"

"Because, look here: what if we do this? What if I come up with three thousand in front and we carry off in six years? I mean, you come down to ten percent on the carry too. But no maintenance."

Frankie smiled. "That's what you want, you black bastard. Now I get it. You got government money for conversion and you're going to take over the maintenance. So you get me out of the picture and you do it all."

Willie returned the smile. "You ain't so dumb for a honky."

"So we get sixty grand in front and then we get the mortgage money every month," Mick said.

"Now you figuring it," Willie said. "See? We don't have no call to fight each other. We be friends in this thing, ain't that right, Frankie?"

"Whatever you say, Willie."

"See, you be calling me a black bastard but I see where you're coming from."

"And you call me a honky and I know what you are," Frankie said.

"We the same, Frankie, you and me, we the same thing."

"Is that right?"

"Rub your white color off and you be a nigger underneath, same as me."

Frankie Coolin exploded into laughter and Mick smiled. Willie looked from face to face. "Dig?"

They talked some more about the deal.

"Well," Willie said at last. "I talk to my man and get my lawyer on this case."

"Who's your lawyer, Willie?"

"Dude downtown."

"Is that right? Who is it?"

"Well, I got his name from this man I know."

"He know about the deal?"

"Not yet but he be a good lawyer, he arrange everything. He Jewish."

"That's the best kind."

"You know that white dude comes by in the neighborhood? Sells juice and eggs and all that? White dude named George? He put the man on me. I check around, this dude is all right, this Jewish lawyer."

"Well, tell him to call me," Frankie said, getting up.

"Name is Klein. Arthur Klein," Willie Oboe said.

Just like me all the time, Frankie Coolin thought.

26

What happens tomorrow?"

Rose asked the question as she stood on the footstool and placed a cardboard star wrapped in aluminum foil on top of the tree.

"Who knows? I called up Klein and he just says show up at court and he asks me for a millionth time if I want to plead something. I got nothing to plead. I'm so sick of this fucking business."

"I don't think I'm going to put tinsel on this year, the stuff just gets caught in the branches and I'm cleaning it out of the rug in July."

"Don't then. It looks all right without tinsel."

"Remember this star, Frankie?"

She asked the same thing every year.

"Yeah," he said, as he said every year.

"I made this star the first year we had Christmas in the old apartment."

"Yeah."

She got down off the footstool and put her hands on her hips and looked at the finished tree.

"I don't care what you say, Frank, but this tree looks more real than a real tree."

"It cost a lot more too."

"Remember when they first came out with artificial trees? They didn't cost anything."

"I hate them."

"You get nervous with a real tree in the house, if there was a fire."

"That's propaganda."

"You always read in the papers about a Christmas tree causing a fire."

"Propaganda," he muttered.

"Well, this tree is ten years old, think of all the money we saved not buying real trees."

"Think of all the money we'd save never having Christmas in the first place."

"Frankie." She sat down in her easy chair across from him. "I'm going to make this a nice Christmas. You'll like it: Andy and Two will come over, I got a turkey from the butcher. . . ."

"I'm not going to prison tomorrow," he said.

"Frank." Tears welled in her eyes.

"I'm sorry," he said. "Jesus." He picked up the sports section of the *Tribune.* He looked at the headlines and realized he had read all the stories. He put down the paper and looked at the tree. Christmas to Christmas, he thought. Brian had spent two Christmases in the joint. Maybe it would be two years or three years. Or maybe he'd beat it. But no; he didn't really believe that.

"I wish to fuck Klein would talk to me."

"Frank."

"I'm sorry. Pay that fucking Jew five Gs and he don't want to give you the time of day. It's like your towel-head doctor. They don't want to tell you anything, like you were a dumb animal or something. Maybe I ain't that smart but I ain't that dumb."

"Frank, you're just making it worse, worrying like this with Christmas coming—"

"The hell with Christmas coming. I'm talking about going to the joint."

"I know. God. I don't know what to say or what I can do."

"Don't say nothing."

"Frank."

"One Christmas I would like not to be here. I'd like to be in Florida or California. Someplace that wasn't here with all this snow and all this bullshit about the tree and people coming over."

"I thought you like Christmas."

"It just reminds you."

"What?"

"That you had one last year and that the Christmases are all piling up on you."

"I don't want you to be sad."

"I'm not sad." He got up from his chair and went to the window and looked out at the failing, dusky light. The short day was receding into a winter's night. Snow lay on the ground. Tomorrow was the twentieth.

"At least I took care of the buildings," he said. "You don't have to worry about that. Mick and I took care of that." He was surprised by what he said. "Mick," he repeated aloud. "I didn't know what I was going to do about the buildings. You figure it out and you go with your gut. I had my mind set on Joey and he finked out on me. You never figure it out right, never. It was Mick all the time."

"What about Mick?"

He turned and looked at her. "Nothing."

"Don't be sad."

"OK."

"No. Really."

"You want me to sing Christmas carols."

"I love the lights. It's worth it all. The mess."

"We could go to an Italian restaurant and look at Christmas lights, they got them year-round."

"You're teasing."

"No, I'm being serious." He thought Christmas was getting sadder every year.

"You bought presents yet?"

"Yeah. My sleigh is in back. Rose. I haven't even thought about presents."

"You know what Peg wants?"

"A doll?"

"Frank. You got to be serious."

"The only serious thing is going to court tomorrow. That's serious. And I can't get word one from my five-thousand-dollar lawyer."

"Frank. I got to tell you, I got a call from the secretary. In the law office. She said one of the checks we gave for the five thousand bounced twice."

"What? What check was that?"

"You had those checks in the drawer. From the two plastering jobs. So I endorsed them over with our own check for the five thousand dollars. And it bounced twice, the woman from

Mr. Klein's office said. She said it was the Kamen check."

"Kamen? The woman I did the plastering for last month? I'm a son of a bitch. You can't trust anyone. If ever I thought a check was never going to bounce it was her check."

"They're sending it back to us. They want the money."

"How much was it?"

"Seven hundred and fifty dollars."

"I was in that house for a week, I gave her a break."

"What should I do?"

"I'll take care of it."

"We got money in the bank, I can write out a new check."

"Look. I told you I'll take care of it."

"Frank. Don't get mad at me."

"I'm not mad. Shit."

"Frank. Frank, what are you going to do?"

"I'm going to court tomorrow."

"But what are we going to do?"

He looked at her and clenched his fists and then unclenched them. "Look, Rose. I don't know what's going on. I really don't. Klein don't tell me nothing, he just asks me questions. But I got an indictment against me, seven counts and I got your cousin running around with a tape recorder trying to trip me up—"

"You didn't do nothing wrong."

"Rose. Conspiracy. They got me on conspiracy. Conspiracy is what they say it is. You think a jury is gonna believe that I rented that space in the warehouse and didn't know what the fuck Kennedy was putting in there? Especially when Kennedy decides to do me in? What the fuck do you think is going to happen? Rose, I don't want that, I don't want no tears. You got to listen now." He came over to her and squatted in front of her and held her arms at the wrists.

"I'm gonna do time. I been thinking about it and worrying about it but now that's over. I fixed up with the buildings and Mick is going to be all right. Really. He's gonna be all right. We got some money and that's that. We'll make out the best we can. But I ain't gonna plead for less time and I ain't gonna turn pigeon like Kennedy and I ain't gonna kiss nobody's ass for it. If I gotta do the time, I'll do it. So I'll work out in the joint, I'll join the football team—Brian said that they had a

football team at Sandstone—and I'll read some books I wanted
to read once. I always wanted to read *Huckleberry Finn* because
I heard a lot about it. And Alaska. Maybe I'll read up on Alaska.
Remember when I wanted to go to Alaska? And when I get out,
we'll just start up again, it won't be that tough, Peg will be
married to some spade by then—"

"—don't say that, Frank, you should never kid about that—"

Coolin smiled. "Maybe it'll just be another Polack. The
point is, Rose, you got to face it. I never told you this like this
but now you got to face it. Mick can handle it, that surprised
me. But you. You got to handle it."

She stared at him and her eyes were bright. "I can. Don't
worry, Frank, I can. I don't want you to go away but I can take
it. I'll be here, and I'll be there in the courtroom with you
tomorrow."

"No, Mick is going down with me. It's better that way and
I want you home." They were quiet for a minute. The lights
of the tree illuminated the half-darkened living room. Night
cloaked the house.

"OK. Now we don't talk about it no more," Frankie said.

"It'll be a nice Christmas, I promise."

"Yeah."

"Remember, Frank? When Mick still believed in Santa
Claus?"

Frankie got up and his joints snapped as he rose. "Yeah. He
was seven years old and still believed in Santa Claus." He
made a face. "It's a handicap growing up in the suburbs."

27

You aren't going to do time," Mick said. He sat on the passenger side of the truck cab. They were following the stop-and-go river of cars and trucks pouring into the Loop in rush hour on the Eisenhower Expressway.

"Don't kid yourself. I just about figured you know how to handle yourself with shines at least. Don't start reverting on me."

"Those counts are bullshit," Mick said.

"Those counts on the indictment are on a sheet and the sheet was good enough for the U.S. Attorney so don't tell me what bullshit you think sitting in law school."

"I'm not even in law school yet."

"It doesn't matter. You got to play the hand the way it lays. They got my name. They got tapes. They got Kennedy. How the hell do I know what I ever said to Kennedy? They must of seen something in those tapes to figure they got me. I don't even know how long Kennedy was wired."

"What does Klein say?"

"He don't say shit. You give him five grand and he suddenly clams up."

"You just got to ask him."

"You're gonna tell me now how to do it, is that right? I take you out to the shine neighborhood once and you don't get queasy on me and right away you're running the show, right?"

"Look, maybe I know how to talk to a lawyer a little better than you do."

"You do? What does it take, a college degree to talk to a fucking sheeny lawyer? For five grand, he ought to give me singing lessons on the side."

"I just mean—"

"I ain't in the joint yet, Mick. Don't start running the show until I'm safe inside."

"Look, Dad, you're getting yourself worked up and you want to dump on me, go ahead, make yourself feel better."

"Is that psychology or something?"

"Look, I'm on your side."

Stupid, Coolin thought. He hit the steering wheel with the flat of his hand. What was he yelling about? But he thought the loud words kept down the cold and darkness creeping at the edge of his thoughts. He had felt the cold in the morning, when he realized it was court day.

The Great Seal hung on the plain wood wall of the courtroom, behind the bench. The two oak tables on each side of the bench were occupied, two young men in gray suits at the right, and Klein at the table on the left. Klein was writing something on a white sheet of paper.

"Klein."

"Sit down, Mr. Coolin," the lawyer said without looking up.

"What's going on?"

"Going on? This is a courtroom, isn't it? The law is going on." Klein finished writing, looked up and said to Mick, "And who are you?"

"Mick. Michael Coolin."

"Son? Brother?"

"My kid," Frankie answered. "What the fuck is going on, for five grand you can tell me that."

"Yes. Five grand. I thought I should point out to you that you stiffed me with a bum check. A large bum check. That is a felonious offense."

"Stick it up your ass, Klein. I been trying to get you for two weeks to give me some fucking idea of what the fuck is going on—"

"Complex matters of law, Mr. Coolin, why trouble yourself with them?"

"Because it happens to be my fucking life is why."

"Negotiations, if you must know, with the United States Attorney."

"I got nothing to negotiate."

"I wouldn't say that."

"Hey, look," Mick said, "I don't know where you get off but I know—"

A middle-aged man beckoned from a doorway beside the bench. Klein rose without a word and followed the man into a vestibule behind the court.

"I thought you knew how to talk to lawyers," Frankie said.

"He's arrogant."

"You noticed that too?"

Klein emerged from the vestibule, returned to the table and sat down. "Fatuous," he said.

"What's going on?" Coolin said.

"Morons and imbeciles, compounded arrogance, stupidity squared."

"What kind of a deal are you cooking me into? I ain't going to plead."

"Be quiet, Mr. Coolin."

"What's going on is what I want to know—"

"All the problems I have this morning and now I have an inquisitive client. Will you just be quiet while I set this up?"

Frankie Coolin stared at him for a moment in silence and then, deliberately, shoved the lawyer's briefcase on the floor. The two attorneys at the other table turned and stared. No one else was in the room.

"Look, Klein, I been running into jagoffs like you all my life except now it's important to me. Don't give me that attitude, don't give me that I'm-too-busy, don't give me that look they give you in the clerk's office when I get my license or at the truck-testing station. The whole world is full of jagoffs like you who think that people like me are some kind of shit you got to put up with. Well, motherfucker, you got my money and now I want your attention."

Klein gazed quietly back at Coolin. "You knocked my brief-case on the floor."

"It's better than me knocking you on the floor. You were fucking around with Willie Oboe and you told him to try to stick me on the buildings and now you're fucking around with the G and for all I know, you're going to stick me again. I ain't a chump, Klein."

"I am trying to help you avoid incarceration."

"Is that right? What kind of a deal are you making around me that you can't talk about?"

"Don't you trust me?"

"Shit, no. I don't trust nobody, that way nobody gets disappointed. You want trust, buy a dog."

"Buy a dog," Klein repeated and smiled.

"This is not a fucking joke," Coolin said. "I ain't going down on my knees and I ain't kissing nobody's ass and you can tell the U.S. Attorney that in front. I don't care if they're willing to give me six months at Lexington and hot and cold running whores."

"Tough guy," Klein said. "I told the Attorney you were a tough guy. There's been a snag in the negotiations. I await the pleasure of the prosecution."

"What negotiations? I ain't negotiating nothing. I didn't do nothing."

"So I said," Klein answered mildly. He got up and walked around the table. With effort, he bent and picked up his briefcase and put it down on the table. "I said you were a stubborn man."

"And they didn't believe you."

"Not at first."

"What's going on? I want to know what's going on?"

"Do you realize how many times Mr. Kennedy was wired? For you? He was wired six times, Mr. Coolin. Six times. You suspected correctly that the federal officers who questioned you were wired. But Mr. Kennedy. Did you ever suspect he was wired all that time?"

So that was it, Frankie thought. He felt stunned and sick, suddenly. It was all over. He sat down on the hard chair next to the table. This time the cold and darkness inside him overwhelmed him. So that was it. There was nothing to do. "I won't plead," he said, but his voice was not strong. Mick stood behind him, looking down at him.

One of the gray-suited men came over to the table and looked at Coolin as though he were surveying a dead rat at roadside. He spoke to Klein, but stared at Coolin. "This is your man, huh?"

"What about the Attorney?"

"He put it through. This is your man, huh? He said he's sending down Roberts, in just a minute."

"Well, what's it to be then?" Klein said.

"I don't know until Roberts comes down."

Frankie Coolin looked up at the young attorney. He saw the contempt in the eyes. Yes, he thought: he wanted to be afraid, to fall down on his knees, to beg them not to send him to prison, to let him stay free. Yes. He would beg and plead and lie and do whatever they wanted him to do. He had done it all his life, he had always lived by other people's rules, he had always played the hand he was given. Yes, he thought, he would beg them.

"Who's the kid?" he said to Klein instead.

"A representative of the government."

"Yeah. He looks like a mailman."

The young man did not blush but his face became paler. "If this is up to me, I'll push him into Marion. Hard case. How'd you like ten in Marion, hard guy?"

Klein held up his hand. "Please. This is my client and you are intimidating him."

"No he isn't," Frankie Coolin said. He thought, shut up. Shut up now. He said, "If he was intimidating me, I'd be afraid of him."

At that moment, the clerk of the court emerged at the side door and said, "All rise, now. All rise. Honorable Thomas R. Foley."

A short man in a black gown mounted the three stairs at the side of the bench and sat down.

The gray-suited man returned to his table and Klein muttered to Coolin: "When he calls your name, stand up and go up to the bench."

Fear again. Cold and darkness. I don't want to do the time, he thought.

"Francis Joseph Coolin."

Frankie stood up. Before his arrest, he had not been called Francis since he was a child, when Sister Mary Clothilde would call him to the front of the class and punish him. She made him hold out his hands and they did not tremble when she whacked him with the ruler. Once. Twice. Three times. "Have you had enough?" she would ask and he would never answer. Never.

And she would whack him three more times until his fingers were cold and numb.

A child again.

He walked to the place in front of the bench. The gray man stood on one side, Klein on the other. The judge peered down at him over half-rimmed glasses.

"Well, do we have this settled now or what?"

"Yes, your honor," the gray man said.

"It's about time. I've wasted half the morning on this. The next time the Attorney wants to change the deal, let him notify my clerk. As it is, I'm late now for an appointment. All right, go ahead."

"There were last-minute procedural snags," the gray man said.

Frankie Coolin stared at Klein and at the judge and thought again he was a child caught in a ritual. Standing before the nun in sixth grade, waiting for the smack of the ruler on his knuckles.

"Government is ready, your honor."

"And I want to say—"

Frankie was not following the exchange of words. He could see Sister Clothilde so clearly and yet he had not thought of her for forty years.

". . . Justice is a sword with two edges, Mr. Coolin—"

The judge was talking to him. He tried to stare at the words coming out of the old mouth, the yellow teeth bared at each sound. He stared at the watery eyes. He felt cold and distant now from all of them; he was in the joint now and it was morning or it was evening or it was Christmas or summer, it didn't matter. He could do the time. He would stand it and he wouldn't beg them or plead with them.

The old man in black robes rose and walked down the three steps and disappeared through the doorway into the vestibule.

The clerk came to him. "You have to sign this."

"Sign what?"

Klein said, "Mr. Coolin, for once in your life, do what is best for yourself. Sign here and here."

"What am I signing?"

"Just sign."

Coolin stared at the papers but did not comprehend them.

He signed his name: Francis J. Coolin. Once and then again.

Klein returned the papers to the clerk and the lawyer then turned to his briefcase on the table.

"Hey, what the fuck is going on?" Frankie said.

"Nothing more. That's it. Now about the seven-hundred-fifty-dollar check. I have a Xerox copy here—"

"When do I got to come down again? What was going on? What was I signing?"

"They'll send your bail check in the mail. About ten days."

"What do you mean?"

Klein sniffed. "The indictment has been quashed."

"You just said they had me on tape. That Kennedy was wired six times."

"Exactly. Six times, Mr. Coolin. Six times the government wired your friend in an effort to entrap you and six times, Mr. Coolin, you failed to be trapped. You failed to satisfy the ambitious plans the prosecution had for you."

"What are you talking about?"

"Conversations, Mr. Coolin. And over and over Mr. Kennedy, in his eagerness to serve his masters in government, found himself incriminating himself shamelessly but you failed to join him. Entrapment. Yes, I thought so from the first and when the government failed to bring forth the tapes in any of our conversations, I was certain of it. All such matters must be approved by the court and the tapes existed. But where were they? How could I get them? I am a man of resource, Mr. Coolin."

"You mean they're letting me off?"

"How perceptive of you, Mr. Coolin. It finally penetrates, does it?" Klein closed his briefcase. "I told them we would not bargain, that if the matter went to trial, they faced the prospect of destroying the credibility of Mr. Kennedy. And if Kennedy fell, their case against the theft ring fell. You were a mistake, Mr. Coolin, from the first. The government thought you were involved and then they had to prove you were involved. If we had gone to trial, we would have made mincemeat of their case and the character of their prime witness."

"You mean, I never said nothing on those tapes?"

"For once, your inarticulate self saved you. You might say

you were the means to your own salvation. And now we must
speak of that seven hundred fifty dollars."

"I was ready for it," Frankie said, half to himself. "I was
going inside, I knew it. I was going to stand it and I wasn't
going to beg them for anything. It was like dying. I knew I was
going to die."

"Dying? Then you have borrowed time, now, Mr. Coolin.
Like Lazarus."

"Jesus," Frankie said. Mick had come up to stand beside
him.

"Money," Klein said. "You owe me seven hundred fifty dollars. You gave me a bum check."

"No," Frankie said, snapping out of it. "That was a check
somebody gave to me. I got to collect on it. You'll get your
money."

"I am not in the credit-lending business. I want a check from
you now for seven hundred fifty dollars."

"I don't have a check on me."

"What are you going to do?"

"Look. I'll mail you a check when I get home."

Klein stared at Coolin's eyes and then shrugged. He said,
"The check will be in the mail."

"This afternoon, I promise, as soon as I get home."

"I will be expecting it."

"Don't worry about it, you'll get it. I'm sorry I got hot at you
but you could have told me what was going on."

"No. I do not raise false expectations. And I expect the
check."

"It'll be in the mail."

They didn't speak to each other in the pickup all the way out
to the suburbs. It was snowing again and the salt trucks from
the state were on the expressway, dumping white crystals on
the roadbed, slowing traffic as their orange lights circled lazily
in the grim half-light.

"You want a beer?" Frankie said at last as they pulled along
the side road and neared the Bohemian's tavern. The Old
Style beer sign in the parking lot was lit and the windows of
the bar were trimmed with Christmas lights.

"Sure," Mick said.

They trudged through the snow of the parking lot and went inside. Emil came up and Frankie said, "Two beers."

Emil went down to the far end of the bar to pull the drafts.

"Everything's different now," Frankie said. "You can go to law school and I don't have to condo those buildings—"

"Fuck law school," Mick said.

"Hey, you want to end up a bum—"

"Yeah. Just like you. And don't give up on those condos. Listen to me, that's going to work out. You get the money from Willie and you can buy into some other buildings. Rehabbing is very hot now. Look what they done around DePaul in the last ten years."

"Tell me about it. You keep talking to me like I was born yesterday. But maybe you're right about the condos. What the fuck: we get our money out of the buildings and Willie gets the grief."

"And no law school," Mick repeated.

"You don't have to do nothing you don't want to do."

"Besides. There's no money in it."

"Tell that to Klein."

"You aren't going to send Klein that check," Mick said and smiled.

"Sure I am. Hey, Emil, how about a little less head on that beer. I don't want seventy cents' worth of foam."

"There's a lot of gas in this barrel."

"There's a lot of bullshit in this bar too," Frankie said. Emil poured off a little foam and filled the mug with beer.

"You aren't," Mick said.

"Well, he got four thousand two hundred and fifty bucks already. I mean, at an hour rate, he's made about two grand an hour. Even electricians don't get that yet."

"You never stop hustling," Mick said. "I'm just beginning to understand it."

"There's a lot of things you got to learn."

"Like how to talk to lawyers," Mick said. "With loud briefcases."

"Yeah. You got to get their attention."

Mick laughed out loud. Emil brought the beers and put them down.

Frankie sipped his beer. "It tastes good today," Frankie said.
"You guys been at a funeral the way you're dressed?"

"No funerals today," Frankie said.

"OK. Who pays for this? How come I always got to ask?"

"How come you never buy a drink, you wouldn't have to ask so much?"

"The same reason you don't do free plastering jobs."

Frankie touched his trousers and then the pocket of his sport coat. He looked at Emil with innocence in his eyes. "Hey, I must of left my wallet in my other trousers. I was driving downtown without even a driver's license."

"Who pays?" asked Emil, not smiling.

"Hey, Mick," Frankie said, turning to his son.

"I got it," Mick said, and he pulled out a bill and put it down on the bar. He was still smiling at both of them.

"I see I got to pay tuition in this school," he said.

"Now you're learning," Frankie Coolin said.

ABOUT THE AUTHOR

BILL GRIFFITH is the pen name
of an award-winning writer.
Obviously, he lives in Chicago.